"My lady?"

"I'm not a lady."

"Miss, then?"

Violet managed a nod, even as her gaze remained fixed on the stranger's boots.

"Tell me, miss, is there a spot of mud on my boots? Or is there something else fascinating down there that has kept your attention?"

Preparing herself, Violet lifted her gaze—and found herself staring up at the most striking pair of blue eyes the color of glittering sapphires. The crinkling at the corners told her the smile he flashed her was genuine, but unable to hold his gaze, she focused her attention on the rest of him, starting with the sharp cheekbones, down his straight, aristocratic nose, then his full, firm lips.

He was unlike any person she'd ever seen before, which prompted her to blurt out the first words that came to her mind.

"You're beautiful."

His mouth opened as he threw his head back and barked out a laugh.

Author Note

Numerous women have made great contributions to mathematics—too many to mention, in fact, but I'll try to name notable ones who have inspired this book or me personally throughout my research.

M. Lenoire was not a real historical figure, but she was inspired by Sophie Germain. In 1816, after three attempts, she became the first woman to win a prize from the Paris Academy of Sciences for her paper "Recherches sur la théorie des surfaces élastiques" published under the pseudonym M. Le Blanc. Her later work was also crucial in proving the first case of Fermat's Last Theorem.

Ada Byron, Lady Lovelace, is perhaps one of the most famous mathematicians in history and considered the first computer programmer in the world. While translating an article about Charles Babbage's work on his "analytical engine," Lovelace provided additional notes that theorized machines could do more than crunch numbers, like follow instructions. These notes were eventually published in a science journal in 1843, and her revolutionary ideas paved the way for the use of computers outside mathematics.

In 1943, Euphemia Lofton Haynes became the first African American woman to earn a PhD in mathematics. She taught at public schools in Washington, DC, and was the first woman to become chair of the DC Board of Education in 1966. While there, she argued against the "track system," which discriminated against African American students. Thanks to her efforts and contributions, the system was eventually abolished in 1967.

Thank you, ladies, for your persistence, vision and inspiration.

The Marquess's
Year to Wed

PAULIA BELGADO

Recycling programs
for this product may
not exist in your area.

ISBN-13: 978-1-335-59614-7

The Marquess's Year to Wed

Harlequin Enterprises ULC
22 Adelaide St. West, 41st Floor
Toronto, Ontario M5H 4E3, Canada
www.Harlequin.com

Printed in U.S.A.

Born and raised in the Philippines, **Paulia Belgado** has worn many hats over the years, from office assistant, flyer distributor, singer, nanny to farm worker. Now she's proud to add romance author to that list. After decades of dreaming of seeing her name on the shelves next to her favorite romance authors, she finally found the courage (and time—thanks, 2020!) to write her first book. Paulia lives in Malaysia with her husband, Jason, Jessie the poodle and an embarrassing amount of pens and stationery art supplies. Follow her on Twitter @pauliabelgado or on Facebook.com/pauliabelgado.

Books by Paulia Belgado

Harlequin Historical

The Lady's Scandalous Proposition
Game of Courtship with the Earl
May the Best Duke Win

Look out for more books from Paulia Belgado coming soon.

Visit the Author Profile page at Harlequin.com.

This book is dedicated to my nieces and nephews,
Dana, Mikk, Martine, Raj, Yssa and Sophie.

You make my world better and brighter.
Love always,
Tita P

PS: You're still kids to me no matter how old you are,
so chapters seven, eight, nine and eleven
don't exist to you, okay?

Chapter One

Surrey,
Autumn 1843

Archimedes once said, *'There are things which seem incredible to most men who have not studied Mathematics.'*

While she greatly admired the ancient Greek mathematician's work, Miss Violet Avery doubted this particular piece of wisdom. While she had studied the discipline of numbers and formulas since the tender age of nine, there were many things that Violet still found incredible.

Or at the very least inexplicable.

Indeed, there were many, many things she could not explain.

Number one: Why was it necessary for ladies like her to wear numerous layers of itchy and uncomfortable clothing—a dress over a petticoat, over a camisole, over a corset, over a chemise, over drawers, not to mention stockings and shoes? Not that she would have liked to be naked, but surely one or even two layers of clothing were enough to retain one's modesty?

Number two: why were dinner parties such long, tedious affairs? Course after course of various foodstuffs, brought into the dining room by liveried footman who uncovered each dish with a flourish. Food was nourishment—nutrients to keep the body and mind alive—not entertainment. A simple meal could be finished in minutes. And then there was the social aspect of it. So much chatter and conversation and discourse that extended what should have been a perfectly normal biological function.

And number three—

'Violet, I cannot express how important this event is.'

Ah, yes, number three.

Lady Avery.

Violet's incredible, inexplicable mother.

Since Archimedes had never met Lady Avery, perhaps Violet had to forgive his error.

Her mother marched towards the dressing table where Violet currently sat as she waited for her maid, Gertrude, who was bent over the fireplace, heating up a pair of curling tongs. 'This is our first dinner party at Highfield Park. You must make a good impression on our hosts.'

Why they had even travelled all the way to Surrey from their home in Hampshire to attend a dinner party, Violet did not know. Well, it wasn't just to attend a dinner party, of course. They'd been here for over a week, as guests of the Dowager Duchess of Mabury, an old acquaintance of her father's. Violet and her mother were staying at the dower house, located on the estate of their hostess's son and daughter-in-law, the current Duke and Duchess of Mabury, but tonight was the first formal event up at the main house.

'Did you hear what I said, child?'

Violet turned her head up, focusing on Lady Avery's forehead before forcing her gaze to meet her mother's.

'First of all, Mother, I am not deaf, therefore I did hear you. Second, the word "important" usually signifies something consequential, substantial and life-changing. Yet you have called every dinner, ball and occasion we have attended in the last six months "important". Therefore, if every event we go to is important, then doesn't that dilute the significance of all those occasions?'

'I have not called all of them important,' Lady Avery protested with a huff.

'You have. All twenty-three of them, if you count tea with the vicar and his family.'

Her eyes slid to the heavens. 'Oh, Sir Gregory, whatever am I to do?'

'Papa is dead,' Violet said flatly. 'He's been dead for over two years. I doubt very much he'll hear you.'

Her mother's face crumpled like a balled-up piece of parchment. 'Violet!'

'What?' She shrugged.

'He was your father!' Lady Avery cried.

'He was. One day he was alive, then he went to sleep and didn't wake up.'

'Violet!'

'It's the truth.'

And why people didn't like hearing the truth was, perhaps, the *most* inexplicable thing to Violet. The truth was pure, inescapable and inevitable.

But for some reason many people did not like hearing the truth. In fact, when Violet pointed out the truth, they often acted horrified.

Or offended.

Or both.

Perhaps that was why Mother preferred to forget that tea with the vicar.

Lady Avery shook her head and sank down on the stool next to Violet. Turning her head, she dismissed Gertrude, who scuttled out of the room, hot tongs in hand. 'You want the truth, child? Allow me to lay it out for you. If you don't find a husband, you will learn the *true* meaning of consequential, substantial and life-changing.'

'Husband?' Mama could not be *serious*. 'What are you—'

'I have not finished.' Straightening her spine, Lady Avery continued. 'In the past two years I've been indulging you, as you father did, but I can no longer hide the truth from you. Violet, we are in dire straits.'

Violet knitted her brows together. 'What do you mean?'

Lady Avery's lower lip quivered. 'Wh-when your father died, he didn't leave us with much. Not much. Very little, in fact.'

'Very little? How little?'

'Probably not enough to keep our home.'

'We've lost Oakwood Cottage?' A feeling crept into her chest—a tightness that made it difficult to breathe.

'Not yet, but we will.'

'B-but Papa…he was a scholar! One of the most celebrated of his generation.' Her hands tightened into fists. 'He wrote so many papers…published four books. He had invitations to speak at all the top universities in England and on the Continent.'

'Just because he was intelligent, it does not mean he was wise.' Lady Avery's shoulders sank. 'I only found out we were deep in debt after his death.'

'I don't understand. What happened? And Oakwood Cottage!' Violet shot to her feet. 'Did you know we weren't going back when came here? Is that why we have brought so many clothes? Is someone else living in our house? What about our things?' The very thought of strangers pawing through their things—especially her father's study and his books—made Violet's stomach lurch. 'What if they touch his books and don't return them—'

'Calm yourself and have a seat—'

'No, I will not,' she shouted, then grabbed the first thing she could—a hairbrush.

Lady Avery grabbed her arm and tugged her back down. 'Violet Melissa Avery, you are no longer a child. You will control yourself this instant.'

Violet put the brush down. When she was younger, she'd been prone to fits, especially when frustrated. Often those episodes had turned violent, with her throwing things at the walls or even herself to the ground. Numerous nannies and governesses had given up on her—everyone had.

Everyone except her father.

One day, after a particularly ferocious tantrum when she was eight—which had caused another governess to resign—her father had walked through the door of the nursery. At first, she hadn't been sure who he was; she hadn't really seen much of him in her younger years, and could barely recognise him except for his bushy white beard and eyebrows.

But on that day… She could picture him clearly—his hair dishevelled, cravat loosened, shirtsleeves rolled back to his elbows as he knelt down next to her to place a calming hand on her back. Pure shock at seeing him had quieted her outburst and she could remember the sensation of weightlessness as he picked her up and took her to his study. Violet had never been there before, but there had been something about it—the smell of paper and leather and tobacco, the dark wood furniture, the massive desk piled with books and ledgers and scattered pens—that had comforted her. To this day, she had never felt more at home in any other place than Papa's study.

'Violet,' he'd begun as he'd sat her down on a massive overstuffed armchair by the fireplace. *'Look at me.'*

She hadn't been able to. She'd always had a hard time looking people in the eye.

'*It's all right, my Vi.*'

The pet name had sent a strange sensation through her, and so she'd forced herself to lift her head, even though the very idea of meeting his gaze had sent her skin crawling.

'*Like me, you are different, my Vi.*'

His voice had been like the softest silk brushing against her.

'*The world is unkind to different people like us, but even more so to the female sex. So you must control your emotions. Learn to act like them. And mimic their ways.*'

'*Who's "them"?*'

The corners of Papa's mouth had stretched back. '*Them, my dear child. Everyone but* us. *Do not worry. I will help you.*'

And so Papa had. Every day, he would take her to his study to teach her how to quiet the outbursts that seemed to come out of nowhere. He'd never given up on her. He had taught her tricks to mask how different she was. How to copy the way other girls walked, talked and acted. How she could be like everyone else.

How to be…normal.

As he'd taught her these tricks, however, he had also discovered her interest in mathematics and philosophy, and soon she had begun to spend hours with Papa, solving equations or reading through the works of Aristotle and Socrates, Descartes and Hume.

Papa's study had been an oasis from an outside world that she could not understand and which could not understand her.

And now—

'Are you finished?'

Mama's hands, clawing over hers, startled Violet. She hated unexpected touches, but fought the urge to pull away as she needed to know more.

She nodded.

'Now, there is a way to save Oakwood Cottage. You must—'

'Find a rich husband.'

'So you do understand?'

Papa had had some geographical dissected puzzles in his study that he'd let Violet play with. She'd enjoyed putting the pieces together to make one whole map, loved the way the wood clicked when they snapped into place.

And once she'd seen all the pieces, Violet's mind had always quickly put them together.

Dead father.

Click.

No money.

Click.

Attend parties and balls.

Click.

Push Violet towards any available gentlemen.

It all made sense now.

Violet should have had her coming out four years ago, when she'd turned seventeen, but her mother had delayed it.

'Perhaps she needs more time to…er…mature,' Mama had said.

Violet hadn't cared one way or another—only that she didn't have to disrupt her routine or take time away from her readings. Another year had gone by with no mention of her coming out and then Papa had died…

'Why have you never said anything before?' Violet asked. 'All this time you've been forcing me to go to balls and meeting all these strangers…you should have told me when Papa passed away.'

'We were in mourning,' Mama reminded her. 'And it was only after everything was settled that the solicitors told me about our…situation. The only thing we had left was your small dowry, and—'

'Me,' Violet finished. 'Yet you didn't say anything about the need for me to find a husband.'

'You would have fought me. I could barely get you out of the house to attend all those events. I thought perhaps some gentleman would offer for you once you'd had enough time to…settle yourself.'

It took all Violet's strength and all the training from her father not to scoff at Mama.

'You see, Violet,' Papa had said, *'it's often the ones who love us most who can be hurt by our frank words and re-actions.'*

Mama squeezed her fingers tighter, making Violet's chest tighten, as if her mother's hands were wrapped around her lungs instead.

'I've done my best in the past year to find you a gentleman to wed, but alas we've had no luck on our own.'

Of course what Mama truly meant was that Violet had somehow managed to offend—or, in the case of the vicar's son, horrify—any eligible man who came within hearing distance of her.

Lady Avery continued. 'We are so fortunate that the Dowager has agreed to sponsor you for the Season. With her influence, I'm certain many men will overlook your… flaws.' Her lips pursed. 'Do your best, Violet. You are such a beauty you can capture any gentleman's attention even without a sizable dowry.'

Violet had been told on numerous occasions that she

was, indeed, beautiful. She often stared at herself in the mirror, sometimes for hours a day, but not because she was admiring her supposed looks—no, it was another of her father's lessons. He would practise different expressions with her, teaching her how to smile 'sincerely', or look surprised or shocked when called for. Unfortunately, it was one of the more difficult of his teachings, as the range of human emotions was wider and more complex than all thirteen books of Euclid's *Elements*.

'You just need to control what you say…think before you say anything.'

Violet had heard it a hundred times before from her mother, as well as from her governesses and tutors. The only problem was, she *did* think before she opened her mouth, and yet there were still times when she simply could not stop herself from saying what was on her mind.

But Oakwood Cottage… Papa's study…the furniture… the books and ledgers and scattered pens.

We haven't lost it, she reminded herself. *Not yet.*

'I…I will do my best, Mama.'

Lady Avery's smile widened into what Violet could tell was a genuine, happy smile—one that caused the lines at the corners of her eyes to crinkle.

'Wonderful, my dear. Let me call Gertrude so she can continue with your hair.'

Once her mother had left the room, Violet stared at the mirror, forcing herself to look into her own light blue eyes. 'This is for the best,' she said aloud, her voice sounding even more flat and loud than usual.

Papa had always said she had to learn to control the volume of her voice and her tone and…

Papa.

Long dead and gone.

It seemed illogical to miss him or even grieve for him. The time of mourning was over. One year, they said, and then she was supposed to be finished with mourning. So, after an entire year had passed since his death, Violet had locked up those feelings of sadness and grief. Yet they still escaped somehow, lingering in the corners of her mind.

The door opened and Gertrude crept in, those torturous tongs in hand.

This is for Oakwood Cottage, she told herself silently as she prepared for the upcoming torment.

Find a rich husband.

Save Oakwood Cottage.

Save Papa's books and study.

After what seemed like hours, Gertrude proclaimed that she was ready. A quick glance at her reflection showed Violet the familiar young woman everyone proclaimed was beautiful—dark sable curls piled elegantly on top of her head, heart-shaped face, light blue eyes, and a small mole just above the corner of the left side of her lip.

The light violet silk gown was her best, or so Mama said. She'd last worn it at a ball five months ago, given by Mr William Hollister, a wealthy widower who lived twenty miles down the road. Violet recalled how uncomfortable she had been—more than usual—as Mr Hollister's gaze had slid over her, and how he had said he was surprised at how she'd grown into a lovely young woman. Violet had retorted by reminding Mr Hollister that time worked in a forward motion, and then asked him how old he was—though she'd guessed he was probably older than her father had been. Her mother had turned the most unusual shade of purple and hurriedly ushered her away, much to Violet's relief.

She pressed her lips together, thinking of that encounter and all the others she'd had before that, as it dawned on her that they had all been attempts to find her a husband.

Mama should have told me.

But then again, she was correct in her thinking that Violet might have resisted.

She did not want a husband.

A husband meant leaving Oakwood Cottage for ever.

A husband would expect many things of her, like attending balls and parties and perhaps listening to whatever boring things he had to say.

A husband also meant having children…and the begetting of children.

Unexpected touches. Contact with bare skin. Possibly kissing.

Some time ago, when she had started her monthly flow, Papa had given her a book that explained the process. It had all sounded dreadful to her, and she had put that book back on his shelf and never touched it again.

But to save Oakwood Cottage and Papa's library she would endure anything. When the time came, she would just lie back, close her eyes, endure her husband's unwanted touches and think of something to distract her—like the Pythagorean Theorem or the Euler-Lagrange Equation.

'How lovely you look,' Mama said as she re-entered Violet's room, then escorted her out. 'Now, come. The Dowager has gone ahead to the main house, but she has sent her carriage back to fetch us.'

Due to her busy schedule, Violet had only met their host a handful times in the past week. She'd rather liked Miranda, the Dowager Duchess of Mabury, from the moment they were introduced. When Mama had first announced that they would be visiting the Dowager, Violet had pictured a stern matron with steely white hair. She'd imagined such a high-ranking member of the Ton would look down her nose at Violet and her mother, and perhaps dismiss them with a cold word or two. To her surprise, the Dowager had turned out to be warm and welcoming, and Violet found looking directly in her kind, dark eyes only mildly disconcerting.

'I'm so delighted to finally meet you, Violet,' she had said. *'Your father told me so much about you through our letters. I hope you enjoy your stay here.'*

During the few meals they'd shared together, she'd never treated Violet as if she was different. She'd asked Violet questions, and if she had found any of her answers offensive, she'd never shown it.

Now that Violet knew the real reason she and Mama were at Highfield Park, she wondered what the Dowager truly thought of her. And how she could possibly have agreed to sponsor her after meeting her. Except for Papa, most people dismissed her for her oddness.

'We're here,' Mama announced as the carriage stopped.

Violet blinked. Time had seemingly moved without her noticing, and now they were outside the main house. As they alighted from the carriage Violet stared up at the imposing structure before them. Though they had driven by the manor on their way to the dower house, seeing it up close was quite different. It was nothing like Oakwood Cottage—no, this manor projected opulence and wealth, with its four-columned entrance, high archways, imposing stone walls and perfectly manicured lawn. Having such a large home seemed impractical to Violet—how long did it take to navigate such a place, for one thing?—but then again the Duke was likely a very important and wealthy man, and society dictated that important and wealthy men had significant and large homes.

'Fiddlesticks!' Mama exclaimed when they were half-way towards the door. 'I've left my reticule in the carriage.' She hesitated and looked back. 'I should—'

'Don't be silly, Mama.' Violet picked up her skirts. 'I shall go and fetch it.' Night had fallen and the air around them had cooled considerably. 'You should go inside before you catch a chill.'

Before Mama could protest, she hurried back towards the end of the torchlit walkway where the carriage awaited. She could at least delay the inevitable, even for a few minutes. The thought of being inside an enclosed, stuffy room surrounded by strangers making all kinds of chewing and slurping noises made her want to crawl out of her skin. How was she supposed to find a husband with all those distractions?

Slowing her steps, Violet loosened the shawl around her shoulders, took a deep breath and recalled her father's words.

'One step at a time, Violet. Be methodical. Logical.'

Retrieve Mama's reticule.

Return to the manor.

Sit through a torturous dinner.

Find a husband.

Step one first.

As she reached the end of the pathway, however, she saw the Dowager's carriage was gone, and another stood in its place—a sleek, shiny black carriage, trimmed in crimson, with a team of all-black stallions in the lead. Two liveried footmen dressed in red and black stepped off the rear and made their way to the side.

Violet froze, unsure what to do as she blocked the path. At any moment a stranger would come out of the carriage and she would have to subject herself to said stranger's scrutiny. Her only other option was to turn around and run back into the manor. Before she could make a decision, however, the doors opened and a shiny black boot landed on the carriage step, then a second boot met its twin on the gravel.

For some reason Violet could not keep her eyes off the glossy leather tips of the shoes, not even as they came closer.

'Oh, hello.'

The sound of the stranger's voice was not unpleasant, Violet supposed. In fact, there was a rich, deep quality to it that sent a warm feeling across her chest and warded off the chill of the evening air.

'My lady?'

'I'm not a lady.'

'Miss, then?'

Violet managed a nod, even as her gaze remained fixed on the stranger's boots.

'Tell me, miss, is there a spot of mud on my boots? Or is there something else fascinating down there that has kept your attention?'

Swallowing, she slowly raised her head, tracing her gaze up his dark trousers to the well-fitting waistcoat under his coat, up the snowy white shirt and cravat, until it reached a chiselled jaw. The next part was the most difficult—staring people in the eye. But Papa had said it was one of the most important skills she had to learn. And so, no matter how uncomfortable it was, she always looked people in the eyes.

Preparing herself, Violet lifted her gaze—and found herself staring up at the most striking pair of eyes the colour of glittering sapphires. The crinkling at the corners told her the smile he flashed her was genuine but, unable to hold his gaze, she focused her attention on the rest of him, starting with the sharp cheekbones, then his straight, aristocratic nose, then his full, firm lips.

He was unlike any person she'd ever seen before, which prompted her to blurt out the first words that came to her mind.

'You're beautiful.'

His mouth opened and he threw his head back and barked out a laugh.

No one ever laughed when she spoke the truth.

'Why is that funny?'

'I've been called many things, but this is the first time I've been described with that word.'

'Surely that can't be true.' With a quick intake of breath, she briefly locked eyes with him, before focusing on the point between his eyebrows. 'You're probably the most beautiful man I've ever seen.'

'No one calls me beautiful. Handsome and attractive, yes. But never beautiful.'

'Not to your face, perhaps.'

Your beautiful face.

It reminded her of angels painted by the Italian Masters.

'But people say all kinds of things when they think no one is listening.'

'Really?' He leaned forward. 'What kinds of things?'

'Well…mostly what they truly think about a person. It's baffling to me that people only say the truth when they think no one is listening.'

'I should like to know more of these truths. But we should probably go inside. I assume you are a guest of His Grace, the Duke of Mabury?'

'I am.'

'Excellent—as am I. He's one of my best friends, you know.'

'One of them? You have more than one?' Her mouth twisted. 'But the word best implies a superlative—the leading, the top-ranking. How can you possibly categorise His Grace as your "best" friend if there are others sharing the position with him?'

'Yes,' he replied, as if that single word offered any explanation to the paradox she'd laid before him.

When the corner of his mouth quirked up, Violet quickly rifled through her mental catalogue of facial expressions, trying to find its meaning—and coming up short.

'I must say, you are quite refreshing,' he said. 'And since we are both guests at Highfield Park, would you do me the honour of allowing me to escort you inside?'

She stared at the arm he offered. Courtesy would dictate that she take it, and, so she did. Contact with someone else was not always uncomfortable, as long as she did the touching. 'All right.'

His arm was surprisingly firm underneath the fabric of his coat.

'Tell me,' he began as they made their way towards the manor, 'what other truths would you like to share with me?'

'You really want to know?'

He chuckled. 'From the expression on your face, I can guess no one else asks you to share such things.'

She shook her head. 'No. And when I do… Well, it often ends in disaster.'

'Disaster? How so?'

'I danced the quadrille with Mr Jonathan Eldridge a few months ago at a ball. When we had finished, and he asked me if I enjoyed myself, I told him that while the dancing had been tolerable, the stench from his person had not.'

He burst out laughing. 'I hope my scent isn't as unpleasant as Mr Eldridge's?'

Violet lifted her nose and sniffed. 'Not at all, my lord.'

Most manufactured scents offended her senses, but as long as they did not emit a foul smell like Mr Eldridge she had learned to tolerate them.

'I'm glad.' He stopped when they reached the door, which promptly opened. 'Ah, Eames,' he greeted the butler on the other side of the threshold. 'No need to announce me. I'll make my way in. Refreshments in the drawing room?'

The butler's eyes landed briefly on Violet before he spoke, 'Perhaps I should inform—'

He waved him away. 'Thank you, Eames.'

'You've been here before,' Violet observed.

'Sebastian *is* one of my best friends after all,' he said. 'I was best man at his wedding.'

'And I assume there was more than one best man at this wedding?'

He barked out a laugh.

A tight, hot ball formed in Violet's chest. She supposed she should be used to people laughing at her—and in some ways, she was. But coming from him it made her want to run away and hide.

'Lord, I can't remember the last time a woman made me laugh so much.'

Her steps faltered.

He wasn't laughing *at* her.

He was laughing at something she'd said.

She made him laugh.

The most curious warmth spread across her belly, and for a brief moment she didn't quite find looking into his sapphire eyes so excruciating.

'Ah, here we are,' he declared as he steered them towards an open entryway just to the left of the front door.

Violet's chest tightened and sweat built on her palms inside her gloves. The din coming from the room, the mix of smells, and the thought of being among so many strangers made her want to jump out of the window. No matter how many times she'd been in such situations, the initial assault to her senses always threw her off.

Remember what Papa taught you, she told herself.

Briefly, she closed her eyes, then took a deep breath, and then, using her free hand, she began to touch her thumb to each finger as she counted.

'Are you all right?'

She blew out a breath. 'I…yes.'

'You seem a tad pale.' He frowned. 'I did not even think… Surely you didn't come alone? Do you have a companion… a husband?'

She shook her head, tried to speak, but her throat was too dry.

'Would you like a drink? Perhaps some water?'

She answered with a nod. 'P-please.'

'Wait here.'

Her protest remained stuck in her throat as he walked away. Violet wanted to go after him, but he strode into the crowded room. Seconds and then minutes passed by, but she could not bring herself to proceed. It was as if she was stuck in time while the rest of the world continued to move.

'There you are.'

Spinning around, she found her mother behind her, along with the Dowager. 'Your Grace,' she greeted her, curtseying to their hostess.

'Good evening, Miss Avery, how lovely you look,' the Dowager remarked.

'Did I see you speaking with a man?' Mama asked, her gaze narrowing. 'Who was that?'

'I…I don't know.' How on earth had she had an entire

conversation with a man whose name she didn't even know? 'I was chasing after the carriage when he appeared. Then he escorted me inside. He said the Duke is one of his best friends.'

The Dowager's face lit up. 'Ah, that must be Ash.'

'Ash?' Mama asked.

'Devon St James, the Marquess of Ashbrooke,' the Dowager explained.

Mama's eyes turned as large as saucers. 'Your Grace, does the Marquess have a wife?'

'Er...no.'

'An unmarried marquess.' Mama's fingers steepled together. 'And do you think he's suitable for my Violet?'

The Dowager hesitated. 'I suppose... But I'm not sure if he's in search of a wife. Not at this time.'

'Why not? He's a marquess, isn't he? Surely he must need to produce an heir. And my Violet would be suited to such a task.'

'Me?'

Married to that beautiful man?

The very idea had Violet's heart lurching, though not out of terror. No, this was a different feeling altogether, and just the thought of his handsome face was enough to soothe the anxiousness in her.

Mama laughed aloud. 'Yes, and why not? Violet, what great luck—catching the eye of a marquess before the night has even begun.'

'Mama—'

'Soon people will be calling you "my lady". My daughter...the Marchioness of Ashbrooke! You can have all the fine things in life.'

Before she could protest that the only thing she wanted was to save Oakwood Cottage and her father's library, someone clearing his throat caught their attention. Slowly, she turned her head, her gaze briefly meeting twin sapphire jewels.

'Your Grace,' he murmured, bowing his head towards the Dowager. In his hand was a glass of water, but he didn't offer it to Violet. Instead, his gloved fingers tightened around it.

'Ash, how lovely to see you here tonight. I don't believe you've been introduced to our guests,' the Dowager said. 'This is Lady Avery and her daughter Miss Violet Avery. Lady Avery, Miss Avery, this is Devon St James, Marquess of Ashbrooke.'

Violet wasn't sure what had happened, but it was as if all the air in the room had been siphoned away. Ashbrooke's entire body stiffened as he briefly glanced at her. His expression, however, was one Violet could easily read, because she'd seen it many times before—disdain.

'My lord,' Lady Avery fawned. 'My daughter tells me you found her outside all by herself. I had sent her to retrieve my reticule, and when she didn't return I thought I'd lost her. Thank you for finding her. We owe you a debt of gratitude.'

'I'm sure Miss Avery would have found another saviour,' he muttered.

'My lord—'

'If you excuse me, I see someone I must speak with,' he said, cutting her off by turning on his heel and then walking away.

He was barely out of earshot when Lady Avery exclaimed, 'Oh, he's so handsome—and young too. He will make a fine husband.'

'Um…shall we move inside for refreshments?' the Dowager suggested.

'Do you think Violet could be seated next to the Marquess?' Mama asked. 'Surely now that he's acquainted with her, he'll want to be near her?'

'I believe Eames has already settled the seating arrangements,' the Dowager explained. 'And he does work so hard on these things.'

'Perhaps we could switch with someone…'

Violet watched as Ashbrooke continued to walk way. He hadn't even given her the glass of water in his hand. What could have changed in the time since he'd walked away from her and then come back?

As she followed her mother and the Dowager into the drawing room, she couldn't help but search for him amongst the throng of guests. When she did find him, she almost regretted it. The Marquess was standing by the fireplace mantel, drink in hand, as he spoke to a pretty blonde woman in a blue satin dress. As she continued to stare at them he turned his head towards her, then frowned, his lips twisting into a cruel line, before resuming his conversation.

Anxiety rose in Violet, growing three, four, five-fold as the evening dragged on. But it wasn't the people, the noise, or even the smells that caused her nerves to fray.

No, it was the presence of a single man, seated all the way at the other end of the table with their host and hostess, that caused the discomfort in her.

'How are you supposed to continue your acquaintance with the Marquess from all the way down here?' Mama said with a pout. 'Really… I was the wife of a gentleman. We should be seated further up. Violet, you must do something.'

Violet looked down at her roasted pheasant. She didn't dare look towards the Marquess. She could not bear to see the scorn on his face again.

I suppose I should be used to it by now.

But it was difficult to ignore this time, and even harder to brush off—like burrs stuck on the hem of her dress.

When dinner was finally over, the Duke announced that the men would head to the library for cigars and port and the women would go to the parlour for tea and sherry. As the guests began to file out, Violet breathed out a sigh of relief, thinking she was finally being granted a reprieve. Mama, however, had other thoughts, and she dragged Violet away, blocking the remaining gentlemen—and effectively Ashbrooke—from leaving.

'My lord!' Lady Avery exclaimed. 'You did not get a chance to converse with Violet during dinner.'

The Marquess, who was flanked by a group of equally well-dressed gentlemen, lifted a blond eyebrow. 'You must be lost, Lady Avery.' Someone behind him guffawed. 'The parlour is that way.' He gestured behind Violet.

Lady Avery's cheeks turned pink. 'Ah, yes, indeed. I must have been mistaken.'

She sidestepped, tugging at Violet's arm. And as the gentlemen passed, she couldn't help but feel their gazes upon her. One of them even poked his elbow into Ashbrooke's side, whispering loudly enough for Violet to hear. 'They do grow more desperate each year, don't they, Ash?'

'All the more reason not to let their hooks get into you,' another replied—which caused the others to agree, with mocking laughs.

A sinking pit opened up in Violet's chest and she desperately wished for her entire body to shrink until it turned into a minuscule speck of dust, imperceptible to the naked eye.

Mama's fingers grasped at her hand, but she was too numb to pull away.

'I think you've made an impression.'

'That is one way to put it.'

But Violet had a feeling that the Marquess would never look her way again. He would never give her another genuine smile, nor laugh at something she said.

'Come, we should make our way to the parlour with the other ladies.'

Violet allowed her mother to lead her towards the parlour, though she desperately wanted to run back to the dower house and hide in her room.

'There you are,' the Dowager greeted them as they entered the parlour. Thankfully, it was only half as raucous as it had been in the dining room, which was a relief for Violet. 'I want you to meet my daughter-in-law. Kate, this is Lady Avery and Miss Violet Avery. Lady Avery, Miss Avery, this is Kate, Duchess of Mabury.'

'What an honour to meet you, Your Grace,' Mama greeted her as they curtseyed.

Violet sneaked a quick glance at the pretty Duchess, who was much younger than she had imagined—perhaps only a year or two older than herself—with dark brown hair and blue eyes. Her hand lay on top of the noticeable bump of her belly.

'It's my pleasure,' the Duchess said. 'Are you enjoying your time here at Highfield Park? I do hope you're comfortable at the dower house. If there is anything at all you need, you have only to ask.'

The Duchess's canorous tone and rounded, prolonged vowels pricked at Violet's ears. 'You are not English.'

'I am not,' she said with a warm laugh. 'I'm American.'

'Violet…' Mama warned. 'Forgive her forwardness, Your Grace. She is…tired.'

'There is nothing to forgive, Lady Avery.' The corner of the Duchess's mouth tugged up. 'We Americans happen to find candour admirable and efficient.'

'That's what I have always thought,' Violet added. 'Why waste time using twenty words when you can convey the same meaning in ten?'

The Duchess looked at the Dowager, who smiled back at her. 'I regret that it has taken me so long to meet with you. I have been occupied for the last few months.'

'Of course, Your Grace. Quite understandable.' Lady Avery's eyes quickly darted to the Duchess's middle. 'I'm sure His Grace insists you take as much rest as possible.'

The Duchess let out a burst of laughter. 'Sebastian *wishes* he could tell me what to do,' she said wryly. 'But I can't possibly stay in bed—not when I'm so close to finishing my prototype.'

'Prototype?' Violet asked.

'My daughter-in-law is a locomotive engineer,' the Dowager began, and then proceeded to tell them about how the Duchess's family owned the most successful railway company in America, and that she and the Duke had their own locomotives factory just outside London.

'I've been around steam engines all my life,' the Duchess declared. 'I helped my grandfather, Henry Mason, design his greatest creation—'

'You helped design the Andersen?' Violet interrupted.

The Duchess's jaw dropped. 'You've heard of it?'

'I read about the Andersen in a journal from a few years ago. It's supposed to be one of the most advanced steam locomotives today. And you had a hand in making it?'

'It was mostly Pap's work—that's my grandfather—but he taught me everything I know. He worked as an engineer in the coal mines in West Virginia, you see. Once my father had made his fortune in real estate, he brought us to New York and financed the factory. And, well… Pap had this idea for a steam engine, and after a few years of working on it together we were able to build a prototype, and then eventually it went into production. And now I'm building my own—bigger and better than the Andersen.'

'Oh, I wish I could see it,' Violet said. 'How are you planning to maximise efficiency in the engine?'

The Duchess flashed her a genuine smile, then looped her arm through Violet's. 'Miss Avery, I think we are going to get along quite well. It will be nice to have a new friend around.'

Friend. The word was not something Violet heard often—especially not being applied to herself.

'How wonderful.' Mama clapped her hands together. 'And perhaps we could accompany Her Grace to various functions around London sometimes? For example, a ball?'

Violet's elation quickly deflated at Mama's words, reminding her that she had to find a rich husband in order to save Oakwood Cottage. That sinking pit in her chest returned too, as she remembered the Marquess's sudden cold demeanour towards her.

'There will be plenty of time for that,' the Duchess said diplomatically. 'But, come. Let's sit down for some sherry and we can talk more about my prototype.'

There's nothing you can do for now...not about the Marquess or Oakwood Cottage.

So Violet decided then and there that she would put thoughts of saving Papa's library aside for now, and of the Marquess—permanently.

Violet had thought that the whole business with the Marquess was well and truly over and she would never see him again.

Hours and hours of discourse and debate with her father had honed Violet's logical mind. While there were many mysteries in the world she did not comprehend, she did lean towards the belief that man created his own fate instead of the idea that fate controlled man.

But perhaps, just this once, fate—or some higher power—did indeed control Violet's life. Because she encountered the Marquess of Ashbrooke once again, not even a fortnight later, this time in Hyde Park.

Violet had got along splendidly with the Duchess—Kate, as she had insisted on being called—in the days since they'd met. And when Kate and the Duke had returned to London, the Dowager had suggested they come along and stay at Mabury House, much to Mama's delight. Violet had been to Town once in her life and vowed never to return. The smells, sounds and general chaos there made her want to pull out her hair. This time, however, she had looked forward to it, as Kate had promised to take her to see the locomotives factory.

Alas, as soon as they'd arrived Kate and the Dowager had been called away, as a dear friend of theirs had been injured in some kind of house fire. That had been days ago, and due to Kate's busy schedule and her visits to her injured friend, Persephone, there had been no time for Violet to visit the factory. So today, tired of being inside, Mama had decided they should go Hyde Park.

'Finally, some fresh air,' Mama declared as they walked along one of the tree-lined paths inside the lush parkland. 'We've been indoors for so long… This will do wonders for your health.'

'The air here is hardly fresh compared to Surrey or Hampshire.' Violet's nose wrinkled. Still, Hyde Park was one of the more peaceful places in raucous London. 'And isn't the sun bad for my complexion?'

'That's why you should carry— Oh! What luck.'

'Luck?'

Mama's eyes gleamed, then she nodded ahead. 'Look who it is.'

Violet followed Lady Avery's gaze—and nearly stumbled as she spotted the familiar tall and lean form of the Marquess of Ashbrooke.

'Oh, no.'

He was not alone, either. No, he was surrounded once again by a group of well-heeled people, with servants and chaperons trailing behind them. Most of them were men, but a beautiful young blonde woman dressed in an emerald-green gown embroidered with peacock feathers clung to Ashbrooke's arm. She leaned close as she whispered something to the Marquess, causing him to throw his head back and laugh.

Violet was too far away to confirm if his laugh was genuine or not, but still an unknown emotion stabbed her in the chest, reminding her that when they'd first met she herself had been in the same position as the young woman—before the Marquess's countenance had changed.

'He's coming this way,' Mama announced. 'We must meet him head-on.'

Violet's inner voice screamed in protest, but it was too late as Mama dragged her forward. Violet nearly toppled over as her mother practically threw her at the unsuspecting Marquess. His sapphire eyes grew wide as she collided with him. His arms darted out to catch her. Firm hands wrapped around her bare upper arms, keeping her upright. The unexpected contact sent a jolt through her.

A murmur grew among his friends, and some of them were whispering amongst themselves as they stared at Violet.

Ashbrooke quickly released her. Though his hands had been gloved, they left a brand on her she could not explain.

'Are you mad?' he muttered.

She could understand why he would think that. Most people thought she was. Papa had said it wasn't her fault, but sometimes she thought...maybe it was. Perhaps there was something fundamentally broken within her and she just couldn't understand the world around her.

'My lord, once again you have saved my daughter!' Mama tittered. 'She might have fallen and hurt herself.'

'She does seem to be in the habit of getting in people's way,' someone quipped.

Violet recognised the speaker as one of the guests from the dinner party at Highfield Park.

The young woman who had been on Ashbrooke's arm covered her mouth and giggled. 'Oh, is this *her*?' She eyed Lady Avery. 'And this is the mother?'

Violet's gaze snapped to her and she blurted out, 'Did you know in some cultures peacock feathers are considered a bad omen?'

Mama's face turned a deep shade of red. 'Violet!'

She bit her lip. She couldn't help it, after all. When faced with a situation that she could not easily comprehend, she tended to spout random facts she'd recalled from Papa's books.

The Marquess's expression had turned inscrutable. 'Perhaps we should be on our way, or else the best areas for our picnic shall be occupied.'

Without even a nod, he sidestepped Violet and Lady Avery, then continued down the path, his entourage trailing behind.

Violet stared after them, wondering if she'd done something wrong. But it wasn't her fault; Mama had been the one to fling her at him.

'Well, I never,' Mama said with a click of her tongue. 'And I thought he was a lovely young man… Don't worry, Violet, we are in London now, and there will be plenty of eligible gentlemen vying to court you.'

Unfortunately, Mama's prediction did not come true—not even a little bit.

Violet attended a few more events over the next few days—tea at Lady Highbridge's, the opera, a play at the Adelphi, and even a ball—but she had no gentlemen callers. That would usually have been a relief for Violet, except Mama's constant reminders of their dire situation were difficult to ignore.

'I don't understand,' Mama cried, wringing her hands together. 'We've been here two hours and you've only danced once.'

This evening they were attending a ball at the fashionable home of Viscount and Viscountess Walden, with not only the Dowager, but also the Duke of Mabury and Kate. Many members of the Ton had approached their group, but mostly to speak with Mabury. A few had glanced over at Violet and her mother, murmuring greetings when they were introduced, but all of them had quickly found excuses to leave.

Despite her aversion to touch, dancing did not pose a problem for Violet. In fact, she found it rather soothing: she knew what to expect and could anticipate where her partner's hands would rest upon her. But, more importantly, dancing had rules in place, steps to follow, and everything was based on counting. Papa had once declared it as just another way numbers and maths kept things in order.

Even so, while dancing at balls did not unnerve her, she had only danced twice since coming to London. The one gentleman she had danced with was an old acquaintance of the Dowager. And Lord Hornsby was indeed old—Violet guessed he was at least seventy—and had seemed offended when she'd asked if he would be able to finish the reel, seeing as he seemed to be suffering from stiff limbs. As soon as the dance had ended he had brought her back to her mother and limped off in a huff.

'Violet has only been London for a little over a fortnight,' the Dowager reasoned. 'Perhaps the gentlemen require some time to…to warm to her presence.'

Violet had counted seven men who'd asked for an introduction at Lady Highbridge's tea, five at the opera, three at the Adelphi, and two dances at her last ball. With each outing in London, it seemed, the amount of gentlemen who approached dwindled. Seeing such a downward trend, Violet suspected she could radiate the same heat as the sun and the Ton's shoulders would remain frozen as snow.

'If you will excuse me? I require the retiring room,' she announced.

'As do I.' Kate looped her arm through Violet's. 'Come, let us go together.'

The two women made their way together across the room, and when they reached the parlour which had been assigned as the ladies' retiring room a footman opened the door for them.

Please be empty. Please be empty.

When she stepped in and found the room unoccupied, Violet let out a sigh of relief, then plopped down on the nearest settee. 'It's hopeless,' she declared. 'I will never find a husband.'

Kate blew out a breath. 'Oh, Violet, don't say that. Like Mama said, perhaps you just need some time.'

'I'm not upset. At least, not about the lack of suitors.'

The Duchess sat down next to her. 'You're not? But you have just said you'll never find a husband.'

'I don't *want* a husband,' she declared flatly.

'You don't?'

'No. But I need one. Preferably with means.'

Very substantial means.

Frowning, the Duchess said, 'Explain.'

And so Violet did, starting with the death of her father and finishing with the dire straits she and Mama were now in.

'She will not tell me how much time we have, exactly, but I suspect it is not a lot. That's why I require a husband, a rich one, so that I may save Oakwood Cottage.'

If she did not find a wealthy husband she would completely lose the last links to her father.

'I didn't realise…' Kate straightened her shoulders. 'Then we must do what we can to find you a husband. Mama was able to help me find one, and she'll do the same for you.'

'The Dowager wouldn't happen to have another son hidden away somewhere, would she?'

'I'm afraid not.'

'I didn't think so.' Crossing her arms over her chest, she blew out a breath. 'It is hopeless.'

'Don't give up yet; you've only just started your London Season. There's plenty of time. I do hate to see you like this, Violet… How about we go to the factory tomorrow?' Kate suggested. 'Would that lift your spirits?'

Violet took a deep breath. 'Truly?'

Her friend's head bobbed up and down vigorously. 'Yes.

Persephone's on the mend, and I've finally caught up with my work. We could spend the afternoon there, if you like.'

For the first time in days, Violet's spirits lifted. 'That would be wonderful.'

Perhaps, just for tomorrow, she could put aside all thoughts of searching for a husband and distract herself at the factory.

Chapter Two

London,
New Year's Eve, 1843

Devon St James, Marquess of Ashbrooke—Ash to those who considered him a friend and an assortment of names that could never be uttered in polite society to those who did not—stepped into the grand hall of the large house on Upper Brook Street as soon as the door opened. To his surprise, his host was waiting on the other side, tapping his foot impatiently.

'What a magnificent house, Your Grace,' Ash teased. 'You truly have moved up in the world. Or should I say up from The Underworld?'

'Hello to you too, Ash,' replied Ransom, Duke of Winford, with a sardonic lift of a dark eyebrow. 'And Happy New Year.'

'I know you and Persephone value your privacy at home—even this temporary one.' Ash removed his coat and handed it to the footman standing by the door. 'So imagine my surprise when I received your invitation to this party. I didn't think you'd invite *me*, of all people.'

'Well…' Ransom crossed his arms over his chest. 'You are my best friend after all.'

Ash stumbled on the marble floor, nearly toppling forward, but managed to find his footing. He'd expected Ransom would bite out some cynical reply, or imply Ash hadn't been invited, but his actual words had caught him off guard. However, when he saw the corner of the other man's mouth lift, he barked out a laugh.

'You did that on purpose.'

Ransom, out of the three men he considered his best friends, would be the last one ever to admit the existence of their friendship.

Ransom merely smirked. 'Come. You're fashionably late, as usual, and everyone is waiting.'

As he followed Ransom down the corridor, Ash let out a whistle as he glanced around the sumptuous surroundings. 'This truly is a magnificent home. How did you manage to snag it? Did some degenerate who owed you thousands of pounds hand it over?'

Aside from holding a prestigious title, Ransom also owned a popular gentleman's club in London, making him perhaps one of the richest and most powerful men in England. Not that Ash resented him for that—after all, he himself had a respected title and, while not as rich as Croesus, like Ransom, was wealthy enough to indulge in all the activities a peer like himself needed and wanted to pursue.

'Something like that,' Ransom answered immediately. 'We couldn't keep staying at a hotel after the fire.'

A few weeks back Ransom's home and his club, The Underworld, had burned down, when the kitchen boiler had exploded. Thankfully, no one had perished during the incident. Despite not being in Town when it had happened, Ash still felt a knot tighten in his chest at the knowledge that both Ransom and Persephone had been inside during the disaster.

'Ransom, I truly am glad you and Persephone are safe,' he said, his tone sombre.

The Duke's back stiffened, then relaxed. 'Thank you, Ash.'

Clearing his throat, he clapped Ransom on the shoulder. 'And how *is* your lovely wife?'

Ransom's face lit up at the mention of his duchess. 'She's well and fully recovered. And for some reason she's looking forward to seeing you, so we should hurry along.'

That only made him chuckle. 'I've been told I have that effect on women.'

Ash wasn't blind, of course, nor dull-witted. He knew he was handsome and charming, and it was a fact he fully exploited, allowing him to seduce any woman into his bed. Indeed, no female below the age of eighty could resist his charms, and he wasn't ashamed of his 'accomplishments'. In fact, he fully intended to take advantage of his bachelorhood until his hair and his teeth fell out. And, while all three of his best friends seemed happy enough with their wives, Ash knew he would never find himself shackled in the bonds of matrimony.

A memory from long ago threatened to rise up.

A vivid image of a beautiful summer day.

The swish of cotton and silk.

The slamming of a door.

Ash quickly quashed the image. 'Where is everybody?' he asked as they entered the empty parlour.

'Already seated for dinner.' Ransom gestured to the doorway across the room. 'Kate, Sebastian, and the Dowager arrived over an hour ago.'

'Such a formal affair for six people?'

Ash had guessed that it would just be their hosts, Kate, Mabury and the Dowager tonight. The last grand affair

Ransom had hosted had been his own wedding, and he had hardly been able to stand being around the members of the Ton then. No, judging from the handwritten note he had received a few days ago, this had to be an intimate affair.

'Eight, actually,' Ransom corrected him. 'The Dowager has invited her protégée and her mother.'

'Protégée? I didn't realise the Dowager had taken another debutante under her wing.'

In past year or so the Dowager Duchess of Mabury had sponsored a few young misses for the London Season. Kate and Persephone had been two such debutantes.

'And who—'

Once again Ash found himself nearly stumbling as he missed the small step leading into the dining room because his gaze had landed on the familiar woman sitting at the dining table, staring up at him with those mesmerising eyes before quickly turning away.

Miss Violet Avery.

A roaring sound filled his ears and his heart slammed into his chest at the sight of her, just as it had the first time he'd seen her that night on the torchlit pathway at Highfield Park.

Even now, the damned organ trapped behind his ribcage was beating out a rhythm not unlike the drums of the young men out wassailing tonight, hoping to ward off evil spirits before the New Year arrived.

He had never encountered anyone so breathtakingly lovely. Despite his years of experience and countless lovers over the last decade, he could not remember a single woman who could compare to Miss Violet Avery's beauty—thick sable hair, light blue eyes ringed with dark navy, a sensuous pink mouth and that tempting beauty mark over her lip. She was so achingly beautiful he'd thought he must be hallucinating.

But more than her physical attributes, there was something else about her that he just couldn't put his finger on. She had made quite an impression on him in the short time during that walk between his carriage and the door. Her wit and unique charm had made him laugh—truly laugh aloud, not pretend to for the sake of trying to lure in a beautiful woman. For the first time in his life he'd found he was actually listening to what she was saying and wanting to hear her talk.

But as it turned out she was just like any other debutante on London's notorious marriage mart and had her sights set on him. Why, her audacious mother had practically declared him in the bag, calling her 'the Marchioness of Ashbrooke' to everyone within earshot.

Had she known he was coming tonight? Perhaps she'd waited for his carriage to arrive so she could position herself at the right place to bump into him that night they met. It wouldn't be the first time some brazen husband-hunter had schemed to entrap him.

'You're beautiful.'

Those had been the first words she had said to him.

It had caught him off guard, to say the least. Was that part of her plan? It irritated the hell out of Ash that she'd fooled him—*him*, of all people—into thinking she was different from all the other women of the Ton.

But what the devil was she doing here?

'Ash,' Persephone, Duchess of Winford, greeted him. 'I see you've finally arrived,' she said playfully, in her lilting Scottish burr.

He tore his eyes away from Miss Avery and turned to

the Duchess. 'Persephone, you look ravishing tonight. For-give me for my tardiness. Thank you for the invitation.'

Of course, had he known who else was on the guest list, he would have instantly declined.

Ransom cleared his throat. 'Perhaps we could get back to eating? My dinner is getting cold.'

'Of course. But first, do introduce our guests to Ash.'

Ah, so Miss Avery was the Dowager's new protégée. *What a pity.*

'We've met, actually,' he said curtly. 'At Highfield Park. Lady Avery... Miss Avery.'

'My lord,' Lady Avery chittered, her cheeks puffing ex-citedly. 'How wonderful to see you again after all this time.'

Miss Avery, on the other hand, seemed to find something on her lap riveting as her head lowered to avoid his gaze.

Ah, so she does feel some shame.

'I'm sure it is,' he replied coolly. 'Now, where shall I sit?'

'Beside Mabury,' Persephone instructed. 'We're not seated formally for tonight. I missed having cosy family New Year's Eve dinners like we did back in Scotland with my brothers and I, so I told Ransom I wanted a small affair with just all of us.'

'And I, for one, am glad we don't have to sit through a boring, stuffy dinner with people we don't even like.' Kate raised a glass. 'Come, Ash, have a seat.'

'Kate... Sebastian,' he greeted them. 'Congratulations on the birth of Henry. How is the little one? I apologise for not coming to visit yet.'

Sebastian glowered at his wife. 'He's at home, sleeping. Unlike *some* people.'

'Don't look at me like that, Sebastian,' Kate retorted. 'I don't even know why I'm supposed to stay at home for a whole six weeks when I'm perfectly fine. I simply gave birth, for God's sake. Women have been doing it since the dawn of time. Besides, he's just a few doors away. The nanny will send for us if there's anything wrong.'

'Ah…perhaps I can stop by later to see my godson?' Ash enquired.

'I don't recall asking you to be my son's godfather,' Sebastian said.

'Tut-tut…minor details.'

He took his place at the empty chair between Sebastian and the Dowager. Unfortunately, that meant he was seated across from Miss Avery, but thankfully, throughout the meal, Ash only had to converse with his friends. Lady Avery tried to catch his attention a few times, but Ash pretended not to hear her when she called his name.

Still, when he thought no one was looking, Ash allowed his gaze to stray towards Miss Avery. She looked calm as a millpond, eating her food methodically, almost mechanically, cutting it into even-sized pieces before lifting each morsel to that plump mouth. He scrutinised the way her long lashes cast shadows over her high cheekbones. Even let his gaze stray lower, down to the tempting low neckline—

'Ash, did you hear what I said?'

Ash's head snapped back towards his host. 'Yes?'

'Never mind.'

But Ransom sent him a silent, warning look.

Ash sank back into his seat. It wasn't his fault Miss Avery was so damned tempting—even if she *was* a deceitful little schemer. Why, the chit and her mother had even had the gall to stalk him at Hyde Park.

Ash had planned a picnic outing there, with his old university friends. At least it should have just been him and his friends, but one of them—Lord George Jacobs—had brought his sister Lady Helen along at the last minute. Ash hadn't been able to tell her to leave, even though he'd suspected she had had her eye on him since her coming out earlier that year, and she had clung to his arm as they'd made their way into the park.

As she'd chattered on about nothing, Ash had found his mind and attention drifting away—which was why he hadn't noticed Miss Avery careering towards him until it had been too late. While he should have let her crash to the ground for attempting such a brazen stunt, he'd nonetheless found himself catching her anyway. Besides, it had been a good excuse to prise Lady Helen's claws from his arm.

He had not been prepared, however, to have Miss Avery so close that she'd practically been in his embrace. The smell of her lavender and powder-scented perfume had been enough to send his heart racing like mad once again. When his friends had begun to mock her, he had done his best to steer them away, but of course Miss Avery, her strange behaviour and her outrageous mother, had been a topic of conversation for the rest of the day.

'She must truly be fixated on bagging you, Ash,' Lord George had remarked. *'Twice now she has schemed to catch your attention.'*

Damn George. He'd forgotten that he had been at Highfield Park and witnessed that incident after dinner when Lady Avery had tried to block his way.

'And what a strange girl,' Lady Helen had said with a huff, plucking an imaginary piece of lint from the blue-green embroidery on her gown. *'Going on about peacock feathers and bad omens.'*

That had actually made Ash want to laugh so badly that he'd had to bite the inside of his cheek until it had nearly bled to stop himself.

'Bizarre,' Lord George had harrumphed.

'But you must admit she is a beauty,' someone else had remarked.

'A bizarre beauty.'

Ash had blurted it out thoughtlessly, but it had nonetheless made his companions break into fits of laughter.

That incident had been weeks ago, and frankly Ash had mostly forgotten about it. But he had not forgotten Miss Avery. Though he hadn't run into her again, she was like a gnat, buzzing around him, and the memory of her eyes or her laugh landed in his mind at random times of the day.

He'd thought that after some time he would forget about her. But now it seemed, because of her connection to the Dowager, if he wanted to spend time with his friends, he must also endure her company and that of her mama.

'That was a splendid dinner.' Kate wiped her mouth with her napkin and placed it on her plate. 'Thank you, Ransom, Persephone, for this invitation.'

'The night isn't over yet.' As Persephone stood, all the men were prompted to follow suit. 'We must now wait for midnight which is…' she glanced at the clock '…only two hours from now. I've arranged treats and amusements for us in the library.'

As Persephone had promised, there were indeed treats in the library. Aside from the usual refreshments—port, sherry, tea and coffee—there was a table laden with sweetmeats, gingerbread, four kinds of pudding, mincemeat pies, sugar plums and wassail punch. The household staff had also prepared board games, parlour games, and a card table was set up in the middle of the room.

Kate, Sebastian, Persephone and Miss Avery decided to sit down to a game of whist, while the Dowager and Lady Avery enjoyed some sherry as they watched on.

Ash joined Ransom by the fireplace for port and cigars,

making sure to keep his back towards the room. From the look his friend had given him earlier, he wouldn't be surprised if Ransom suspected he was gawking at Miss Avery, and he didn't want to give his friend the wrong impression.

Well, he *was* gawking—but it was Miss Avery's fault.

Once they had glasses in hand and cigars lit, Ash launched into conversation, hoping Ransom wouldn't ask him about his non-gawking.

'How are the renovations at The Underworld progressing?'

'Very well.' Ransom took a sip from his glass. 'I'm just glad the clean-up is done now and we can finally start building. Seeing it straight after the explosion was heartbreaking.' His eyes drifted somewhere over Ash's left shoulder—most likely towards his wife. 'Persephone was inconsolable for days. But moving here and planning our honeymoon has been a good distraction for her.

'When do you start building?'

'As soon as we can. I need to get The Underworld back in business as soon as possible. But finding the right company is exhausting and no one can get—' He frowned.

'No one can get what?'

Ransom didn't answer. Instead, his hawk-like gaze focused on something behind Ash.

'Ransom?'

'Hmmm…' The Duke's lips pressed together. 'Card-counting.'

Ash glanced over his shoulder towards the card players. 'Oh, yes. Mabury's good at that.'

'Not him.'

Ransom brushed past him and strode off towards the players.

Not him?

Intrigued, Ash followed suit, walking to where Ransom hovered by the card table. Kate and Miss Avery were paired up, while Sebastian and Persephone played together. Normally in such settings, whist was a fun, social activity. However, a thick tension hung in the air as the players rapidly played trick after trick. Or rather it was Sebastian and Miss Avery who were quickly dominating the game, their eyes darting back and forth from their hands to the cards on the table, each one winning every other trick or so.

Damn. Ash didn't play much whist, but it was dizzying watching them play. He'd only seen this magnitude of intensity in gaming halls, where whole fortunes were at stake.

Once the last trick was played and all the cards were gone, Sebastian turned to his opponent. 'Good game, Miss Avery.'

Kate looked at the young miss, then at Sebastian, with disbelief. 'But we haven't tallied the points yet.'

'I assure you, your team has won, my love.' Sebastian flashed her a smile. 'Isn't that right, Miss Avery?'

She nodded.

Kate's jaw dropped, then a grin spread across her face. 'I can't believe it. Someone has finally beaten you at cards. Splendid job, Violet. I knew you could do it.'

Ash scrutinised Sebastian, searching his face for anything that might indicate that he had let the girl win, but found no such clue. In fact, the Duke looked amused that he'd been defeated by a woman.

Lady Avery scrambled towards her daughter. 'Your Grace, you must forgive her...'

'There is nothing to forgive, Lady Avery. Your daughter won the game.'

Horror crossed her face. 'Violet, you should not have done that.'

'Done what, Mama?'

The low, husky voice jolted Ash into attention, and he realised this was the first time he'd heard her speak all evening.

'Defeated His Grace at cards. It's...unladylike.'

She blinked up at her mother. 'How so?'

'Oh, child, this is exactly why you...' She drifted off, then shook her head. 'A wife must humble herself to her husband. If you hurt his pride, no man will want you.'

A protest rose in Ash, but before he could say anything Miss Avery spoke up. 'First of all, Mama, His Grace is already married, so there is no need for me to "humble" myself to him.'

Ash found himself mesmerised by the throaty, smooth quality of her voice...like dark velvet brushing on his skin.

'And secondly,' she continued, 'why should I hide my skill and knowledge just to save a man's pride?'

'What good is skill and knowledge if you end up as a spinster?'

Without a beat, she retorted, '"There is only one good, knowledge, and one evil, ignorance."'

'Socrates,' Kate and Persephone said at the same time.

Lady Avery pressed the back of her hand to her forehead. 'Violet, you will be the—'

The doors opening to admit two footmen carrying trays of champagne flutes interrupted them.

Persephone glanced at the clock. 'It's almost midnight.' Walking over to the pianoforte, she waved at the Dowager. 'Your Grace, would you do us the honour?'

As everyone gathered around when the Dowager played the first few notes to 'Auld Lang Syne', Ash couldn't help but study Miss Avery once again, his mind drifting back to that torchlit path that very first evening they'd met. For a moment it was as if everything that had happened between that short conversation and now had never occurred, and he was once again staring at the breathtaking beauty who had made him laugh and captivated him with her refreshing wit.

Ash shook his head mentally and took a swig of champagne.

No, that couldn't be right.

He could not allow himself to think that way. She might be a beauty, and perhaps possessed an ounce more intelligence than most, but Miss Avery was no different from all the opportunistic husband-hunters in London. He would be damned before he allowed himself to be caught in her trap. His reaction to her was merely a case of lust from not having had a woman in his bed these last few weeks.

Yes, that was it, Ash thought to himself as he took another sip of champagne. This was simply a case of pent-up frustration.

'Happy New Year!' everyone shouted as the clock struck twelve and began to chime.

As all the guests cheered and clicked their wine glasses, Ash decided that now it was the New Year, it was time to seek out some new, friendly company.

'There must be something amiss. Or perhaps something we haven't done yet to attract a suitable husband for Violet,' Lady Avery said. 'It just doesn't seem right that my daughter hasn't had a single suitor in all this time.'

The Dowager placed a comforting hand on Lady Avery's arm. 'Not every girl is a success in the first few weeks of her Season.'

'But we've been in London for nearly four months now, and we've attended dozens of events. And aside from a few conversations here and there, no one has paid her a call or even shown interest in courting her. There *must* be something wrong.'

While Lady Avery did not always act within the bounds of reason and logic, Violet found herself agreeing with her mother because the evidence did seem to support her theory. By her count, in almost four months in London, she had attended fifty-two events, including ten balls.

She had been introduced to thirty-seven gentlemen, although only twenty-three of them were unmarried, and danced thirteen and a half times—the half was due to the fact that her partner during ball number eight, the Honourable Gregory Talbot, had seemingly lost his way after changing partners during a quadrille and had not returned to her. She could only assume he was still out there, wandering about London.

And she had exactly zero prospects.

To Violet, the numbers simply did not add up. Surely by this time she should have had at least one call from a gentleman.

Perhaps Mama was correct: something was definitely wrong.

Kate sent her a sympathetic look. 'Do not fret, Violet. I'm certain you will find a suitor. Maybe even tonight. There are so many more gentlemen here, and now we've expanded our search to include a few international prospects.'

Tonight, she, Mama, the Dowager and the Duke and Duchess were in attendance at a gathering at the Spanish Ambassador's house. Violet had dreaded the prospect of attempting to mingle with the diplomatic set. After her months in London she was now able to observe the rhythms of London society, making it less daunting to navigate. The people tonight, however, with their own ways and pace and patterns, were an entirely new variable to her. However, she'd had no choice in the matter.

'Violet, please be careful with what you say,' Mama warned her. 'You cannot risk offending more people.'

'Only half the guests here can even understand me, so I'm quite certain that there is a lower chance of me offending anyone.'

Mama let out an impatient breath. 'Still, you must try to keep your thoughts to yourself.'

Violet tried. She really, truly tried. Each time a thought popped into her head she kept it to herself. And it worked—most of the time. There were instances where she just could not help herself, however—like when she'd asked Lady Katherine Pearson to please stop playing the pianoforte because it sounded like a dying warbler being trampled by a cart. The noise had been unbearable, and had driven her to breaking point.

Mama continued. 'And Violet, don't forget to—'

Kate cleared her throat and stood up. 'I must visit the necessary. Violet, would you be so kind as to accompany me?'

'Yes.' Violet practically leapt up from her seat. 'I would very much like that.'

Once they were out of earshot of Violet's mother, Kate said, 'I don't really require the necessary. But I thought maybe you'd like a few minutes away from your mother.'

'Thank you.' She breathed a sigh of relief. 'I really am trying, Kate.'

'I know.' She bit her lip. 'I mean…if I may be frank?'

'Always.'

'Violet, you're a stunning beauty. You may not be perfect, but I still cannot fathom why you have no prospects after all this time. Even if they aren't rich or titled, surely at least one man should have shown interest in you.' Her dark eyebrows furrowed. 'While I know I was not raised here in England, some things work the same way in New York. If a marriageable woman out in society has not had a single caller, then perhaps there is something else at work.'

'You think there are other reasons why I cannot find a suitor?'

'It's possible.' Kate tapped a finger to her chin. 'For example, in my case, I was simply shut out by the elite of New York society because my father had made his own fortune instead of inheriting it.'

'That seems illogical. Money is money.'

The corner of Kate's mouth lifted up. 'The rules of society are hardly ever logical. But in any case… Perhaps we can investigate and find out what is going on.' She paused. 'I shall write to my former companion and chaperon. She guided me in navigating the waters of London society. She'll be able to help us.'

'Another perspective on the matter? That sounds like a fairly reasonable plan.'

'I shall write to her in the morning. In the meanwhile…' Halting, Kate pulled her aside and lowered her voice. 'I have some excellent news for you. We will be ready to test the locomotive in a few weeks' time.'

The very prospect of seeing Kate's locomotive in action sent a thrill through her. 'That soon?'

'Yes—and it's all thanks to you and your assistance.'

Violet shrugged. 'You did all the hard work in the beginning. All I did was assist with your calculations.'

When she hadn't been attending the aforementioned fifty-two events, Violet had spent most of her time at Kate's locomotives factory—Mason & Wakefield Railway Works. During their initial visit the Duchess had shown her the initial designs, as well as the prototype, and while Violet did not know much about steam engines, she had noticed that a few of Kate's figures in one of the plans were inaccurate. Initially, she had feared her friend would be insulted when she pointed out the error, but Kate had been ecstatic.

'I've been going mad trying to figure it out. Thank you, Violet.'

That had led Kate to ask her to look over other plans and calculations—and that had meant she was at the factory nearly every day. It was her place of solace—not even the loud noises and all the people milling about bothered her. No, when she was sitting down and working on torque diagrams and calculating tractive force formulas, the world outside simply disappeared.

'There's one more thing I want to speak to you about, Violet.'

'What is it?'

Kate hesitated. 'I have had a thought… What if…? I mean, just on the small chance you can't find a husband… What if you stay in London and work for me? At the factory?'

Violet inhaled a breath. 'W-work for you?'

'Yes. I would pay you a salary, of course. I'm afraid it won't be enough to save your Oakwood Cottage, but you and your mother could have a comfortable life. And this first locomotive is just the beginning. We could work together, and you would co-own any patents we create. What do you think?'

Stunned at the offer, Violet couldn't form the words to speak. 'I…'

A movement—no, a presence—caught her attention from just over Kate's left shoulder. It was the Marquess of Ashbrooke.

After their encounter in the park, she'd been certain she would never see him again. When he'd arrived at the Duke and Duchess of Winford's New Year's Eve dinner less than a fortnight ago, Violet had thought she was hallucinating.

Truth be told, the Marquess had always been there…just at the edges of her mind. How could she forget the beautiful man who'd said she was refreshing and had wanted to hear the truth from her? Who hadn't laughed at her, but at something she'd said?

Violet had tried to completely banish him from her mind, because it was evident from his dismissive behaviour that he didn't think much of her. And it had worked for a time—especially when she'd tried hard not to think about him.

Now here he was again…reminding her of his existence.

And he was not alone.

The Marquess stood in an inconspicuous corner of the room, next to a stunning brunette.

Violet wanted to turn away, but she couldn't. So she watched as Ashbrooke leaned over and whispered in the woman's ear, his hand disappearing behind her. Narrowing her gaze, she scrutinised the woman. There was something familiar about her…as if she'd seen her before. But from this distance Violet couldn't see her features.

The woman's lips curled up into a smile and she nodded at the Marquess, then he caught her hand and dragged her towards one of the glass doors leading out to a balcony.

A strange, stabbing sensation pierced Violet's chest, making it hard to breathe—just like that day in Hyde Park, when the blonde woman in the peacock dress had clung to his arm.

'Violet?'

'I…I need the necessary.'

Her stomach turned, and suddenly everything around

her was too loud, the lights overhead too bright. She rushed away from Kate and quickly crossed the room to her intended destination. Pushing at the door, Violet took one step in—but stopped when voices from inside filtered out.

Drat.

'I'm quite sure that's her…the strange one,' a voice said. 'She was wearing the same pink gown at the Adelphi.'

Violet's eyes darted down to her own pink evening gown.

Surely they couldn't mean…?

'And that's the mother?'

'Who else could she be, Lydia? Do you see her eyes light up like some poor street urchin peering into a sweet shop each time a man approaches her daughter? She's probably imagining their wedding day. How utterly desperate!'

A hand squeezed her shoulder. 'Violet…' Kate whispered. 'I'm sure they don't mean—'

'Me?' Violet pursed her lips together, resisting the urge to shrug off what Kate probably thought was a reassuring gesture.

The chatter continued. 'Apparently during the intermission at the opera she went on and on about whale oil.'

Now she was certain those women were talking about her. She recalled that conversation. She'd been talking with Lord Banks when he'd complained about his opera glasses being broken and she'd suggested he clean them with whale oil. Then she'd proceeded to tell him about how the oil was harvested, from the spermaceti organ, and the way sailors persevered it during the long months at sea.

'She spouted something about peacock feathers when we crossed paths at Hyde Park,' a new speaker said.

'Peacocks? Why would she say anything about that, Lady Helen?'

'Who knows? No wonder Ash thinks she's bizarre. The Bizarre Beauty,' she added with a sneer.

Ash.

The Marquess of Ashbrooke thought she was bizarre.

Despite his cold indifference to her, she could not help but still find him beautiful. Out of all the gentlemen she'd been introduced to, none could compare to him. She had decided that perhaps it was better just to admire him for his looks. He didn't care for her, so why should she care for him?

But hearing these words made something fierce pierce her chest.

Mad, he'd called her.

Strange.

And now bizarre too.

'Word about her has spread, and no man will even go near her,' Lady Helen guffawed.

'You mean, *you* helped spread the word?'

Lady Helen harrumphed. 'It's all true—and her continuing to act in such peculiar ways does not help her at all.'

'Such a waste, really. She is stunning. What I wouldn't give to have her complexion.'

'Or her eyes. Mine are just plain brown.'

'Mama says blondes are no longer in fashion. Do you think that's true, Lady Helen?'

'Blondes will always be in fashion,' she replied snidely. 'But odd girls who cannot fit into society will never be.'

Without a word, Violet took a step back, spun on her heel, then marched away from the door.

'What those women said...it simply isn't true,' Kate assured Violet as she walked beside her. 'I had a difficult time too, when I first came to London. I was too different. Too American.' She wrinkled her nose.

'But that's not the same, is it?' Violet stopped short and faced Kate. 'I'm not just different. I am *bizarre*.'

She could practically hear the Marquess's deep, rich voice uttering the word.

'No, you're not—'

'Yes, I am, Kate. Please, I thought we admired each other's candour. Except I am not just candid. I lack restraint and I simply cannot act normally.'

'Do not talk like that.' Kate placed her hands on her hips. 'Violet, you are brilliant and lovely, and if "normal" means you'd be just like all those snooty Englishwomen who acted like I was dirt under their heels when I first arrived here, then I'd rather have you abnormal.'

Abnormal.

Yes, that was what she was.

Bizarre.

Mad.

Not normal.

Never normal.

Kate's eyes widened. 'No, wait…that's not what I meant.' She clicked her tongue. 'And Ash… I can't believe he would say something like that. And in front of other people too. Perhaps they misheard him?'

Violet blinked as once again the puzzle pieces began to click into place.

Bizarre Beauty.

Click.

The Marquess had called her that and now everyone called her that.

Click.

Fifty-two events, twenty-three unmarried gentlemen, thirteen and a half dances.

Click.

Exactly zero prospects.

Click.

It was *him*.

Ashbrooke was the reason she had no suitors. Because of him she would be unable to save Oakwood Cottage and Papa's library.

A cold, silent rage rose up in Violet. Try as she might, she couldn't stop it. It was a like a wave, washing over her. Even her father's words rang hollow in her mind, unable to penetrate the fury wrapping around her.

'Violet? What are you— Where are you going?'

Her hands forming into fists, she spun on her heel and marched off, devouring the space between her and the balcony door across the room. Grabbing the handle, she flung it open.

'You!'

Ashbrooke and his companion—whose hair looked mysteriously dishevelled—jumped away from each other.

'What— Miss Avery…?'

The brunette shrieked. 'How *dare* you come out here?'

Ignoring the woman, Violet marched towards until she stood toe to toe with the Marquess. Craning her head back, she somehow found the resolve to look him straight in the eye.

'This is all your fault.'

'My fault?' He raised his palms. 'Whatever do you mean?'

'It's because of you that I don't have any suitors!' She poked him in the chest.

'I have no idea—'

'Violet? Where have you— Ash…?'

Violet spun her head and saw Kate in the doorway.

The Duchess gasped. 'What's going on here?' Her gaze darted from Ash, to Violet, then to the brunette. 'Ash, what in God's name are you doing out here?' Slamming the door behind her, she strode over to him. 'I can't believe you'd plan a tryst here, of all places.'

'The Spanish Ambassador's house is one of the best places to plan trysts,' he said casually. 'So many balconies.'

Kate narrowed her eyes at the brunette. 'Mrs Bancroft?'

It dawned on Violet why the woman seemed familiar. They'd been introduced the previous week at a charity function.

'Ah, I see you're already acquainted with Emma,' the Marquess said cheerfully. 'That should save me the awkward introductions.'

'Yes, we are acquainted indeed.' The Duchess's nostrils flared. 'We both attended that fundraising event for war widows. She was there—along with her husband. How *is* Mr Bancroft, by the way?'

The woman's face turned pale.

'Husband?' His expression shifted completely. It was like storm clouds swooping across a sunny sky. 'You're married?' His voice was measured and controlled, with a knife-like edge.

'M-my lord.' Mrs Bancroft let out a nervous laugh. 'This is merely a misunderstanding—'

'You lied to me.' His teeth ground together audibly. 'You said you were widowed.'

'Well, she was at a war widows' charity event,' Violet stated. 'Perhaps she was trying to imagine herself in their place.'

Ashbrooke's head snapped towards her, his sapphire eyes blazing.

Was he angry with her? When she was the injured party here?

Mrs Bancroft's face flushed. 'Miss Violet Avery,' she sneered. 'You truly are as ravishing as they say. I thought as much when we were introduced. And then you insulted our hostess by asking her to stop playing the pianoforte—in her own home.'

'She was a terrible piano player,' Violet stated. 'No sense of rhythm, and her fingers landed on the wrong key with every fifth note.'

'Everyone was talking about you afterwards—you and your desperate mother. I hear she's been flaunting you all about Town, trying to get you married off.' She clicked her tongue. 'It's such a tragedy that no man will come near you because you're truly…what do they call you? Ah, yes. The Bizarre Beauty.'

'Emma!' the Marquess barked.

The cold fury that had earlier fuelled Violet drained away as the other woman's words confirmed everything she had learned tonight. The entire Ton did, indeed, consider her a laughing stock. A mad, bizarre woman whom no man would ever want to marry.

Slowly, she turned to face Ashbrooke.

'I hate you.' Violet once again managed to look him straight in the eye. 'I hate you and I never want to see you again.'

An arm slipped around her shoulders. The unwelcome touch made her flinch, but the arm didn't move.

'Violet,' came Kate's soft voice. 'We should leave.'

'Kate—'

'Ash, for once in your life, keep your mouth shut,' the Duchess hissed.

'But—'

'Shush!'

Everything from that moment on passed in a blur for Violet. She had a vague memory of being led off the balcony, of people staring and whispering, and being whisked away to a carriage.

The one thing she knew she would never forget from that night was her feeling of loathing towards the Marquess of Ashbrooke. She had truly meant the words she'd thrown at him, and if she ever did see him again it would be far too soon.

Chapter Three

Ash had had some terrible evenings in his life, but tonight was undoubtedly the worst.

After he'd escaped the Spanish Ambassador's party, he quickly found his carriage. Upon reaching his home, he stormed in without even waiting for his butler, Hargrove, to open the door and then proceeded to his study to retrieve the bottle of aged Glenbaire Whisky he'd hidden under his desk. His best friend Cam, who owned the Glenbaire Whisky Distillery, had told him it was one of the finest bottles they had produced and to save it for a special occasion or—this added jokingly—for an emergency.

Well, if this wasn't an emergency Ash didn't know what was, so he uncapped the bottle, took a healthy swig, then collapsed on the leather chair behind the desk.

Christ Almighty.

The evening had begun smashingly enough. After days of heavy flirting and getting to know each other, he had set up a meeting with his potential new paramour at the Spanish Ambassador's party. Everything had been going splendidly, and he'd managed to find an empty balcony where they could continue their 'acquaintance'.

Then Miss Violet Avery had come along and it had turned into a disaster.

Ash took another gulp of the whisky, the smooth liquor sending a warm path to his gut. When they'd met at Covent Garden the week before, Emma Bancroft had told him she was a widow and that her husband had been gone five years now. There couldn't have been a misunderstanding, and nor did he misremember because, despite his appetites, there was one kind of woman he didn't touch—one line he did not cross.

Ash did not sleep with married women.

At least that was one consolation from tonight's debacle. Miss Violet Avery had saved him from breaking his own cardinal rule. He should thank her—except he would never get the chance.

'I hate you and I never want to see you again.'

Tossing his head back, he tipped the bottle up and allowed the liquid fire to burn his throat until his eyes watered.

'Blasted...hell,' he spat, slamming the bottle on top of his desk.

Slumping back in his seat, he blew out a breath.

What did I do to deserve this?

He'd never done anything to her—had barely interacted with her since that first night. After the champagne had been drunk at Ransom's New Year's Eve party he'd left right away.

But tonight, when she'd charged out onto the balcony, she had said something about her lack of suitors being his fault.

'How in blazes am I to blame for that?' he muttered.

But another more pressing thought niggled at him—how could she not have any suitors? Between her scheming and her good looks, surely by now she should have roped some poor, besotted fool into proposing? Were the men of London blind? The young, healthy bucks of the Ton should all be falling over themselves and elbowing each other to fawn over her—Miss Avery was gorgeous, after all. Even if her dowry was small, some rich old lord looking for a young, healthy third or fourth wife to parade on his arm should have snapped her up. Miss Avery's standards couldn't be that high, considering she was not wealthy nor the daughter of a peer.

A knot formed in his chest as he imagined her married to some man who probably wouldn't be able to appreciate her wit.

Shrugging, he put it out of his mind. In any case, it was not any of his concern—though the very thought of her in someone else's bed had him reaching for the bottle and chugging down another healthy measure of whisky.

Dong! Dong! Dong!

Ash glanced up at the grandfather clock as it chimed away the hour—midnight.

It was a new day.

His thirtieth birthday, to be precise.

He had hoped to ring in *his* new year between the sheets with the luscious Emma Bancroft.

Happy birthday to me.

Taking one last pull from the bottle, he leaned back, closed his eyes, intending to rest for a few minutes before he called his valet to help him prepare for bed…

'My lord!'

Ash shot up to his feet. 'What the blazes—' His head felt as if it had been split open with a dull axe, and he fell back onto his chair.

Chair?

Glancing around, he saw that he had, indeed, fallen asleep in his study. He dropped down again, closed his eyes, and reached back to massage his nape with his fingers.

That crick will be there all day.

'My lord?'

Bleary-eyed, he cracked an eye open. 'Yes, Hargrove?'

The white-haired butler was standing in the doorway, posture stiff as a board. 'My lord, you have guests.'

'Guests? Who?'

'I don't know all of them, my lord, but Mr Madison accompanied them here.'

'My solicitor?' What the devil was *he* doing here? 'Did he say what this is about?'

Hargrove shook his head. 'No, my lord. Only that it is of the utmost importance and that you must see them right away. Mr Madison said that I should haul you out of bed as if your life depended on it.'

Arthur Madison was a stodgy old chap who never minced words. Ash only saw him at most twice a year, so if he was knocking on his door this early it must truly be important.

With a frustrated groan, he hauled himself upright. 'Invite them into the parlour, then send Holmes to me with a strong pot of coffee.'

Thanks to the miraculous work of his valet, Holmes, Ash appeared presentable within fifteen minutes and found himself walking into the parlour just a short time after that.

'Good morning,' he greeted his guests.

Madison spoke first. 'My lord.' The solicitor's face was drawn into a grave expression as he stood up. 'Forgive me for imposing upon you at home at such an inconvenient hour. The Canfields and Mr Gallaway came to my office this morning with a concerning matter and I thought it best to come straight to you.'

'I see.' He glanced over at the other three occupants. 'Good morning.'

An older woman, perhaps in her late fifties or early sixties, sat in the middle of the settee. She was dressed in pink velvet and fur, with a garish feather hat on top of her head and several strands of pearls wound around her neck. To her right was a tall, skinny young man who was probably just out of university, wringing his hands in his lap, and across from them was a balding man in a flashy wine-red coat.

'My lord, allow me to introduce Mrs Alberta Canfield, her son Mr Richard Canfield, and their solicitor, Mr James Gallaway. Madam, sirs, this is Devon St James, Marquess of Ashbrooke.'

'Now, now, no need to be so formal.' Mrs Canfield rose up and walked over to him, then—to his utter surprise— enveloped him in a hug. 'After all, we're family.'

'Family?' Ash gently wriggled away from her embrace. 'I have no family. Only a distant relative who lives in Shropshire. My father's second cousin, twice removed.'

And the only reason he even knew about said cousin was because he would eventually inherit the marquessate, since Ash did not plan to marry.

'We're from a different branch of the family, my dear.' Mrs Canfield smirked. She turned to her solicitor. 'Mr Gallaway, if you please?'

The solicitor cleared his throat as he retrieved a sheaf of papers from his briefcase. 'My lord, are you aware of the marriage contract between your great-grandfather, the Third Marquess of Ashbrooke, and your great-grandmother, Mrs Hannah Canfield?'

'A contract three generations old? Why would I know of such a thing?' He looked to Madison. 'What is going on?'

His solicitor's bushy white brows drew together. 'Please keep listening, my lord.'

Gallaway continued. 'Allow me to give you a summary, my lord. Your great-grandfather signed a betrothal contract for his eldest son, your grandfather, to marry Hannah Canfield's daughter. Aside from a substantial sum of money, her dowry included all the lands around the marquessate seat, Chatsworth Manor. Upon their marriage, the original estate and the Canfield properties were joined together, and all of it now belongs to the marquessate, to be passed on to the eldest St James son.'

'Yes, that's generally how primogeniture works.' Ash could not help the sarcasm in his tone. The effects of the coffee he'd gulped down were beginning to wear off and the pounding in his temple had resumed. 'But I presume you're not here for a family history lesson?'

Mrs Canfield barked out a laugh. 'No, we are not. Go on then, Mr Gallaway.'

'Er…yes, of course, madam.' He waved the papers he had taken out from his briefcase. 'This is the Canfields' copy of the betrothal contract and the marriage certificate. You should also have one somewhere in your estate, or filed with whomever your great-grandfather's solicitors were at the time. In any case, there is an extra clause here, regarding the lands.'

'And what clause is that?'

'The lands that form the original estate may only be passed on to the first-born male heir, and each future marquess must produce a male heir by his thirty-first birthday. Otherwise, these lands will revert back to the Canfields.'

'I beg your pardon? Is this true?' Ash looked to Madison, who only nodded. 'It can't be. Who— Why would anyone add that clause and why would my great-grandfather agree to it?'

'Hannah Canfield was an eccentric old woman.' It was Mrs Alberta Canfield who answered. 'She grew up poor, scraping by for her entire life. However, after years of saving and scrimping, she and her husband were able to start their own cotton factory, where they made their fortune. Despite all their money, the Canfields were shut out by the hoity-toity people of the Ton, but Hannah was determined that her only daughter should have the respect and status she'd never had herself, so she married her off to the reputable but insolvent Marquess. However, Hannah didn't agree with the way inheritance favours only the male heir. So, to ensure the wealth and lands stayed in the Canfield family, she had that clause added. She didn't want some distant relation of the St James's to benefit from her hard work and sacrifice.'

'That's utter madness.' Ash rubbed a hand down his face. 'Why would she force members of my family to produce heirs?'

'No one's forcing anyone, are they?' Mrs Canfield pointed out. 'You're free to go about as you please—just not with Canfield money. Hannah wanted only those of her blood—' she looked meaningfully at her son '—to enjoy the fruits of her labour. Not some distant relations who have no connection to her.'

Ash turned to Madison. 'And how much of the estate would go to the Canfields?'

'Most of it.'

'Most? Meaning…?'

'All the income-generating portions, my lord. You would, of course, be left with the manor house and the gardens, as well as this townhouse.'

Dread pooled in his chest. Without the lands he would not have enough income for the upkeep of either home. Or himself. Whatever money he had would only last him a few years, and that was if he tightened his belt.

'Madison, is this legal?'

'I assure you, it is,' Gallaway interjected, then shoved the papers back in his briefcase. 'And might I remind you, my lord—with all due respect—that neither the Canfields nor I were legally required to inform you of this. Your great-grandfather should have taken the steps necessary to inform all future marquesses of this clause. Your own father should have told you.'

'Well, my father was busy dying when I was ten years old, so I'm afraid he didn't have the time.'

'My condolences.' He stood up, as did Mrs Canfield and her son. 'Thank you for your time, my lord. We shall see ourselves out.'

'And, happy birthday, my dear.' Mrs Canfield had the look of the proverbial cat that had got the cream. 'We will see you in a year. Come, Richard.' The man—boy, really—who had said nothing the entire time, sprang up like a trained puppy and followed his mother.

'Not legally required to inform me—like hell!' Ash exclaimed once he and his solicitor were alone. He kicked the closest thing he could reach—which was thankfully the padded armchair Gallaway had been sitting on. 'That woman has deliberately waited until the very last year to tell me of that clause! Madison, surely it isn't binding.'

'I'm afraid it is, my lord. I made sure to read every single line before coming here.' Madison clasped his hands together. 'If you want to keep the lands around Chatsworth, you must produce an heir within the next year.'

An heir.

Which meant he needed to get married.

For a moment Ash considered just letting that horrid woman and her milksop son take the lot. It would be worth it so that he didn't have to be shackled to some woman for the rest of his life.

'Damn.'

He kicked the armchair once more before sinking down on it. There had to be a way to get around the clause. But if Madison was correct, there might not be any legal way to do it.

Drumming his fingers on his knees, Ash considered his options.

'For heaven's sake, Ash, I'm leaving for my honeymoon in sixteen hours,' Ransom roared as he charged into Ash's study later that day. He hadn't even bothered to remove his hat and coat. 'What's this life and death situation? And if I miss my honeymoon, someone *will* be dead.' He eyed Ash, who sat behind his desk, menacingly.

Sebastian, who had already made himself comfortable on the chair in front of Ash's desk, gestured to the seat beside him, then poured some whisky into two glasses from a nearly empty bottle. 'Come and sit, Ransom. There's at least enough in here for both of us.'

Ransom plopped down. 'What's this all about?'

'A tragedy, my dear best friends.' Ash sighed exaggeratedly. 'I have the most distressing news.'

He then proceeded to tell them what had transpired that morning with the Canfields.

'And it's all binding?' Sebastian asked. 'There's no way around it?'

'Not according to Madison—though he said he would speak with his colleagues, along with a judge, to see if there's any loophole or legal manoeuvre to invalidate the clause.'

Ransom finished his half-measure of whisky. 'Then what do you need from us?'

'Moral support? Ideas? Someone to kick the stool from under my feet while I hang myself?' Leaning back on his chair, Ash massaged his temples with his fingers.

'Could you not purchase the lands?' Sebastian asked.

'I've already withdrawn all my income from last year, and most of it has been accounted for, with upkeep and salaries and whatnot.'

He'd had his man of business, Mr Bevis, come over that afternoon to explain his current financial standing. The situation was just as he'd thought—if he were to lose the lands he would be left without any means of income to support himself.

'You could get a job,' Ransom pointed out.

'A *what*?' Ash scoffed. 'Marquesses do not work.'

Both men rolled their eyes.

'I should have invested with you, Sebastian.'

The Duke had been in similar straits when his father had passed away, but through smart investments Sebastian had not only paid back his father's debtors but increased his wealth tenfold.

'All this wasted time...'

Ash was not the type to worry about the future. Indeed, as long as his tenants were comfortable and he had a healthy estate, that was all that mattered. He was used to being wealthy, to having his solicitor and his employees attend to the boring parts of life while he enjoyed the fruits of his lands. He hadn't expected a disaster such as this to strike.

'I don't see what the problem is,' Ransom said matter-of-factly. 'You have exactly one year to produce an heir. So...produce. You're very good at that, or so I've heard.'

Ash let out a breath. 'In case either of you did not re-alise it, to produce a legitimate heir there is another crucial step. Marriage.' The word left a bitter taste in his mouth.

'So?' Sebastian tutted. 'Every woman of marriageable age in London is after you. Choose any one of them. I'm sure many would be happy to marry you tomorrow if it meant becoming the Marchioness of Ashbrooke and bagging the most elusive bachelor in all of England.'

They made it sound so simple.

And yet it wasn't.

Not to Ash.

He closed his eyes as memory threatened to rise again.

But this time he allowed the scene in his mind to surface...

A vivid image of a beautiful summer day.

The swish of cotton and silk.

The slamming of the door.

'The witch is finally gone.'

The little boy—not little, not really, after all he was nine years old this year—turned around. *'Father?'*

His father stood at the top of the steps. His shirt was open at the throat, hair dishevelled, eyes red and wet. *'Your mama, Devon, has packed up and left us.'*

The boy turned back to the door. *'Mama...?'*

'Has left me—us—for her lover. Joining him on the Continent. She's going to his villa in Italy.'

'No! Mama!'

Mama wouldn't leave me.

He began to run towards the door.

Father moved down the steps, catching him just before he reached his destination.

'Stop this snivelling.' His hands gripped the boy's shoulders tightly. *'You are the future Marquess of Ashbrooke, and marquesses do not cry.'*

'But Mama...'

'She does not deserve any tears. From now on you must learn to live without your mama. You don't need her anyway,' Father sneered, looking towards the door. *'You don't need anyone, Devon.'*

'Ash? *Ash?*'

Ash jolted back into the present. 'Yes?'

'What are you going to do?' Sebastian clasped his hands together and rested his chin on his fingers.

'What the hell else?' He threw his hands up. 'Get married, I suppose. Produce an heir.'

'You know, just because you're married—'

'Doesn't mean I'll be able to produce a male heir?' Ash rose and walked over to the window, then stared out into the busy street. 'And I could be saddled with an unwanted wife for the rest of my life? I know that, of course, but what choice do I have?'

'You don't need anyone, Devon.'

The words had stuck in his mind. They had allowed him to become self-sufficient, even after Father's death a year later.

Ash didn't need anyone and certainly not a wife.

'Not all marriages have to be terrible,' Sebastian said in a quiet voice. 'Having a wife to love and to love you back might not be a bad thing.'

A shudder ran down Ash's spine. If Sebastian thought the idea of love would encourage Ash to marry he was dead wrong. It only accomplished the opposite. Love was even more dangerous than needing someone. His mother had loved his father, yet it hadn't been enough to stop his fits of jealousy that had eventually consumed their relationship and pushed her to have affairs. And his father had loved his mother so much that when she'd left it had destroyed him.

Ash had vowed never to make the same mistake.

'I'd rather have a wife who won't fall in love with me and with whom I will never fall in love.'

Never fall in love.

Never...

'That's it!' Ash spun around so fast he knocked over the bust of Shakespeare behind him, but caught it in time. 'Oops, my apologies, Will.' He replaced the Bard on his pedestal.

'What's "it"?' Ransom asked.

'If I must wed, then it must be to someone with whom I will never fall in love. Someone I don't particularly like, maybe am even repulsed by.' He stuck out his tongue. 'No, no, she needs to be pleasant enough if I must beget an heir. Young and healthy. Someone like...'

Well, truly there was only one person in his mind.

Perhaps she'd been lurking there all this time, ever since he'd found out about the clause.

Sebastian slapped his hand on the table to catch his attention. 'Someone like who?'

'Gentlemen, I know exactly whom I shall wed. Miss Violet Avery.'

'The Dowager's protégée?' said Ransom.

'Miss Avery?' Sebastian exclaimed at the same time, in a louder voice. 'You can't be serious, Ash.'

'I am. It's perfect. She's perfect.'

Miss Avery was looking for a husband and Ash was certain he would never fall in love with her.

'She's the one.'

'Aren't you forgetting something, Ash?' Sebastian narrowed his gaze at him. 'Last night? The Spanish Ambassador's party?'

'The what?' Ransom scrubbed a hand down his face. 'Ash, what have you done this time?'

Sebastian rolled his eyes and explained the events of the previous night to Ransom.

'Ash, you monster!' Ransom roared. 'Did you drag the

poor girl into scandal because you couldn't keep it in your trousers for one night?'

'Excuse me, I did not drag her into a scandal. And I certainly stayed within the confines of my trousers.' Ash pursed his lips together. 'Though apparently it's my fault the chit doesn't have any suitors. I don't even know why she would accuse me of such a thing.'

'I do,' Sebastian offered. 'Kate told me. She said you had started rumours about her and given her the nickname of the Bizarre Beauty. Now no man will go near her.'

'I did no such thing,' Ash retorted indignantly. Certainly he had not particularly enjoyed being deceived by her and her mother, but he couldn't care a whit who courted her. 'And nickname? Where would I come up with such...? *Oh.*'

Hyde Park.

Lady Helen.

Bizarre Beauty.

Unease crept across his chest. 'Oh, dear.'

'So it's true?' Sebastian's tone did not denote a question. He had obviously deduced the answer from the expression on Ash's face.

'Not on purpose.' *Hell.* No wonder she was furious. 'Of course, there is an upside to all this.'

'And that is?'

'I don't have any competition for the girl.'

'Thanks to your thoughtlessness.'

'I'll take that as a compliment.'

'It was not meant to be one,' Sebastian replied, exasperated.

Ash straightened his shoulders. 'In any case, it's the best solution.'

'She hates you, Ash,' Sebastian pointed out.

'You don't know that.'

'I was standing on that balcony. She said, and I quote, "I hate you and I never want to see you again."'

Ash waved a hand dismissively. 'Pish-posh…minor details.'

He was confident he could overcome this small matter—after all, he was Devon St James, Marquess of Ashbrooke. No woman could resist him. Besides, all they needed to do was marry and conceive, which he could accomplish quickly.

'Sebastian, are you headed back to Highfield Park?'

'Tomorrow, yes. Kate and the rest of the ladies left this morning, thanks to you and your antics. We'll be staying for at least a fortnight, or until the gossip dies down.'

'Excellent. Invite me to stay with you.'

'What? Why?'

'So I may woo Miss Avery, of course.'

'Kate will not allow it.' Sebastian folded his arms over his chest. 'She was there last night too, remember?'

'You're the Duke of Mabury—why would you allow your wife to dictate who can and cannot stay at your estate?'

'Ash…'

'Think of it as your birthday gift to me,' he pleaded. 'You've never given me one, ever, by the way.' Planting his hands on the table, he leaned forward. 'Besides, if I become destitute and lose my homes, you know you'll have to deal with me? I'll become your permanent house guest and sponge off you.' He grinned at Sebastian. 'For ever.'

Ransom smirked. 'Why don't you let him try, Sebastian? You're not forcing the girl to marry him. I almost wish I wasn't leaving for my honeymoon. I'd pay good money to watch you pursue a woman.'

'I suppose it would be an amusing sight.' Sebastian smiled wryly. 'I will not invite you to stay, as I already know Kate will never forgive me. However, I know better than to try and dissuade you, Ash. So, if you somehow find a way to invite yourself, I won't stop you.'

'Now I really am tempted to cancel my honeymoon.'

'What? Have you no faith in me?' Ash blew out a breath. 'Some best friends you are… Besides, the two of you have already done it. How hard could it possibly be to convince one woman to marry me?'

The two men looked at each other and laughed.

Chapter Four

Violet was deep into her calculations on the required boiler pressure for varying locomotive engines sizes when Mama burst into Kate's office.

'There you are.' Mama hurried to her side. 'It's nearly dinner time—hurry up...we must get you dressed.'

'Dinner?'

'Yes, dinner.' She tutted. 'What in the world are you doing here in the Duchess's private sitting room?'

Glancing down at the desk, Violet considered hiding the papers strewn about. Mama shouldn't find out what she was doing. But, then again, she didn't seem concerned about the scribblings. 'The Duchess is teaching me how to...' she scrambled to find something that would placate her mother '...to balance chicken accounts.'

'Chicken accounts?'

'*Kitchen*. I mean, kitchen accounts.'

Chickens were found in kitchens, weren't they? That sounded logical, at least to her ears.

'Oh, I see. How thoughtful of Her Grace to train you in such matters.' Mama clapped her hands together. 'Yes, soon you will be running your own household—perhaps even one as grand as this one. You must be prepared, so as not to disappoint your husband.'

'Of course, Mama.'

By some miracle, Lady Avery did not have any inkling about what had happened during the Spanish Ambassador's party. As Kate and the Duke had whisked Violet off, the quick-thinking Dowager had hidden Lady Avery away in her own carriage before whispers spread among the guests. They had further delayed any gossip from reaching her ears by fleeing to Highfield early the next day, citing the foul air in London as their primary reason for leaving.

As soon as they'd arrived, Violet had joined Kate in her office and immersed herself in her work.

It was the only way she could stop from thinking about *him*.

She couldn't even bear to say his name.

'Still, we must be off, child. Dinner is in one hour, and I cannot allow you to miss another one. I know you were feeling poorly after the long journey yesterday, but you must pull yourself together and make an appearance at dinner, lest we offend our hosts.'

Violet knew she could barricade herself in the office for ever and Kate and the Duke would never be offended, but she couldn't let Mama become suspicious. After all, she'd already made her decision. In between all the calculating and measuring, she had concluded that there was only one logical solution to her predicament: accept Kate's offer of a job to save herself and her mother from a life of genteel poverty.

But Mama couldn't know about her plan because Violet knew she would try to force her to marry. She might even attempt to take Violet away from Highfield Park, and then they truly would have no other option.

No, the only thing she could do was wait. Wait for their creditors to take hold of Oakwood Cottage, along with

Papa's books and other things. There was no denying it: her father's library was lost to her. The pain of it was indescribable, as if she was losing him once again.

'Violet,' Mama began again as she dragged her out of the office and towards their rooms. 'That new gown you were fitted for last week has just arrived. I cannot wait for you to wear it at your next ball. You do look so stunning in blue.'

Violet swallowed the lump in her throat as moisture formed on her palms. How she hated lying—and yet it was only now she understood that perhaps telling a few fibs was not a bad thing, especially if it meant protecting someone you loved.

So all she said was, 'Yes, Mama.'

After her bath, and half an hour of torture with dressing, and pulling hair and corset strings, Violet was finally ready, so she made her way down the main floor. Thankfully this was just the usual dinner with Kate and the Duke, and the staff at Highfield Park already knew how she liked her food prepared and her routines when dining. It would be a nice, quiet dinner with no surprises.

'My lord, you are here! I didn't know you were invited—what a wonderful surprise!'

Violet halted as she neared the bottom of the stairs. Who was Mama speaking to?

'Good evening, Lady Avery. Is that a new gown? It does suit your complexion. But then you are always the epitome of style and grace in any room.'

No.

'Oh…you flatter me, my lord.'

Violet shook her head.

No, no.

'Only because you deserve it.'

No, no, no.

Air rushed out of Violet's lungs.

Not him.

The need to flee was overwhelmed by shock, forcing her feet to stay in place. It was far too late, in any case, as the Marquess of Ashbrooke had stepped out of the doorway and into the main hall. His head immediately snapped up, and he flashed her a bright smile.

'Violet, look!' Mama yelped. 'The Marquess of Ashbrooke is here.'

'Miss Avery.' He bowed his head. 'Good evening to you.'

She stared at him, unable to speak or to move. What was he doing here? Had Kate and the Duke invited him? After what had happened?

'Child, don't just stand there.' Mama laughed nervously. 'Come down and greet His Lordship.'

Fearing her mother would drag her down by force otherwise, Violet pushed herself to walk down, taking each step slowly and deliberately, as if delaying the inevitable.

'My lord,' she managed to murmur, lowering her gaze.

'Miss Avery, you're as lovely as the day.' His smile did not waver. 'I'm happy to see you.'

Violet jerked her head up. The crinkles at the corners of his eyes told her the smile was genuine. But why was he here?

'Will you be joining us for dinner?' Mama enquired.

'Oh, is it dinnertime?' Ashbrooke turned to the butler, Eames.

'Yes, my lord. His Grace and the Duchess are already in the dining room.'

'What are you doing here?' Violet asked, finally finding her voice.

'Don't be rude, Violet,' Mama said.

'It's quite all right, Lady Avery.' He grinned at her. 'I'm

afraid a tragedy has befallen me. My carriage has broken down, you see. My coachman has said we will not be able to find a replacement, and it was getting dark, so I took one of the horses to find an inn for the evening. But then I remembered that my best friend the Duke of Mabury's home was only five miles down the road, so I thought I would come here instead.'

'How fortunate.' Mama sighed. 'And it's a good thing too, as you could have been set upon by bandits at this hour.'

He would have deserved it, Violet sulked silently.

'So, Eames, do you think I could impose upon you for dinner? I hate to disrupt your carefully planned meals...'

'Not all, my lord. Please follow me and I'll announce—'

'No, need.' The Marquess waved a hand. 'I shall announce myself.'

'Very well, my lord. I'll instruct Chef Pierre to prepare for an additional diner.'

'Lady Avery... Miss Avery...' Ashbrooke offered them one arm each. 'Shall we?'

'Yes, my lord!' Mama tittered. 'Violet?'

Violet would have rather cut off her own hand than touch him.

'Violet.'

Defeated, she gingerly placed a hand over his arm and allowed him to lead them to the dining room. She continued to fume as they entered.

'Lady Avery, we were just— Ash?' Kate's lips pressed together tightly as her gaze landed on the Marquess, then she turned to her husband. 'Sebastian, what is he doing here?'

The Duke leaned back in his chair. 'I'd love to hear an explanation too.'

'Ah, Kate, Sebastian...good evening to you too,' Ashbrooke said. 'Well, you see there has been an unfortunate incident.' He went on and explained the situation with his carriage. 'And now I must impose upon you for the evening. I hope you don't mind? Seeing as we're friends and such. You wouldn't want me to ride back to London on my own. I could be set upon by bandits.'

'Oh, you really could,' Lady Avery added.

The Duchess's nostrils flared, but she remained silent.

'I suppose it's just for one night.' The Duke motioned for one of the footmen to add a setting for Ashbrooke, which unfortunately meant he was placed beside Violet.

'Thank you.'

Everyone sat down to dinner, and the footmen brought in their first course.

'I always look forward to meals at Highfield Park.' Ashbrooke took a spoonful of the soup. 'Ah…my compliments to Chef Pierre. Miss Avery, are you not hungry?'

Violet had kept her hands under the table as she continued to touch her fingers to her thumbs one by one. 'What part of your carriage had broken?'

'I beg your pardon.'

She turned her head to face him. 'What. Part.' She could feel Mama's stare burning into her, but she ignored it.

Ashbrooke's eyes widened. 'You know…the thing…'

'What thing?'

'The *thing*.'

She straightened up and placed her hands on the table. 'The axle?'

'Yes, exactly that.'

'Which one?'

'Which what?'

'Which axle?' She narrowed her gaze at him. 'The topside or downside?'

'The downside.'

He said it with so much confidence that Violet might have believed him—if she hadn't known there was no such thing as a downside or an upside axle.

'Tell me, Ash,' the Duchess began, eyeing him. 'What business brings you to Surrey in the first place?'

'The smog in London was getting far too thick. I needed some fresh country air,' he replied cheerfully.

'Thirty miles from London? Surely there are places much closer...like Stratford?'

'It's a very thick smog, Kate.'

'That's why we left,' Lady Avery informed him. 'All that smoke was making Her Grace ill.'

'Ah, I see we are of the same mind, Kate.' Ashbrooke winked at her.

Violet gripped the edge of the table so hard her knuckles turned white. She would rather die than have to exist in the same space as him. Her fury from the other night began to build in her, and she opened her mouth to tell him to leave, but Mama interrupted.

'How wonderful it would be if you could stay,' Lady Avery fawned. 'Isn't that true, Your Grace? I'm sure you will very much enjoy the Marquess's company, seeing as you are best friends.'

Ashbrooke raised his wine glass to the Duke. 'The very best.'

Drat.

Violet couldn't very well tell Ashbrooke off—even if the oaf deserved it. It would be rude to shout at a guest in the Duke's own home. Besides, if Mama found out the reason she abhorred the Marquess, she would also eventually discover Violet's plan to work at the factory with Kate.

So she would have to stay silent, at least for now.

Besides, he couldn't stay here for ever, could he?

Chapter Five

'I think it went well,' Ash said to Sebastian as they enjoyed their after-dinner cigars and port in the library.

'The girl hardly spoke to you, and when she did she interrogated you and caught you in a lie.' Sebastian sat down on the wingback chair by the fireplace. 'Only you would think this evening has gone "well".'

'I can always chalk it up to the fact that I don't know a damn thing about axles.' She was smart—he had to give her that. 'And now I have an excuse to stay here for a few days.'

'A few days? Ash, you do know we have at least three carriages that could take you back to London.'

'And? Just say all your coachmen are indisposed.'

'So now I'll have to lie to my wife about why I can't send you packing in the morning?'

'It's not a lie… You're just withholding the truth from her for a little bit.'

'That's the same, Ash.' Sebastian shook his head.

'If it makes you feel any better, you may tell her the truth of why I'm here.'

'Because you wish to force her friend into marriage after you destroyed her reputation?'

'When you put it that way…' Ash took a seat opposite him. 'But I'm running out of time, Sebastian. With each day that passes, the possibility of that horrid woman and her son taking my lands and impoverishing me increases. Besides, it's not like I'm some fortune-hunter, trying to get my hands on Miss Avery's dowry. In fact, with this marriage, I'll be elevating her status and making her into a wealthy woman.'

'If you produce an heir.'

'Which I will. But you must help me now.'

'If Kate demands an explanation of why I'm letting you stay, I won't lie to her.'

'In the first place, the decision will be Miss Avery's,' Ash pointed out. 'I plan to ask her to marry me, and if she rejects my proposal then I'll leave and find someone else.'

His gut twisted at the thought.

'Promise me you'll court her properly and you won't force or trick her. And if she says no, you will leave her be.'

Ash sniffed, indignant. 'I do not force or trick women. I promise you, if she accepts, it will be of her own free will.'

Sebastian finished off his port. 'Then I suggest you work as fast as you can.'

Ash took Sebastian's words to heart. The following day he avoided the breakfast table and skulked around the manor—lest he run into Kate and receive an ear-bashing—then went in search of Miss Avery.

That, however, proved to be a monumental task in itself, as no one could seem to find her. According to Eames, Lady Avery was feeling tired and had retired to her room, but as far as he knew Miss Avery had not followed suit. He checked the sitting room, the library, the morning room, the drawing room, the gardens and even the orangery—still no Miss Avery. He supposed he could find out where her bedroom was and seek her out, but he had promised Sebastian he'd be on his best behaviour.

'You,' he called to passing footman as he found himself circling back to the hall for the third time. 'Have you seen Miss Avery?'

'Miss Avery?'

'Yes—you know. His Grace's guest. There can't be many young unmarried women scurrying about here, can there?'

'I…er…' The young man gulped. 'I think I've seen her.'

'Where?'

'Her Grace's office?'

'Are you asking me or telling me?'

'T-telling you, milord. I mean, yes… I believe that's where she is. I heard the maids say they were bringing her tea.'

'Excellent. Show me.'

Ash followed the footman as he led him to a room on the east side of the manor. It could only be accessed through the drawing room, which was why he'd missed it.

'Thank you,' he said, dismissing the footman.

Once he was alone, he raised his hand to knock at the door, but stopped.

What should he say to her?

It hadn't occurred to him to prepare a speech, but there was no time to sit down and outline a plan now. Should he declare his intentions?

No, that would scare her off.

Besides, if last night was any indication, she was still miffed about the whole Bizarre Beauty thing.

He had never proposed to a woman—propositioned them, yes, but never actually offered marriage. For a moment he thought to forget the whole thing altogether, but then he reminded himself that he was not built for poverty.

Screwing up his courage, he knocked on the door. No one answered, so he rapped his knuckles on the wood once again, this time much harder.

There was a pause before a familiar husky voice said, 'Who is it?'

'It's me. I mean, Devon. Er… Ashbrooke.'

Lord, he sounded like a fool. But for some reason his heart raced like a thoroughbred at Royal Ascot.

'Go away!' came the muffled reply.

'Can I come—'

'I said, go away.' Loud footsteps told him that she was coming towards the door. 'And don't come back.'

'Miss Avery, I only want to speak—'

'No, I am not speaking with you. Besides, I'm alone in here and we have no chaperon. It's not proper.'

Ash thought that sounded like a great idea—if they were discovered then they'd be forced to marry—but then he recalled his promise to Sebastian.

Damn.

'I only want to—'

'No!'

It was obvious that unless he barged in he would not be able to coax her out of the room. So he decided to change his tactics.

'Perhaps I will fetch Lady Avery? Then she could chaperon us.'

'You wouldn't dare.'

Ah, so she didn't want her mother around. He had to admit charming the older woman had been much easier, and he knew she would be on his side once he'd pleaded his case to Violet.

'She did seem genuinely happy to see me here. Let me fetch—'

'No!' The door was flung open. 'Do not fetch my mother.'

Once again, blood roared in his ears and his heart careered into his ribcage at the sight of her. She looked especially ravishing this morning, in a light blue gown that matched her eyes. Her cheeks were flushed pink, and a long sable lock had loosened from the knot in her hair and now curled over the low neckline that revealed the tops of her bosom, as her shawl had loosened and fallen away.

'What do you want?'

The low, husky tone of her voice sent a sharp rush of desire though his body. 'Huh…?'

'I said, what do you want?'

He could only think of one thing he wanted right at this moment. 'Um… A walk in the orangery. With you.'

'And then you will leave me alone?'

'Yes.'

At least he would until luncheon, at least.

The door slammed in his face, but moments later it opened again and—much to his disappointment—he saw she'd secured the shawl around her shoulders and swept up a stray curl back into the knot and under a warm hat.

'Let's go.'

'Where is your cape?'

'No need.'

She marched through the parlour and down the corridor to the glass doors that led out into the garden. Once they were on the path, he caught up with her.

'What a lovely winter day—'

Miss Avery continued on, blazing through the hedgerows like a soldier on the warpath, moving towards the brick and glass building at the top of the garden. Warm, humid air greeted them as they stepped inside, and exotic plants surrounded them, bringing them into a lush, tropical garden. However, they barely had time to enjoy the greenery as she stamped down the tiled path, crossed over to where a beautiful fountain stood in the middle, circled around, then brushed past him.

Blowing out an exasperated breath, he followed her as she left the orangery. The blast of cold air slapped his face. She was already halfway back through the garden.

How the devil did she move so fast?

He ran across the garden, catching up with her again as she re-entered the manor. 'Miss Avery!'

She continued on, stopping only once she had reached the door outside Kate's office.

'You walk fast for a woman,' he commented as he caught up with her. 'Wait, please,' he said as she put her hand on the door. 'Just one moment, Miss Avery.'

Blowing out a breath, she spun to face him. 'What do you want, my lord? Why are you here? And please do not insult my intelligence by repeating that story about your carriage—we both know there is no such thing as a downside axle.'

She refused to meet his gaze straight on, but he didn't need to look into her eyes to know that she was deadly serious. And so, having no plan or strategy in place, he decided on the one thing he hadn't tried yet: the truth.

'Miss Avery, I would like to court you.'

'I beg your pardon?' She inhaled deeply. 'No, you're lying...this is a cruel joke.'

'It's not. And I'm not lying—well, I am. I don't want to court you. I want to marry you. And—'

The door slammed in his face.

Ever the optimist, he thought to himself, *It could have gone worse.* Besides, she hadn't said she *wouldn't* marry him. As far as he was concerned, as long as the word *no* did not leave her lips, he could continue his pursuit without breaking his promise to Sebastian.

Still, wooing Miss Avery was proving to be a more challenging task than he'd anticipated. And time was running out. Even if they married at the end of the week, and conceived on their wedding night, it would take another nine months for an heir to be born. There was scarce room for error, and there would be no second chances. He would have to find a way to woo her—and quickly.

I must intensify my efforts.

Yes, that was it. His gestures needed to be grander and more opulent, to show her that he was being serious about courting her.

Ash didn't believe in miracles but, considering what he had accomplished in a single day, he could, in fact, categorise what he'd achieved as miraculous.

'Is everything set?' he asked Holmes as he looked around the ballroom.

'Yes, my lord.'

His valet had worked all night, then travelled from London to help him put together his grand proposal for Miss Avery. After his 'walk' with her yesterday, he'd sat down and devised a plan, written down everything he required and paid someone from the nearby village to rush the letter to his staff back in town. Sure enough, by noon, everything—and everyone—was in place.

He just needed to lure Miss Avery out of that damned room.

Ash hadn't seen her since she'd slammed the door in his face. She hadn't shown herself at dinner, and when he'd enquired about her Lady Avery had said Violet was at the dower house, as the Dowager was feeling under the weather but didn't want to dine alone. Kate, on the other hand, had looked ready to skewer him with the knife and fork in her hand. Obviously she had heard about his plan to marry Miss Avery, and possibly his failed proposal.

Ash had spent the night with a chair propped against his door.

'All right, Holmes, wait here. As soon as she's inside—' he pointed to the main doors leading into the ballroom '—I want everyone to start right away.'

'Yes, my lord.'

'Excellent. I shall fetch Miss Avery now.'

Ash had barely stepped out of the ballroom when he saw Sebastian marching towards him.

'What in the world is going on, Ash?' Sebastian's dark eyebrows slashed downward. 'Eames says you have had the ballroom—*my* ballroom—locked up and forbidden any of my staff from entering this entire wing?'

'And a good day to you too,' Ash greeted him. 'Don't worry, I just need your ballroom for…oh, the next fifteen minutes or so. Then I'll be out of your hair.'

Sebastian blocked his way. 'Ash, Kate informs me that Miss Avery has told her that you proposed yesterday. You promised me you would leave her alone if she refused your suit.'

'But she didn't refuse it.'

He blocked Ash once more when he tried to sidestep him. 'Yes, she did, otherwise Lady Avery would be shouting from the rooftops with joy.'

'Miss Avery didn't say no. I didn't hear the word.'

'Ash, you need to stop the wooing.'

'I swear to you she didn't reject me. Yes, she slammed the door in my face, but until I hear her say *I don't want to marry you* then the wooing shall continue.'

'Ash, she doesn't want you. Accept it.'

Damn Sebastian. But, then again, perhaps his friend was

right. Miss Avery didn't want to marry him. There were dozens of girls who would say yes to his proposal in a heart-beat. He should leave now and stop pursuing Miss Avery.

But for some reason he just couldn't.

With a determined shrug, he feigned a step to the right, prompting the Duke to obstruct him, then quickly moved around Sebastian's left side to escape.

Sebastian let out a furious grunt when he realised he'd been fooled, but it was too late as Ash sprinted away.

'Besides,' he called back, 'the jugglers have already been paid!'

'Jugglers? What jugglers? Ash!'

Chapter Six

Violet had re-read the formula exactly twenty-three times and she still couldn't process it. *L equals the length of the stroke in inches... D equals the diameter of the driving wheels in inches...* How could she focus when a single sentence continued to intrude into her thoughts?

'I want to marry you.'

Slamming the book closed, she knocked her forehead on the cover three times, then let out a groan.

It didn't make sense. Nothing made sense any more. But, then again, ever since she'd met the Marquess of Ashbrooke logic and her life had become incompatible.

I wish everything would go back to the way it was.

That, however, made even less sense. Time moved forward, not backwards. Things couldn't go back to the way they had been.

Pushing herself away from the book, Violet sat up straight. This was all a joke—because how could Ashbrooke change his mind so quickly? He hadn't been able to stand the sight of her all the way up to New Year's Eve and now he wanted to marry her? Was he ill in the mind? Or did he perhaps have a head injury? She recalled reading an article in one of her father's journals about men returning from the war with Napoleon who had suffered head trauma and whose personalities had completely changed. However, as far as she knew, the Marquess hadn't participated in any battles between New Year's Day and today.

A knock at the door shook her out of her thoughts. 'Who is it?'

No answer.

'Who is it?' she called, a little louder this time.

Violet drummed her fingers on top of the desk. Who could be knocking and why weren't they answering?

Rising to her feet, she cautiously crept towards the door. 'Who's out there?'

Still no answer.

Oh, it must be that new maid.

Yesterday, Violet had rung for a pot of tea. However, she'd been so caught up in her work that she'd failed to hear the knock on the door. The poor thing had been so painfully shy that she'd stood outside the door with the tray for thirty minutes, until Violet had got up to check that the kitchens had received her request.

Shrugging, she opened the door—but there was no one there.

She was about to close the door when she noticed a slip of paper on the floor. Glancing around, she bent down and picked it up, then unfolded it.

Come to the ballroom.

'The ballroom?' she said aloud.

Who would send her such a note? She flipped the paper over but found no other writing. Was it Kate?

The Duchess had been furious when Violet had told her about Ashbrooke's sudden proposal. 'You don't have to see him again,' Kate had promised, and had then made an excuse for her so she could stay in her rooms during dinner. When she hadn't found him at breakfast this morning, she'd breathed a sigh of relief. Kate had not appeared either, but the Duke had told her she was feeling ill and was still in bed.

Perhaps she had recovered and was up and about?

So Violet made her way to the ballroom.

She knocked before opening the door. 'Hello? Kate?' When no one answered, she waited a few seconds before turning the handle. 'Kate, are you in here?' she called as she entered.

The room was empty and silent, but there was something not quite right. For one thing, an enormous curtain had been drawn across the room, effectively halving the space and blocking out the light from the windows.

What on earth—

The curtain dropped to the floor, revealing a horde of people on the other side.

But they weren't just ordinary people.

A small orchestra began to play the overture to *The Marriage of Figaro*, and the blast of trumpets and drums and scurrying violins and flutes sent an unpleasant jolt of shock through her body.

Then groups of dancers filed in through the door, surrounding her. Their colourful bejewelled costumes bombarded her vision along with their frenzied, frantic movements.

Her palms began to sweat at the overwhelming display, but she somehow found the will to weave through the dancers and find a route of escape. However, as soon as she escaped that circle of hell something else exploded from one side, nearly jolting her out of her own skin.

Were those men blasting fire from their mouths?

Violet raised a hand to block out the blaze and prevent it from burning her eyes. All the sights and sounds were proving too much. Terror and panic overwhelmed her and her heart hammered in her chest. An acrid, burning sensation rose up her throat as her stomach turned, threatening to expel that morning's breakfast.

Slowly, she took deep breaths as she methodically touched her thumbs to each finger, counting from one to ten repeatedly. The harsh, abrasive sensations receded and her breathing evened. However, all her progress was lost as a horrid squawk blared into her ears.

Was that a—

Squawk! Squawk!

She could only stare as the gigantic bird—a peacock—spread its magnificent tail. But that only proved to be a momentary distraction as four jugglers began to descend towards her.

The noise and the spectacle crescendoed, but time seemed to stand still. Her body swayed as the ringing in her ears made it difficult to find her balance. Despite the cacophony, she heard a distinct male voice behind her. She managed to swing around.

'Miss Avery,' Ashbrooke began, reaching out to her. 'Will you do me the honour of becoming my wife?'

Violet opened her mouth, but nothing came out, and Ashbrooke's handsome face swam before her eyes as her vision darkened. Her chest constricted, making it difficult to breathe. Her attempt to inhale some air only seemed to make it worse.

'What the blazes is— Violet!'

Someone caught her as she toppled forward.

'Violet—dear God!' Kate cried. 'Violet, what's wrong? What do you need?'

'Need...to...leave...'

Without another word, the Duchess put an arm under her and hauled her out of the ballroom, away from the insanity of the Marquess of Ashbrooke's circus.

'What the blazes were you thinking, Ash?' Kate berated Ash once she'd found him hiding out in Sebastian's study.

'I wanted to give her a proposal she couldn't ignore and show her how serious I am,' he retorted.

'Well, she received your message—and now you need to leave.'

'But she didn't say no.'

Kate's nostrils flared as she sent him a death glare. 'That's because you nearly killed her, you imbecile. Not to mention you woke Henry from his nap with that commotion.'

'I'm sorry for waking my godson.' Ash cowered away. 'Is she...all right?'

His heart had dropped when he'd seen the abject terror on Miss Avery's face. It was at that moment he'd known he had made a terrible mistake.

'No thanks to you.'

'May I see her?'

'Absolutely not.'

Ash swallowed the lump in his throat. 'I'm sorry. I truly am.'

How had he been supposed to know his grand gesture would send Miss Avery for her smelling salts? She didn't seem the type to have a weak constitution. But he supposed the peacocks had been a bit much.

'Ash, there are about a hundred women back in London who would be willing to marry you. Why are you pursuing Violet when she clearly wants nothing to do with you?

Is it guilt? Because you think it's your fault no man will marry her? And now you're giving her a pity proposal?'

Ash hadn't even thought of that. It would have saved him the trouble of hiding his real reason for proposing to Miss Avery from Kate.

'That was hardly a pity proposal, Kate. I brought in fire eaters, for goodness' sake. Do you know how difficult it is to find them in the winter? Poor Holmes must have roamed half of London searching for them.'

'You thick-headed buffoon.' Kate threw her hands up in the air. 'She doesn't need your proposal. She doesn't need *you*.'

For some reason the words hit their mark like an arrow, right in the chest.

'My love,' said Sebastian, wrapping an arm around his wife's shoulders. 'Would you mind giving us some privacy? I'd like to speak with Ash alone.'

Kate crossed her arms under her chest and huffed. 'Fine. I'll check on Henry.'

While she accepted Sebastian's kiss on her temple, she glared at Ash before marching out.

'You idiot!' Sebastian bellowed. 'Give me one good reason why I shouldn't toss you out right now.'

'I haven't broken my promise, Sebastian. She still hasn't said no. Perhaps I went overboard and—'

'Overboard? You capsized the entire boat!' Sebastian rubbed a palm down his face. 'Have you thought about perhaps considering *her* wants? Finding out what she wants in a husband and in a marriage so you may appear more amenable to her?'

'Amenable to her? I'm rich and titled—what more could she want?'

Sebastian clicked his tongue. 'All your experience with

women and you haven't learned a thing. Ash, for once in your life, use the intelligence that I know you possess. If you can't figure out how to make her accept your proposal, then you don't deserve her. Have a think. I'm giving you one last chance, but after this I'm afraid I'm going to have to ask you to leave Miss Avery alone.'

And with that, he left.

Ash placed his hands on his hips and expelled a breath. It was obvious his usual tactics for pursuing a woman— dazzling them with his wit and charm—weren't working. Perhaps Kate was right. He should just give up.

'Never,' he said aloud.

He was the Marquess of Ashbrooke. Renowned rake and seducer of women. He was not admitting defeat so easily.

But how the hell could he figure out what Miss Avery wanted in a husband when he couldn't even get her to speak with him? And even if he did, it wasn't as if he could ask her outright.

He had to find a way to learn more about her.

An idea struck him.

'Ah!'

It was underhand and unethical—so it just might work.

Chapter Seven

Miss Avery had stayed abed the whole day and night after the proposal debacle, but the moment she was feeling well enough to leave her room Ash sprang into action. Thanks to a few well-placed bribes amongst the Highfield Park staff, he knew exactly where she and Kate were throughout the day. He saw his chance when a footman informed him that Miss Avery was scheduled to leave with the Duchess to visit the village. Knowing the two women would be gone for the day, he made his way to the east wing and let himself into Kate's office.

The Duchess would truly kill him if she found him there, so it was a good thing Ash had no plans for getting caught.

Ash crept inside, then made a quick assessment of the room. It looked as if it had been a ladies' sitting room at some point, with light pastel pink wallpaper, lace curtains, and cosy, plush furniture, but all the comfortable chairs had been pushed to one side. Instead a large oak desk and a drafting table dominated the middle of the room.

Curious, he circled around the table to the front, where various sheets of papers were stuck to the top. Leaning forward, he attempted to read what was on them, but there were no words—or at least not in English. There were numbers and symbols written in clear handwriting, seemingly in some semblance of order that Ash could not decipher. But what were they?

He was about to pluck one from the table for a closer look when he heard the noisy squeak of the door handle as it was turned.

Damn!

Panicked, he dived towards the curtains and managed to hide behind them just as the doors flew open. He pressed his body against the window, ignoring the cold draught filtering through the cracks and through his thin shirt.

I should have worn my coat.

'It's a pity the poor road conditions forced us to turn back,' Kate said. 'I was looking forward to showing you the White Horse Inn Brewery.'

'And I was looking forward to seeing it,' Miss Avery replied, then she shuddered. 'Brr... I am glad to be inside. The cold is brutal today.'

Ash swallowed the panic building inside him as Miss Avery walked towards him. She drew the drapes on the other side to slide them closed, coming but mere inches from him.

She's going to find me. Then I'll be dead.

'There, that should keep out the draught.'

He relaxed once she'd walked away.

'At least we can finally finish our work,' she continued. 'I'm sorry for the delay, Kate. I promise I'll work on those figures for you today.'

Work?

What kind of work was she talking about? Did it have anything to do with those papers on the drafting table?

'Oh, pish-posh, you've only just recovered from your fainting spell.' Kate paused. 'Are you sure you're well enough to be up and about?'

'I told you. I'm fine. It's just something that...happens.

Too much noise or fast movements and colours around me seem to trigger these spells.'

Ash, you idiot.

He smacked himself on the head silently. Somehow he'd managed to find all the things that made her ill and put them together in one space. No wonder the poor girl had been sent to her sickbed.

'I've learned to cope with it over the years,' she continued. 'Small gatherings, parties, and even balls are not so bothersome, although I often need a day or two to recover from them, but I haven't had an episode like that since I was a child. The ballroom…it was just too much.'

Kate harrumphed. '"Too much" is the very definition of Ash— Oh, apologies. I shouldn't have mentioned his name.'

'It's all right, Kate.'

'I should have asked him to leave the moment he arrived. I knew he was lying, of course, but I swear I was as surprised as you when he came.'

'I believe you. And, really, he is the Duke's friend and this is his home. You couldn't have asked him to leave— not if your husband wanted him here.'

The Duchess huffed. 'Believe me, we are still having that conversation…'

'I did have something I wanted to tell you, Kate. I've decided to accept your offer.'

'Really? That's wonderful. Oh, we'll make so much progress now. But wait—is this because of Ash? Because of what he said and did?'

'No… I mean, yes.' She sighed. 'The truth is, I would never have attracted any suitor nor made any kind of match in the first place. Why would any man want to marry someone like me? Ashbrooke only verbalised what everyone else would have found out—that I'm bizarre. Too odd. Too broken.'

Indignation—and shame—rose in Ash at those words. Despite the fact that he hadn't mean to call her bizarre in a disparaging way, it was still his fault.

'Don't say that, Violet.'

'It's true, Kate. Oakwood Cottage and the library were lost the moment Papa died and it was left for me to save it through marriage. I've come to accept it. It's all right, really.'

Ash froze at the words.

So that's why she needs to marry.

Her father's death had left them destitute. She needed a rich husband to save them from poverty.

'No. No, it's not. Oakwood Cottage was your home and your papa's library was your solace. If anyone can understand what you are going through, it's me. Whenever I work with engines I feel like my grandfather is alive again and that he's here with me. And when I thought I was losing my freedom to work and my factory it was as if he was dying once more. For you to lose the one place that meant so much to you and to him—it must feel like you're losing your father all over again.'

A dead silence filled the air.

'But at least with your offer of a job Mama and I won't be penniless.'

'I'm so glad you've accepted. You truly are gifted with numbers. I've never seen anything quite like it. And with you as my chief mathematician I'll be able to shorten my timeline for creating new designs and increase efficiency at the factory. I have so many ideas for us to try.'

'I cannot wait. Now I only have to convince my mother. I fear she'll never agree to it.' Miss Avery let out another shiver. 'The fire's gone out.'

'I've instructed the maids not to enter this room unless one of us is around, so no one has come to stoke the fire. Why don't we go to the library for some tea? We can celebrate your new position. But let's stop by the nursery first. I should check on Henry.'

Ash held his breath, waiting until he heard the sound of the door clicking shut before he expelled it. Pushing the curtains aside, he stumbled out from his hiding place. A dizzying sensation threatened to overcome him, so he braced himself against the drafting table. Once the feeling passed, he lifted his head and focused on the neat writing on the paper.

Her handwriting.

This was all Miss Avery's work.

In an instant, he saw the symbols and numbers in a different light. Reaching out, he dragged a fingertip across a line of equations. The beauty and the wealth of knowledge in her mind was in these pages. He couldn't decipher any of it, but now he did understand her.

Miss Avery—Violet—had a logical mind for mathematics. And if Kate—who was quite intelligent herself—said that she was gifted, then Violet must truly be beyond brilliant.

Ash had once had an instructor at university like her— Professor Halston. He'd been a mad old bat, set in his ways, and had liked order and routine. Normally quiet and unassuming, he'd once thrown a book at a student who was tapping his pen on a table. In one instance a few students who'd hated him had chased him around with Roman candles; he'd been absent for an entire week.

Halston had been truly unlike any of his other professors. He had not succumbed to Ash's cajoling or flattery when he'd needed better marks or extra points in his exams.

No, Professor Halston's mind could only be changed with logic and reason.

So, that was how Ash would formulate his next and hopefully final proposal. This time, it wouldn't take him much time or effort to put it together. No, he didn't need pomp and ceremony for this one. He just needed to get Violet alone.

So he implored Sebastian to help him once again, promising that if she rejected him he would leave her alone.

Early the next day Ash headed to the orangery and waited by the fountain. Fishing out his pocket watch, he kept his eye on the time, as he knew Sebastian would be punctual. Sure enough, at eleven fifty-eight, he heard voices and footsteps coming towards them. Ash strained to hear the conversation.

'Such a marvel,' Lady Avery gasped. 'It's like summer in here.'

'There is a boiler underneath us that produces steam and filters it out through the vents,' Sebastian explained.

'I should like to see that,' Violet said.

'Perhaps Kate could show you some time.' The footsteps halted. 'Oh, dear.'

'Your Grace? What's wrong?'

'Lady Avery… I feel incredibly foolish.'

'Foolish?'

'Yes. My wife is with Henry as he's been crying all morning. She thinks he might be ill and has asked me to retrieve… Oh, dear, I can't remember it. Something to help soothe Henry. I was supposed to ask the kitchen to prepare it.'

'Oh, goodness.' Lady Avery's hand covered her chest. 'Did she ask for a poultice of some sort?'

'Yes—exactly. I should have known you'd understand.

You are a mother, after all.' Sebastian tsked. 'I feel so very terrible, not knowing about such things.'

'You are a man, Your Grace, you are not expected to know about these things.'

'Lady Avery, I don't suppose you are knowledgeable about poultices?'

'I... Well, I do recall one that I used for Violet when she was an infant.'

'Lady Avery, could I impose upon you...?'

'Not an imposition at all, Your Grace. It would be an honour. Come, let's go back to the kitchens. Violet, could you—'

'Surely we don't all need to go? I mean, kitchens are hot and dirty, and the staff will be skittish enough having me there with you. Miss Avery, didn't you say you wanted to see the fountains?'

'Yes, Your Grace.'

'They're just up ahead.'

'Your Grace, surely we can't leave Violet—'

'There's no one else here, Lady Avery. She will be fine.'

'Well...if you say so, Your Grace.'

Ash straightened up, smoothing his palms down his coat and trousers. His heart pummelled out an erratic rhythm, but he managed to calm it with deep breaths. A knot tightened in his gut as he spotted Violet coming around the corner. When their eyes met, she gasped.

'Miss Avery—'

'What are you doing here?' Her voice was strained and taut with tension, as if she were going to burst into tears at any moment.

'I just... I wanted to...'

'Stop.' She held up a hand. 'Just say it. Please.'

'You know why I'm here. I want to marry you.'

The colour drained from her face, and from the way her body tensed he could sense she was ready to flee.

'Please, Violet.' She didn't flinch at the use of her name. 'I promise—really promise this time—that if you say no I will never approach you again. But just hear me out.'

She eyed him, those stunning orbs boring right into him. 'All right, my lord.'

'Thank you.' He blew out a breath. 'First, is this place…? I mean, are you comfortable here?'

'I…' Confusion crossed her face. 'Yes.'

'It's not too bright? Does the steam from the vents bother you? If it wasn't so cold outside, I would take you somewhere peaceful.'

'It's fine, my lord.'

'Excellent.' He cleared his throat. 'Violet, I know you would probably prefer I get right to the point, so I shall tell you the truth. I know about your father's death and that you will soon be without a home.'

'How?'

Guilt poured through Ash, but he knew he had to tell the truth. 'Violet, I was spying on you.'

'What?'

'I overheard you speaking with Kate in her office… I was hiding behind the curtains.'

Her mouth formed a perfect O. 'You were hiding? Eavesdropping? Did you see anything in the office?'

'Enough. And I apologise. But I just wanted to know you. Understand you. Please forgive me.'

Her teeth chewed at her lip. 'I supposed you would have found out about my father.'

'Eventually.'

'And you are being honest with me—which I appreciate.'

'Good. So now you must marry me.'

'I beg your pardon? I must?'

'Yes.' He could see the confusion her face. 'You need me, so I can pay off your father's debts, and I need you, Violet.'

She frowned. 'I highly doubt that. I have nothing to give you.'

He chuckled. 'Actually, there is something you can give me.'

'And what is that?'

'An heir.'

Colour drained from her face. 'No—'

'Before you say no, please allow me to continue. Listen, and then you can say no.' His nerves felt frayed at the edges, but he soldiered on. 'A few days ago a solicitor came to my house…'

And he told her everything—the truth about the clause, the Canfields, and his need for a legitimate heir.

'So you see, you can help me fulfil the requirements of the clause before my next birthday.'

'I do not see why it must be me. Surely there are multitudes of women in London who would be more than willing to marry you and produce an heir.'

Why indeed?

But before he could come up with an answer, she spoke first.

'Are you proposing to me out of pity, my lord? Because you have ruined my chances of finding a match?'

'Yes,' he blurted out, hoping that was the right answer. 'I mean, yes, *partly*. And I'm only partly responsible for that horrid nickname, you know. I did not spread it amongst the Ton.'

'But you invented it. Why?'

'Because you are.'

'Bizarre?'

'A beauty.'

Her eyes grew wide and her lips parted.

Taking advantage of momentarily stunning her, he continued. 'There is nothing wrong with being different, Violet. I found you quite refreshing that first night we met. I had misinterpreted your intentions because of what your mother said, but I see now that you are not some scheming debutante. After learning more about you, I've come to the conclusion that you're a logical, reasonable woman. And our marrying makes sense.'

'And that's all you require of me? An heir, to be produced within the next year?'

'Yes. The only other stipulation I have is that you cannot fall in love with me.'

She scoffed. 'I hardly think that's possible.'

He ignored the knot in his chest. 'See? That makes you the perfect candidate. I don't have time for silly games and romance and sweet nothings. I need to secure my lands with an heir, and you need my funds to save your home and your papa's library.'

Her eyes lit up at the mention of her father.

'It makes perfect, logical sense.'

'There is a flaw in your argument, my lord.'

'What is it? And, please, do call me Ash.'

'Ash…' She said the name aloud slowly, experimentally, as if she were testing the way it sounded to her ears. 'There is a chance I could produce no heir at all and then we would both end up penniless.'

'True. But that could happen anyway. You currently have no suitors, and I have no time. There's no way to predict if my chances of begetting an heir would be higher with another woman, but the probability of saving your home increases if you marry me.'

'I—' Her mouth clamped shut. 'I could end up home-less, married to a man with no prospects.'

'Well, there's one more thing.'

'And what is that?'

'Once we do produce an heir, you'll be free to follow your own pursuits. I imagine your mother would never allow you to work with Kate at the factory—not unless you become completely destitute. As your husband, I'll give you my permission to do as you please, even if we don't secure the lands. In a year you'll be free of me, and of your mother.' He paused, allowing the information to sink in before he continued, 'What do you think?'

She stood there, not speaking, not moving for what seemed like a lifetime. 'My lord—Ash,' she began when she finally spoke, 'I appreciate your honesty and this logi-cal solution to our problems. But there is one more thing you must know about me.'

'And what is that?'

'I should not... I cannot...' Colour bloomed in her cheeks. 'You will not want to marry me after I tell you.'

'You need to tell me, don't you, for me to assess that?'

Her gaze lowered. 'I'm afraid I cannot have marital re-lations with you. I'm a virgin, you see, and...'

'I expected as much. Violet, it's normal to fear inti-mate—'

'No, no.' Her arms stiffened at her sides. 'This isn't a virgin's fear. The fact of the matter is, I cannot stand being touched.'

'You can't? Why not? What do you mean?'

'Do you remember the other day? In the ballroom?'

How could he forget? 'Yes.'

'I was overwhelmed. By all the new sensations. Anything new and unknown drives me to panic—to fear. It was too much. Some days, the whole world is too much. I've learned to live with it, through practice and experience. I can cope with nearly all the sights and sounds bombarding me because I've had years of repetition to show me the variables and possible outcomes, so I can make the right decisions. It's not perfect, and sometimes I fail spectacularly—like when I blurt out random facts or my thoughts just come flying out of my mouth.'

She pressed her lips together.

'I've read about what the marital act requires and, frankly, the thought of being touched like that…everywhere… I cannot stand it. It makes me want to vomit. The fluids…the contact…the—'

'I understand. You don't have to elaborate further.'

'You see, that's the flaw in your logic. Rather, *I'm* the flaw. I'm too broken—'

'Stop.' He held up a hand. 'It doesn't have to be that way.'

'What do you mean? Can you fix me?'

Fix her? 'No, Violet. What I'm trying to say is that it's natural to fear sexual relations, especially when you've never experienced them.'

'Is it? Were you ever afraid?'

He strangled the laugh building in his throat. 'Anything new can be overwhelming. But what if it wasn't so new to you?'

She cocked her head. 'What do you mean?'

'You say you need time and practice and repetition to help you overcome your fears. What if you practised?'

'P-practised?' Her eyes widened. 'Is that possible?'

'Of course it's possible.'

'But with whom?'

Without hesitation, he said, 'With me, of course.'

* * *

Violet could only stare at the Marquess's—Ash's—handsome face as she processed his words. 'Practise with you?'

'Yes, who else?'

Her mind immediately focused on the details. 'And when would we begin?'

'Now is a good time.'

'What would this practice entail?'

He tapped a finger on his chin. 'Tell me, how did you train yourself to overcome your panic and fear in other overwhelming situations?'

She bit at her lip. 'My papa taught me some techniques. He was like me.'

'Ah-ha.' The sound of the snap of his fingers reverberated across the room, bouncing off the glass ceiling. 'If you brief me on these techniques, I may be able to adapt them for our practice.'

'So you could be like a teacher? The way Papa was with me?'

'Er…not exactly. I mean, your father…er…' Ash's complexion had turned an alarming shade of grey.

'Are you all right?'

'Um…yes. But let's not speak of your papa at this moment, as I doubt he would approve of my…er…techniques.'

'He's dead, Ash. He won't be here to disapprove.'

He let out a strangled sound. 'Still…in order for me to practise with you, I would prefer we don't mention him.'

'As you wish.'

Hopefully he wouldn't be acting this strangely throughout the practice session, she thought.

'First I must prepare my mind and anticipate all the possible outcomes of the situation, so as to reduce any chance of surprises catching me off-guard. Knowing things in advance allows me to anticipate all the variables and prepare.'

'So, no surprises?' He paused. 'If I tell you what I'm going to do, would that help?'

'Immensely.'

'Understood.' His firm lips pursed together. 'Violet, I'm going to move close to you. Very, very close.'

'Wait.' She processed the information and blew out a breath. 'All right.'

He crossed the distance between them with one step. This close, he towered over her, but she found it didn't bother her—not even the fact that there was only a small gap between them. Knowing he was going to do this had allowed her to prepare her mind and body.

'How are you feeling? Relaxed?'

'More like...unbothered.'

Though her mind was not protesting at his closeness, her body was reacting differently. An unusual tautness had built in her stomach, like a string being pulled. It only increased when she inhaled and received a whiff of something pleasant coming from... Ash?

Curious, she leaned her head forward and sniffed.

'Violet? Is something the matter?'

'Nothing. I mean...that smell.' She inhaled once more, just to be certain. 'Are you wearing a different cologne today?'

It was different from the one he'd had on the first night they'd met.

'I hope I don't smell like Mr Eldridge,' he joked.

He obviously remembered that story from the night they'd first met.

'Um...not at all.'

In fact, he smelled *good*.

Leaning forward, she took in another whiff.

Oh, Lord, it *was* good.

'I'm afraid I didn't have time to put any on as I was in a rush this morning. That's all me, I'm afraid.'

'Oh.'

Was that his natural scent?

'Is it all right?'

'Yes, it's fine.'

Wonderful, actually.

However, she had to restrain herself from continuing to sniff at him, lest he think she were a bloodhound.

'Please continue.'

'As you wish. Now, I am going to hold your hand.'

Her nerves frayed. 'Which hand?'

'Does it matter?'

She nodded.

'The left one. With my right.'

'A-all right.'

Violet closed her eyes and held her breath. Their gloved fingers made contact, then the slightest pressure wrapped around her left hand.

He let go.

'So?'

'It was not…unpleasant.'

It had been over much too soon for her taste.

'I see. Shall I go on?'

'Yes.'

He continued, telling her where he would touch her—her upper right arm, her left shoulder and her elbow—before actually making any contact. With each touch, Violet found she needed less and less time to prepare.

'How are you now?' he asked. 'Are you feeling uncomfortable? Is this too much? Should I stop?'

'No!' That sounded rather emphatic. 'Not at all.'

'All right.' He raked his hand through his golden hair, leaving it tousled. 'So, we've established that when it comes to touch informing you allows you to prepare. What's next?'

'Um…the next technique is exposure.'

'I beg your pardon?' he spluttered.

'Exposure to all the different variables makes them… well, not variable any longer.'

'Oh? So repeated touches should help?'

'Yes.'

'All right. Now, I'm going to touch your—'

'You needn't say it all over again,' she interrupted. 'I mean, you've already established that you're going to touch me, and where. Once you've said it, I don't need it to be repeated.'

'Oh, thank the Lord. Otherwise this would take a very, very long time. So…'

He gave her hand a tentative squeeze, then brushed against the same spots on her arm, shoulder and elbow. Violet did not tense with each one, nor did she find it repulsive. In fact, she was mildly disappointed that it was once again over so quickly.

'I trust my touch was not offensive?' he asked.

'Not at all.'

'May I touch you…more?' he asked, hesitant.

A curious sensation prickled the back of her knees. 'Oh, yes.'

'On other places?

The idea that he wanted to keep touching her on other places on her body took a while longer for her to process, but eventually she bobbed her head up and down.

'Violet, I want… May I touch your cheek?

She drew in a breath. 'Yes.'

Raising his hand, he brushed a thumb across her cheek-bone.

Just as he was about to withdraw, Violet found herself reaching up to stop him. 'You may touch me for longer.'

The corner of his lip tugged up. 'If you say so.'

As his thumb continued its caress, the tingling behind her knees increased and spread up the backs of her thighs. She sighed and leaned into his hand, but when his finger strayed lower to touch her lips, she jolted.

'Apologies.' He pulled away. 'I should have... Violet, I'm sorry.'

Her eyes flew open. 'It's...it's all right. Apology accepted. Please, go on.'

'Are you sure?'

'Yes.'

Once again he caressed her cheek, adding more pressure. This time, his touch was most definitely pleasant. The fabric of his soft gloves was soothing, and the warmth of his skin seeped through. He had leaned closer too, so his tantalising scent tickled her nostrils.

'Violet?'

'Hmm...?'

'May I kiss you?

The request sent a shock through her, and panic rose.

'Violet, are you all right? You seem to be breathing rather rapidly.'

'What?' She slowed her breath, taking deep, long gulps of air. 'No, breathing helps me. Steadies me.'

He didn't move...didn't even take his hand away. And as she took deep breaths she concentrated on the sensation of the fabric of his gloves and his scent.

'I'm sorry. That was a lot to ask.'

'No… I just… I've been learning to tolerate touch since I was a child. But I haven't… I've never—'

'Been kissed? On the lips?'

She shook her head. 'No.'

'No daring young boy from the village has ever tried?' he asked in a light tone.

'I never go out to the village.' It was far too noisy and crowded and smelly. 'I just stay at home.'

'Violet…my sheltered, shy Violet. I can almost picture you at home, surrounded by your books all day. You must look adorable?'

'Adorable?'

'Yes. Spending your days in your father's library, learning about mathematics.'

'And philosophy and nature and biology.' Truly, Papa's library was extensive, and she'd read nearly all the books twice. 'It is my favourite place. I've never felt so safe anywhere else.'

'Think of that place, then, when you're feeling overwhelmed.'

She pictured the library. The smell of paper and leather and tobacco. The feel of the rough paper and soft leather underneath her fingertips. Papa's soothing voice as he read aloud.

'There you go,' he whispered. 'All better?'

She realised her breathing had returned to normal. 'Yes.'

'Now may I kiss you? On the lips?'

'Yes.'

His head moved down towards her in slow motion, his eyes closing. Violet found herself doing the same. The touch of his lips was much lighter than she had expected. His mouth brushed against her for only the briefest moment before he pulled away.

'How was that?'

'F-fine.' Opening her eyes once more, she looked into his sapphire gaze. 'C-could you do that again?'

The request came out much too quickly, but she was unable to stop herself.

'Longer this time?'

'Really?'

'Yes, please.'

His mouth descended on hers, this time with more force. Firm lips pressed against hers, moving in a slow rhythm. It was pleasant, but it felt lacking. Deficient, even. So she pushed herself up on her tiptoes. This caused him to add more pressure to the kiss. And then he drew her bottom lip into his mouth. Something wet and warm stroked over her lip—his tongue. The sensation was new, but she didn't mind it. She whimpered from the sensation.

'I… My apologies.' He pulled away. 'I didn't mean to… It was too much.'

'No, not at all.'

'No? How was it for you?'

Violet struggled to describe it. Perhaps it was because she had never felt anything like it—not on a first touch. Her heart raced, her limbs were loose, and there was a fluttering in her stomach as if a hundred butterflies wanted to burst forth.

'We should stop,' he said. 'I should go— Mmph!'

The idea that he wanted to stop and leave her had caused panic to rise in Violet, and so she'd acted on impulse—lunging up at him and raking her fingers through the back of his hair to pull him down to her lips.

Their mouths met in a frenzied, hurried dance. His arms wound around her waist, but the touch didn't repel her, although she would have slid to the ground had it not been for the support.

Violet parted her lips, hoping he'd understand the invitation. He did, and he dipped his tongue between her lips, darting in quickly. When she moaned aloud and pulled his head closer he plunged in, rubbing his rough tongue against hers.

Lord, he smelled *and* tasted good.

And she wanted more.

Her fingertips raked his scalp. That elicited a throaty moan from him, bringing a strange thrill through her. She wanted to taste more of him, so she pushed her tongue into his mouth, mimicking his earlier movements. Her arms wound tighter around him, pressing her to him, and the sensation sent her to the edge. His hips brushed against hers and she felt a hardened bulge against her belly.

He abruptly pulled away.

'My lord—Ash, did I do something wrong?' Violet could not read his face…could not decipher the look he gave her.

Was it good?

Bad?

Was he angry?

His eyes nearly bulged out of their sockets and his face was flushed. 'Are you sure you've never been kissed before?'

'That was my first. Second, if you count the first one you gave me. Did I do anything wrong? Was it awful?'

'Awful?' A rich laugh escaped his mouth. 'Not at all, Violet. You didn't do anything wrong, and it certainly was not awful. I found myself…overwhelmed.' He adjusted the front of his coat. 'But I'm afraid this practice must cease.'

'Oh…' Disappointment filled her.

'For now.'

He touched her face again and Violet tried not to rub her cheek against his glove—and failed.

'We can continue later, though.'

'There's more to practise?' she asked, incredulous.

'Oh, so much more, Violet. If you are amenable.'

She was absolutely, positively amenable. 'I am. When?'

'How about tonight?' His voice lowered. 'In your room.'

It was a shocking thought. To have a man—Ash—in her room tonight.

But also intriguing.

'Is that too forward?' he asked, his jaw set. 'We don't have to anything you don't want to, but if you want me to come I promise to leave the moment you become uncomfortable. Just say the word.'

Warmth pooled in her chest. Had any man—anyone, really—ever been so thoughtful of her?

'All right. What time will you be there?'

His expression relaxed. 'Once everyone has gone to bed I will come to you.'

'I need a time. So I can prepare.'

'How about…eight minutes past eleven?'

'Eight minutes past eleven?' she repeated. 'Why not make it eleven o'clock or half-past eleven? Even a quarter past would have been preferable.'

The corner of his mouth quirked and she recognised that he was teasing. It was a triumphant feeling, to unlock a new facial expression. She quickly added it to her mental catalogue.

'You are jesting with me.'

'Only because you are so adorable.' He planted a kiss on her forehead, then stiffened. 'I forgot to tell you I was going to do that.'

'N-no, it's fine. As I said, once I've been exposed to a variable, it becomes no longer a variable.'

The touch of his lips to her forehead had been enjoyable, in fact, in a different way from his other kisses.

'I'll remember that.' He tapped a finger to his temple. 'You should return to the house. I shall follow along later, so no one suspects you were here with me.'

'Of course.' She'd forgotten that they were alone, un-chaperoned. 'Good day, Ash.'

'Good day, Violet.'

Violet wasn't sure how she managed to get through the rest of the day. It was as if she was walking in a thick fog, and no information could penetrate the cloud surrounding her mind. Working on her equations was a futile exercise. Dinner was practically a muddle of confusion—especially with Ash just a few feet away from her, acting as if nothing had happened. And having him so near only built the tension inside her, stretching it taut, waiting to snap.

When she was finally in bed, and Gertrude had left her alone, Violet expected the tension would disappear. However, as she stared at the clock, it only grew with each passing minute.

Five minutes past eleven.

Six minutes past eleven.

Seven minutes past eleven.

Eight minutes past.

And nothing.

The second hand continued ticking. It was halfway across the clock face when she heard the door creak open and Ash slipped inside, wearing only a black robe while his feet were bare.

'You're thirty seconds late,' she stated.

'Apologies.' He closed the door behind her. 'Damned candle blew out. Had to grope my way here.'

Violet sat up, then swung her legs over the side of the bed. 'Next time, just say a quarter past eleven, then you'll be early.'

He grinned from ear to ear. 'If I had my way, the next time I find myself in your rooms will be on our wedding night.'

Her heart drummed madly at the thought, and that tingling behind her knees returned.

'Now, I'm going to come closer,' he announced, then strode over to her. 'Is this all right?'

'Yes,' she whispered. 'And I told you—you don't have to repeat telling me about anything that you've already done before.'

'You are referring to all the things we did in the orangery this afternoon?'

'Yes.'

'Did you like it, Violet?'

Dryness permeated her mouth. Unable to utter a word, she nodded.

'Which part?'

Her gaze lowered to the floor. 'All of it.'

'Would you like me to do it again?'

'Yes.'

'Good.'

A hand reached out to cup her chin and tip her head up. She flinched, making him draw his hand away.

'Violet…?'

'Your hand,' she said. 'You're not wearing gloves.'

'Oh, should I go and get them?' Panic filled his voice. 'I can—'

'No!' Her arms reached out to grab the lapels of his

robe. 'Oh…' Distracted, she rubbed her fingers over the soft, furry fabric. 'That's nice. Velvet?'

'It is.'

The smooth nap against her skin was soothing. 'Ash? Could you please continue?'

'Of course. I'm going to touch you now, Violet. With my bare hands.'

Once again he cupped her chin, their skin touching. This time she didn't mind it at all. In fact, she rather liked the feel of his warm fingers pressing on her.

'Can we do what we did this afternoon?'

His head swooped down to capture her mouth in a kiss. This time it was more urgent—demanding, even. She found herself sliding her hands up the lapels of his robe and then pushing her fingers into the nape of his neck—oh, the hair was so soft there! Unable to help herself, she wound the locks around her fingers and pulled.

'Violet…' he gasped against her mouth. 'You're going to be the death of me.'

Releasing his hair, she dropped her hands to her sides. 'What did I do wrong?'

'Nothing. I mean, it's all right. It felt good.'

'I made you feel good?'

'Yes, darling.' He nipped at her lips. 'It was very, very good. Now, shall we continue our practice?'

'That would be best. What is next?'

Ash paused. 'You said you know how the marital act is done?'

She nodded. 'In theory, yes. The…mechanical aspects. The man's member enters the woman's organ and expels its seed to fertilise her.' She frowned. 'Is there more to it?'

'There is so much more to the act of making love. There's touching.'

'Where?'

'Everywhere.'

Surprisingly, the thought didn't repel her. In fact, the most curious warmth pooled in her belly at his words.

'And it will feel good. I promise. May I show you?'

'All right.'

'Lie down on the bed.'

She did as he instructed, backing away until she reached the edge, then climbing in. The mattress dipped beneath her, indicating that he had joined her.

'Violet, I'm going to lift your night-rail.'

The fabric swept up her thighs, exposing her skin to the cool air. Ash pushed it all the way up, over her breasts.

'Open your eyes, Violet.'

She did—and found him looking down at her.

'You're so lovely, Violet. All of you. I'm going to kiss your breast. Your left breast.'

Her body tensed, and she almost protested, except once his warm mouth had wrapped around her left nipple she lost all thought. His tongue circled the hardened bud, lashing it with a wet, warm heat. Her body seemed to have a life of its own as she began to squirm under his touch.

Much to her disappointment, he released her. 'I'm going to kiss the other nipple, then I'm going to caress your thighs and touch you between your legs.'

And he switched his attention to her other breast, while his hand gently landed between her thighs. He teased her, fingers pressing and massaging the soft flesh there.

The sensation made her dizzy—in a good way. She thought that was the culmination of it all—until he reached her sex, his fingers sifting through the tuft of downy hair before seeking out the swollen petals of her most intimate part.

Her hips bucked at the touch. His fingers were working

her like magic. Then he found the swollen bud at the crest and centred his attention there, stroking it in a maddening rhythm that made her cry out in the most unladylike way.

Ash released her nipple. 'I'm going to kiss you here.' His finger pressed hard on her. 'I want to make you come, Violet,' he murmured. 'It should feel good, but if you feel overwhelmed, or uncomfortable, just say the word and I will stop.'

He moved lower, trailing kisses down her body before reaching between her legs. Nudging her thighs apart, he ran his tongue across the crease of her sex.

Her fingers reached for the sheets, curling around them, and her feet kicked out as Ash's mouth and tongue worked her to a frenzy. His movements switched from gentle and teasing to fast and feverish, bringing her to the edge. She writhed underneath his touch as her body exploded with pleasure, and when he pushed a finger inside her she didn't even mind that he hadn't warned her first.

She was too lost in ecstasy to care.

'Violet? How do you feel?'

'I…I…'

Lord, that had been… Well, the words in the English language to describe it had apparently not yet been invented.

'Was it good, at least?' He sat up, then moved away from between her thighs, curling up beside her.

She nodded. Once her heart had stopped racing and her limbs were relaxed, she asked, 'But what about the rest of it?'

'The act to conceive, you mean.'

'Yes. It will be painful?'

'I'm afraid so. But I will do my best to relieve your discomfort and it should only hurt the first time.'

She knew that. After all, if copulation caused agony all

the time, the world's population would have dwindled to nothing.

A soft kiss was pressed to her temple. 'What else can I do to ensure there are no more surprises?'

'May I see you?' She plucked up her courage. 'Touch you?'

His blond eyebrows drew together. 'You don't mind?'

'No, I don't mind it when I do the touching. So, please… may I touch you?'

'You have my permission to touch me.' Rolling onto his back, he untied his robe. 'Anywhere. And you may do anything to me.'

Violet sat up. Unsure what to do, she ran her hands over the lapels of his robe, then parted it, revealing the expanse of his chest. Tentatively, she pressed her palms on it, feeling the hard muscles covered in a soft mat of hair. She rather liked the feel of the soft and hard at the same time. Feeling bolder, she further parted his robe, exposing his naked torso to her gaze, then lower to—

'Oh.'

'Oh?' His head rose from where it rested on the pillow. 'What's wrong?'

'I…' She glanced down again at his stiff member, jutting out from the thick patch of hair between his legs. 'Are you sure that's going to fit?'

He stifled a laugh. 'I'm very sure.' Reaching out, he stroked her arm encouragingly. 'When you're aroused, and after your orgasm, your sex becomes wet.'

She pressed her thighs together, confirming what he said.

'That will help me ease into you. If not, I also have an oil we can use. It should make it hurt less.'

There was still some doubt in her mind, but he'd been honest with her so far, so she had to trust that he knew best.

'May I touch you? Th-there?'

His blue eyes darkened. 'As I said, you have my permission to touch me anywhere. In perpetuity.'

Violet hesitated, then squared her shoulders before extending her hand towards his abdomen. Her fingers brushed up and down his length tentatively, but it didn't really feel different from touching his arm or the rest of him. So she wrapped her hand around it.

Curious.

The hardness was definitely there, like steel, but the warm skin and flesh made it feel so alive.

She wondered what would happen if she stroked it.

Ash moaned as she moved her hand up and down. Her fingers gripped him tighter, moving in a steady rhythm. When she increased the speed, his hips bucked up to meet her hand.

'Yes… Violet… Don't stop.'

She switched her gaze back and forth from his hard shaft, which now glistened at the tip, to his face, which was twisting with an expression she could only guess was ecstasy. It was difficult to decide where to focus her attention, as both sights fascinated her.

'Violet…stop!'

Abruptly, she released him. 'Did I hurt you?'

'No, no, darling.' He heaved himself up, then reached for her hand and squeezed. 'It was marvellous. I just want more.'

'More?'

'Hmm… Will you let me try something else? Something new?'

'Are you going to complete the marital act?'

'No, but we will get as close to it without breaking your maidenhead.' He pushed her down on the bed so she lay on her back. 'Think of it as more practice to get you accustomed to the idea of lovemaking. Do you want to try it?'

She bit at her lip. It was intriguing, this proposition of his. 'Yes, I want to try.'

Placing his hands between her thighs, he spread them apart. 'I'm going to position myself between your legs, and then I'm going to get very close to you.'

Violet braced herself as his body pressed down on hers. She had prepared herself to hate it, but to her surprise she rather enjoyed the feeling of his weight on top of her. His arms snaked around her, which brought her even closer to him.

'Oh…' She pressed her face against his neck. His delicious scent was so much stronger coming from the skin behind his ear. 'You really smell so good.'

If a perfumier ever found a way to bottle that scent, she would buy out his entire stock.

'Now I'm going to move.' His hips stroked up and down slowly. 'Like this.'

'Mmm-hmm…'

She was still rubbing her nose on his neck, savouring his smell, so she didn't pay much attention to the sensation. However, when he shifted his hips, and his shaft rubbed right along her crease, the friction sent a jolt of pleasure up her spine.

'Ash!' Her hands gripped his shoulders.

He grunted and continued the motions, his warm, hard flesh stroking her, spreading her wetness around. Once in a while, his tip would connect with the bud atop her sex, sending the most delicious thrill through her.

His weight, his smell, their bodies sliding together, the sounds they were making—everything was new, and the sensations were overwhelming, yet she was much too distracted to panic. That pressure began to build within her again, and she orgasmed once more as Ash whispered encouraging words in her ear.

He continued his movements on top of her, rubbing himself against her until his body tensed and he let out a strangled cry. Wetness splashed against her belly, and then he slowed his movements before rolling over on his back, his breath coming in gasps.

'Ash…' she began a moment later. 'Did you…?'

'Yes. I had an orgasm as well.'

'Did it feel good?'

'Very much so.'

'Does this practice satisfy you?' he asked. 'Does it reassure you and help you overcome your fear of touch?'

'Yes. But only with you.' Frankly, the thought of doing that with anyone else made her stomach churn.

He grinned. 'And so now you have listened to my arguments, seen the logic of my reasoning, had your objections quelled and your fears allayed, Miss Violet Avery, will you do me the honour of being my wife?'

Truly, she couldn't argue with that proposal. And so she answered without hesitation. 'Yes, I will.'

'Excellent.' He breathed a sigh of relief. 'We will be married in three days.'

'Three days?' She sat up quickly. 'How? Isn't there a procedure we must follow? Banns to be read and such?'

'Indeed there is, but I secured a special licence before I left London.'

Before he'd left London?

'How did you accomplish the paperwork so quickly? And what clergyman would issue you a licence without the name of the bride?'

'I did know the name of my bride—yours.' He flashed her a grin. 'The licence already has our names on it.'

'Our names? You procured our marriage license before you came here to ask me to marry you? What if I had said no?'

'I had my doubts, yes, but I thought I had better be prepared, just in case.' He winked at her. 'But that's all moot now, since you've said yes.'

'But three days... Is that even enough time to arrange a wedding? What about dresses and breakfasts and bridesmaids?'

He paused. 'My apologies, Violet. I didn't consider your preferences.' He kissed her on the temple. 'I suppose we could wait another month. That would be enough time for you to have your trousseau made, plan the wedding, send out invitations—'

'Invitations?' She swallowed hard.

'Yes, for the guests. I suppose you and your mother will want a big affair? With one hundred guests in attendance, perhaps?'

The thought of standing in a room full of people with the focus on her had her palms dampening and her stomach turning.

'No, thank you. Let's get married here. With the Duke, Kate, the Dowager and Mama.'

'Whatever you want, darling. Tomorrow morning, I—*we* will speak with your mama, and then we will announce our engagement at breakfast. Will that be all right?'

It sounded quick and efficient—she liked it. 'Yes.'

'Excellent.' He gave her a quick kiss. 'Now, I should get back to my own rooms before anyone discovers me here.'

Ash left the bed, then hurriedly dressed, bidding her goodnight before he slipped out through the door.

As she lay in bed, all alone in the dark, one thought repeated in Violet's head.

She was going to be married.

To Ash.

Chapter Eight

'Marriage?'

Lady Avery's exclamation made Violet cower. Seeing her shrink back, Ash took her hand and squeezed. He was glad they'd asked her to meet them in the library before breakfast, without anyone else around.

'Yes, Lady Avery. I asked Violet to marry me yesterday and she said yes.'

She looked to Violet. 'Why didn't you tell me?'

'It just…happened.'

'My lord, you haven't courted her properly. There is a process to this…a way to do things.' She tsked. 'Think of her reputation.'

In his haste in attempting to secure Violet's hand in marriage Ash had forgotten a small, yet crucial part of the equation—Lady Avery's permission. She was still Violet's mother, after all. While she might not object to the marriage itself, she would certainly protest against its expeditiousness. He would have to convince her to allow him to marry Violet in three days.

But that was a simple matter for Ash. Charming ladies into doing what he wanted happened to be his speciality.

However, what explanation would a woman like Lady Avery believe?

Think, Ash, think!

An idea struck him.

'Lady Avery, please forgive me.' He mustered his most remorseful tone, even casting his gaze downward. 'I'm afraid I was struck by your daughter's beauty and wit from the first moment I saw her.'

The woman's eyes grew to the size of saucers. 'Are you saying you fell in love with her at first sight?'

He nodded vigorously. 'You see, all these years I have thought myself immune to Cupid's arrows. I've avoided his sights for many years. But alas!' Waving his hand dramatically, he pounded his chest with his fist. 'He found me. I was struck. In love.'

Silently, he sent a prayer to Professor Kingston, his deceased teacher of poetry and literature during his university days.

'Desperately so. I had to make Violet mine.'

'But you have had months to court her. You never even paid her a call.'

'This is my first time being in love, my lady.' He glanced over at Violet, who was now eyeing him suspiciously. He grinned at her. 'I resisted, like…er… Romeo and Juliet.'

'Didn't they die?' Lady Avery's gaze narrowed at him.

'Er…no… I mean, that must have been in a different version you read.' He cleared his throat. 'Anyway, for weeks I was sick with love…unable to eat, sleep, or do much else, really.'

When Violet rolled her eyes, he tugged at her hand.

'So you came here to propose?'

'Yes. I could not stand it any more. I saw her at the Spanish Ambassador's party and I knew I had to confess my feelings before they burst out of my chest. Yesterday morning I came upon her in the orangery and took my chance.

Confessed my love to her on my knees and asked her—no, *begged* her—to marry me.'

'You said yes, Violet? Without telling me?'

'We are telling you now, Mama. And I didn't say yes right away. I had to think about it, and I told him last night.'

'Last night? When?'

'This morning!' Violet blurted out. 'I mean I accepted this morning, which is why we wanted to speak to you.'

'Oh, I see.' Her face lit up, as it seemed to dawn on her what was happening. 'Of course you'll be wed. Violet, I can't believe it. You're going to be the Marchioness of Ash-brooke.'

Lady Avery lunged at her daughter and pulled her into an embrace. Ash could not help but cringe himself as he saw how uncomfortable Violet was with the touch.

'There is one more thing, Lady Avery.' Ash thought he might as well spring it on her now, while she was still giddy from the news. 'I would like to marry Violet in three days' time.'

'Three days? But my lord…that's not…you can't…' she spluttered, releasing Violet. 'Why so hasty, my lord? Surely there must be a proper engagement period, with enough time to prepare a grand wedding. Doesn't a wedding in springtime sound lovely?'

'Yes, but…uh…' He needed a good excuse. Could he tell her he was dying? Being shipped off to war? Prison?

'Mama, he's compromised me,' Violet stated flatly. 'He stole into my room after dinner and we were alone. All night. So, you see, we must marry right away.'

The colour bled from her mother's face—and then she fainted. Thankfully, Ash caught her before she landed on the floor.

'Violet.' He carried Lady Avery to a settee and gently lowered her on it. 'Why did you say that?'

Violet shrugged. 'You were flailing.'

'I was not flailing,' he said, miffed. 'I was thinking.'

'And flailing.' She placed her hands on her hips. 'This was more efficient.

And it was the truth. Mama could not object to an expeditious wedding now.

'Besides, we are running out of time, are we not? I've calculated exactly how many months we have left before the deadline, and as far as I know the gestation period for humans is still nine months.'

The corner of his mouth quirked up. 'Logical as ever.'

'What on earth is— *Ash*.' Despite her miniscule frame, Kate's stature seemed to fill the entire frame of the doorway as she glared at the Marquess. '*Now* what are you doing to poor Lady Avery?'

'I merely saved her from falling to the ground when she fainted.'

Kate raised a dark eyebrow. 'And why did she faint?'

Violet cleared her throat. 'Entirely my fault, I'm afraid. You see, Kate, I told her that the Marquess and I must be married in three days.'

'M-m-married?' The Duchess's face turned scarlet and her eyes widened.

'Yes. Ash has compromised me, and so we must be married.'

'You blackguard!'

Kate lunged for Ash, but Violet managed to put herself between them.

'Kate, please, there is no need for violence.'

She glanced back at the Marquess. 'My lord—Ash, could you please have a footman fetch Mama's maid to tend to her?'

'Of course.' Ash stood up and brushed some imaginary lint from his lapels.

The Duchess opened her mouth and then closed it quickly.

Relief poured through Violet. 'I shall explain everything once we are alone.'

Once Ash had left, and Lady Avery's maid had arrived with some smelling salts, Violet led Kate away to the office.

'All right, we are now alone.' Kate folded her arms over her chest. 'Speak.'

Violet didn't bother to mince words with her friend, so she laid out the entire truth about the clause and her agreement to help Ash produce an heir and save his estate.

'I knew he was hiding something,' the Duchess fumed. 'I thought he was proposing to you out of pity, because of that blasted nickname debacle. Of course he has ulterior motives.'

'As do I, Kate,' Violet reminded her. 'And we will benefit mutually from this marriage.'

If I can birth an heir.

'You must agree his argument makes logical sense.'

'Ash using logic…' She shook her head. 'Despite my objections, I must admire his tenacity. But still…he did not really seduce you or compromise you?'

'I…er…he compromised me, but not fully.'

Kate stared at her, slack-jawed. 'I beg your pardon?'

Violet frowned. Surely the Duchess was well versed in sexual relations? Or perhaps the Duke did not participate in anything other than the marital act.

'Kate, I regret to inform you that, as I have recently discovered, there's more to the marital act than the penetration of the man's—'

'I—I am well aware, thank you very much,' Kate spluttered, her face once more turning an alarming shade of red. 'So you and he were intimate, while still keeping your virginity?'

'Yes.'

Violet explained to Kate how Ash had helped her overcome her aversion to touch.

His touch, anyway.

'Oh, Lord.' Kate blew out a breath. 'Dear Violet, I am well aware that the…er…pleasures a man is able to give you can be…overwhelming. But now that you are not… er…under the spell of…uh…his touch, are you sure you still want to marry him?'

Violet nodded vigorously. 'Yes. It's the best chance I have of saving Oakwood Cottage and Papa's library. And even if we fail to produce an heir I would have the freedom to work for you. Don't you want that?'

'Of course I do. But not at your expense. There's so much more to marriage…' The Duchess clicked her tongue. 'What about love?'

'Oh, we have taken care of that.'

'You have?'

'Of course. I have promised I won't fall in love with him.'

'Promised— Violet, forgive me, but that is the most inane thing I've ever heard.'

'Inane? But it makes perfect logical sense. Love is not a prerequisite for marriage, is it? Most people marry to gain some benefit, and ours will be no different.'

Kate's lips twisted, and then she let out a resigned sigh. 'All right. If this is truly what you want, then I will stand by your side.'

'It is.'

'And if things go awry, you know I will be here as well.'

'Thank you. I appreciate that.'

Not that she thought things would go awry.

Well, they could. No plan was foolproof. And one could only predict an outcome, not guarantee it.

But, then again, there were no guarantees in life. Not even Papa had been able to guarantee that he would live long enough that they didn't have to be in this situation. Life, sadly, was not like mathematics, where there was only a wrong or a right answer. She could only choose the options that would give her the best outcome.

Sure enough, in three days' time, Ash and Violet were married.

'You're really wed,' Sebastian stated as he handed the groom a flute of champagne. 'I can't believe it.'

'Did you doubt me?' Ash scoffed.

The small ceremony had been held at the parish church in the village, with only Sebastian, Kate, the Dowager and Lady Avery in attendance. Afterwards, they'd headed back to Highfield Park, where a beautiful wedding breakfast had been set up in the orangery. Once they'd finished the meal, the footmen had arrived with cake and champagne.

'If I was a betting man...' Sebastian shook his head. 'Well, let's say I would have lost this one.'

Ash placed a hand over his heart. 'I'm hurt,' he said in a mocking tone. 'But it's all done.'

Finally, he'd secured his bride. How he wished he could see Alberta Canfield's face when she saw the announcement in the papers. Ash had made sure every newspaper and gossip rag in London received it.

'This is only the beginning, Ash,' Sebastian said. 'There is still the part where you have to produce an heir.'

'I know.'

He glanced over at Violet, who was listening with rapt

attention as the Dowager explained something about the orchids hanging from the pots overhead. That was his Violet—intense, focused.

His Violet.

His wife.

'And what about the financial side of things?' Sebastian asked, breaking into his thoughts. 'Any news on that? On Oakwood Cottage?'

'Yes, I received a letter from my man of business this morning.' Ash wanted to keep his end of the bargain, so he'd asked Mr Bevis to make enquiries regarding Sir Gregory Avery's accounts. 'The debt isn't substantial or unreasonable. Sir Gregory made a few bad investments and had to take out a mortgage to keep afloat. His scholarly work, book royalties and speaking engagements were enough to support the family and make payments on his debts. Unfortunately, he died suddenly.'

An ache filled Ash as he thought about what Violet had gone through when her father had died. When his own father had passed away, Ash hadn't had time to feel sad. He did, however, remember a profound sense of relief.

'And then what happened?' asked Sebastian.

'He left Lady Avery and Violet with very little. Mr Bevis says that currently they have enough funds to last at least until July, but after that the bank will take possession of the house. I asked him to look into the Avery finances further, to see if there were any other assets left to sell, so they can keep making payments until I secure my lands and pay off their mortgage.'

That was still a few months away, and Ash would deal with it when the time came. For now, he had other things to worry about—that was producing his heir, which might very well be conceived tonight.

His wedding night.

Ash had not touched or kissed Violet since the night she had accepted his proposal, but she—and her sweet, responsive body—had been on his mind the entire time.

This had not been part of his plan.

Well versed in sexual acts, Ash enjoyed women, loved sex, and had spent many a pleasurable night in the company of various lovers. There were few things he hadn't experienced before, and no act he hadn't tried at least once. He rarely bedded the same woman for more than a few weeks, as he fully enjoyed the buffet of available bed partners in London.

Yet, being with Violet…it had been indescribable. At first he had assumed it would be boring, having to tell her what he was about to do, and that it would take away the thrill of sex. However, he'd found it refreshing. Exciting in its own way. He'd marvelled at her reactions to his touch, at her little sighs and moans. She'd been so eager and responsive it had left him wanting more. He wanted to know all the secret places on her delectable body, and gain permission to touch all of her.

He gripped the champagne flute tighter.

Control yourself, Ash. You're not some eager young lad who's had his first taste of a woman.

When he'd first decided Violet would be the one to help him fulfil his duty, he'd thought he would bed her only once or twice. That was all that would be needed? He'd spent most of his life trying to prevent conception—surely it couldn't be that difficult to get a woman with child?

But now—

'Ash, are you all right?' Sebastian eyed him warily. 'You look deep in thought.'

Lifting his flute to his lips, Ash finished the champagne,

then gestured for the footman holding a bottle to refill his glass. 'Fine. I'm fine.'

She might very well conceive on their first try, he supposed. He might only need to bed her once. Maybe two times. *Yes, definitely. Two, maybe three times.*

And once that was done he would never have to bed her again. As he'd promised her, they would go their separate ways. The child would be raised at Chatsworth Manor, and Violet could go and work for Kate at the factory. And he... Well, Ash supposed he would go back to whatever the hell he'd done before his life had been turned upside-down.

Violet's low, husky laugh caught his attention and his head snapped towards her. She was standing in the middle of the path with Kate, and a shaft of sunlight streamed down over her. She looked like an angel in her pearl-white gown.

As if she felt his eyes on her, she turned to face him, and smiled shyly when their eyes met. His gaze dropped low to her lips, moved down her long neck to the swells of her breasts, and he remembered how her nipples tasted.

Breaking away from her mesmerising stare, he finished the second glass of champagne in one gulp.

Chapter Nine

Ash could not remember the last time he'd been nervous entering a woman's room. A meeting with a new lover typically brought excitement and thrill, and had him relishing the thought of the pleasures that awaited him. But this was different. This was his wedding night, and Violet was his wife.

Ridiculous, he sneered silently. She would be no different from any woman he'd bedded. Tonight was about conceiving his heir and saving his lands.

'Come in,' came Violet's reply to his knock.

He slipped into the room, much as he had the last time he'd come. Violet sat on the edge of the bed, staring up at him. His breath caught at the sight of her, hair loose, sable waves tumbling down her back, eyes wide and luminous in the glow of the candlelight.

Two or three times, he reminded himself. *Four at most.*

'I hope I'm not late?'

He hoped his jest would mask the feelings bubbling underneath his relaxed facade.

'We didn't set a time, so that means you can't be late.'

Logical, lovely Violet. 'Ah, but if we did, I would have set it for three minutes past seven.'

Her face scrunched up. 'What is your fascination with imbalance? There is beauty in symmetry.'

'Really, now?' He crossed the room until he stood over her. 'Hmm... I see what you mean.' He cupped her chin with his thumb and forefinger, enjoying the fact that she didn't flinch or seem surprised by his touch. 'Your face is perfectly symmetrical. Even. One side is the precise mirror image of the other. But...' his thumb ran over the beauty mark over her lip '...this mars the symmetry of your face.'

Disappointment crossed her features. 'And makes me less beautiful?'

He shook his head, then leaned down to kiss the mark. 'No, Violet. I think it makes you even more beautiful. And unique. And tempting. I've been wanting to do that since I met you.'

She inhaled a rapid breath. 'You've already kissed me so many times.'

'But not on your beauty mark.'

He pressed his lips to it again, then shifted to capture her mouth. She opened up to him, arms winding around his neck, hands raking into his hair to pull him closer. Did she have any idea how much that affected him? Just thinking of her fingers pulling at his hair made him hard.

He drew away, wanting this whole thing to be done.

And yet, not.

You're doing this to save the estate.

Once Violet was with child he would never have to sleep with her again. Still, he wasn't a monster. Despite her eagerness Violet was still a virgin, and she would not fully comprehend what happened during the sexual act until she had experienced it for herself.

'Are you ready, Violet? Is there anything more I can do to prepare you?'

'Will we do the same things we did the other night?'

'Yes. And more.'

'The sexual act?'

'Yes. I will do my best to ensure you are comfortable and to reduce the pain.'

A vial of the oil he'd promised her was in the pocket of his robe.

'Then I'm ready.'

Taking a step back, he removed his robe and draped it over the headboard. Violet did the same with her silk robe.

'Wh-what are you wearing?' he rasped.

She grimaced. 'This?'

'Yes. *That.*'

The white silk chemise, held up by red ribbon straps, had a low neckline that showed off her breasts. The fabric skimmed over her torso and came down to the tops of her thighs, showing off a good three inches of skin before matching silk stockings covered the rest of her.

'My modiste said I needed to wear this tonight. That you would like it.'

'Very much.' His blood heated at the sight of her wrapped up so daintily in silk. 'But I'd like it better off. The chemise, at least.'

The stockings would stay on.

He pushed the ribbon straps to the sides, then pulled at the fabric, allowing it to fall at her feet.

'Violet, you're gorgeous.'

He'd thought he'd only dreamed about her sensuous body, but no, it was real. Every detail—her high, pert breasts, the soft pink nipples, the dip of her flat waist, the silky triangle between her legs—was real and just as he remembered.

And all mine.

Pushing her back to the bed, he climbed in with her, moving over her. 'You're so beautiful, Violet...'

He caressed her breasts, kissing the flesh around her nipples to tease her before he drew a bud in. She tasted so damned sweet he could feast on her the whole day.

'Ash...' she moaned, her hips wriggling underneath him. She probably wasn't even aware of it.

'Patience, darling.'

He shifted his attention to the right nipple, then used his fingers to gently pinch the other one. For a moment he feared she would object, since he hadn't told her what he was going to do, but she did not seem to notice.

Shifting his position, he moved lower, kissing her bare skin as he trailed down over her stomach and right down to her curls. He nosed at her, then licked up her crease, causing her hips to lift off the mattress.

He steadied her hips with his hands, then spread her wide so he could further access all her soft, pink, secret parts. His mouth pressed up to her and his tongue explored her petals, parting them so he could dip inside to taste her nectar.

Fingers raked into his scalp, sending a jolt of pleasure all the way to his erection. But he continued his feast, lapping at her sensitive flesh. Once she was sufficiently wet, he slipped a finger inside her.

Still much too tight.

Ash had never been with a virgin before—a fact he'd withheld from her lest she changed her mind. But he would do his best to ensure her comfort, even if he had to stop and try again another time. The thought of hurting her made him sick to his stomach.

He wiggled his finger, easing it gently in and out. She responded, pushing her hips against his hand, urging him to move faster. So he did, and as his fingers thrust more deeply into her he drew her swollen bud into his mouth and suckled hard. Her cries of pleasure turned more vocal and guttural as her body trembled with her impending release.

That's it, my Violet.

He guided her through her pleasure, allowing her to peak, before helping her settle back down. Her breath eventually evened out and she lay on the bed, eyes closed, skin covered in sweat, looking more lovely than ever.

'You did well,' he said, pressing his lips to her temple.

Her eyes fluttered open. 'Am I ready?'

'Only you can answer that, darling.' He kissed her gently. 'Physically, I believe you're ready.'

Yes, she was so wet, and more than ready to accept him. He just needed to get on with it. Spill his seed inside her and get her with child.

But she looked, oh, so lovely and tempting. He wanted to tease her more. Play with her. Make this night into something special so that once they parted she would never forget it.

And never forget him.

'Ash?'

'You're very ready, but…'

'But?'

'I do love seeing you climax. Will you let me touch you some more?'

Her pupils blew, the dark pools engulfing the light blue of her eyes. 'I would very much like that.'

'Excellent… Because there is so much more we can do and other ways I can bring you pleasure.'

In Violet's mind, it seemed they had already explored all possibilities of the pleasures of intimacy, save for the act of copulation itself.

'But how else can you pleasure me?'

'Do you trust me, Violet?'

'Yes,' she replied without hesitation.

'As I said, I love seeing you orgasm. And I think it would benefit you too, if you could see just how beautiful you look when you're at the peak of your pleasure.'

'See myself? How?'

He didn't answer her, but slid off the bed, then pulled her along to follow him to the dressing mirror in the corner of the room.

Oh.

'Ash, you can't…'

'You said that you trust me, did you not?' He positioned her so she was at the dead centre of the mirror, her naked body on full display.

Violet was familiar with her body, of course, but seeing herself so fully exposed was a shock to her system. She looked away.

'No, Violet. There's nothing to be ashamed of.' He brushed her hair aside, then nuzzled at her neck. 'Please look at yourself and see how beautiful you are.'

Turning her head back, she glanced at her reflection, swallowing audibly. 'I can't. It's shameful.'

'There is nothing wrong or shameful about the naked body,' he began. 'Look at the symmetry of your form, your curves, your limbs. Just looking at you makes me ache.'

She felt something hard brush against her buttocks.

'I want you so terribly. I want to be inside you. Do you understand what I mean?'

Her throat had gone as dry as a desert, so she bobbed her head instead of speaking.

'But for now I'm going to touch you. I'm going to make you come, and you're going to watch yourself. See what you look like and how you look when you're at the height of your release. Do not look away.'

His last words had a force behind them that sent a thrill through her. 'I won't.'

'Good girl.'

Unblinking, she watched as his hand spread across her stomach, then crept up to her right breast. His thumb and forefinger pinched her stiff nipple, making her gasp.

His hand froze. 'Did I hurt you?'

'No.' She leaned her body into his hand. 'It was good.'

He continued to tease her, rolling the nipple between his fingers, cupping her breasts with his warm palms as if testing their weight. His other hand reached up and mimicked the same motion on her left breast. She watched in fascination, looking at the symmetry of his hands and the way he manipulated her flesh. For some reason she did not understand, seeing him touch her added to the excitement building inside her.

He released the right breast, then lowered his hands between her thighs, cupping her sex and covering the entirety of it.

'Everything about you is beautiful, Violet.' The heel of his palm pressed against her. 'These past few nights I've been dreaming of what it would be like to be inside you.' A finger unsealed her crease and teased at her. 'You're still so wet…so slick and tight.' The digit dipped into her and she clenched around him. 'Violet, you're going to kill me.'

'Kill you? How?'

'With how hot and tight you are. Do you think you can take another one?'

Breathlessly, she nodded.

A second finger joined the first inside her. 'How do you feel?'

'Full…' It sounded terribly depraved, but it was the first word she could think of.

'When I am inside you, you will feel much fuller than this.'

Her eyes rolled back as he thrust his fingers inside, moving in and out of her. His mouth was attached to her neck, sucking at the soft skin there, sending a frisson of pleasure through her.

It was too much, and yet she didn't want him to stop. Her hips met each thrust of his hands, and that tension was once again building inside her.

Too much…

'Don't close your eyes.' He nipped at her neck. 'Look, Violet.'

Her gaze fixed on the reflection—her reflection, her body. Her hips were wantonly shoving against his hand, her mouth was open wide as she cried out, and her breasts were bouncing with the rhythm of her movements, her flesh all pink and flushed. Then she locked eyes with him, and instantly she recognised the look of ecstasy on his face. He truly was excited by watching her being pleasured.

'Ash!'

'Hold on to me. Let it happen.'

Reaching back, she gripped his shoulders as pleasure razed her body. He continued to whisper words of encouragement to her until the sensations ebbed away and her limbs turned limp.

'I have you… I have you.'

The floor disappeared from under her. Ash had picked her up and was now carrying her.

'You did so well, darling.' He kissed her as he slid onto the bed with her. 'Now you are ready.'

She wanted it to happen so badly. Needed it, lest her body expire from the craving he aroused in her.

'Please... Ash.'

He covered her body, just like the last time. 'Spread your legs...that's it.'

She held her breath, waiting, until she felt his blunt intrusion. It felt much larger than she remembered.

'Violet...darling...' His face was scrunched up as he continued. 'So...'

Violet tried to relax—truly she did.

But, Lord, the pain.

It was too much.

She closed her eyes tight, telling herself it was going to be all right. That the searing pain that increased with each push wouldn't increase. That it would be all over soon.

'Violet?'

She hadn't even noticed he'd stopped.

'You're hurting?'

If she said no, he might stop before they'd completed the act.

But if she said yes, he would continue.

'Darling, you're like a wound-up spring.' He slowly withdrew from her. 'Relax your limbs. Unclench your jaw. Open your eyes.'

Relief poured through her as the intrusion left her body.

'Violet, I have hurt you terribly.' A kiss landed on her forehead. 'Forgive me.'

'You didn't mean to,' she whispered. 'Please, just...just get it over with. I won't make a sound. I won't move. I promise.'

A dark look crossed his face. 'No, I shan't let you lie there in agony while I rut you like some animal. Wait one moment.'

Reaching over her head, he reached towards his robe.

'I should have done this in the first place, but I was much too carried away. Here...'

Gently, he rolled her to her side.

'Will you let me try making love to you one more time, Violet? We can stop and try again later, or tomorrow if it proves too painful for you.'

That would only prolong her torture. 'No, I want to try now.'

It was only the first time that it would hurt, he'd said. She would endure it for now.

'As you wish. But if it's too much, just say the word and I shall stop.'

She nodded.

Ash opened the vial and poured a few drops of oil onto his fingers, then spread it over her sex. It didn't feel like anything to Violet, but she did enjoy his gentle ministrations. Once he had finished he moved closer to her, so that his front was pressed to her back.

The contact of their skin was comforting, and her tense muscles loosened. His left hand cupped her left breast, teasing the nipple and massaging her. Then his lips clamped down on her neck, kissing her there, suckling and teasing the flesh. When his teeth nipped at her she gasped, the sensation sending a pleasurable jolt all the way to her lower belly.

His hand moved from her breast to her sex, massaging the flesh, pressing against her. His fingers expertly manipulated the swollen bud above her crease, coaxing a quick release that had her writhing back against him and her buttocks kneading against his organ.

A hand slipped under her left knee, lifting it up. 'Hold

your leg up for me…yes, that's it. Now, I'm going to enter you once more.'

She braced herself, waiting for the invasion. It pushed at her, slowly and the pain returned, though to a lesser degree.

'Is that better?'

'Somewhat.'

He pushed further, but stopped. 'Relax your body. You will adjust, I promise. We will go slow.' His fingers brushed at where they joined, then her bud, rubbing in slow circles. She moaned, moving her hips, allowing more of him inside her. When his mouth found her neck once more, she cried out as the bite of his teeth shot a bolt of pure ecstasy through her. His length slid in, and the pain was unbearable, but just for the briefest moment. Her mind was too busy processing the pleasure from his mouth and fingers to care.

'That's it. You did so well, Violet.' He nibbled at her neck.

'I…' Just as he'd said, she felt so much fuller than she'd expected.

'How are you feeling? Does it hurt still?'

'Somewhat. Wait.' There was a slight soreness there, but that lessened as each moment passed. They lay still for what seemed like the longest time before she spoke again. 'I think I'm all right now,' she whispered. 'Please, Ash. Make l-love to me.'

'I'm going to start moving, Violet. The friction will feel good for you.'

'And for you?'

'And for me. Very good.' He shifted his hips to pull back, then pushed in again. 'Did that hurt?'

'Surprisingly, no.'

'Excellent.' He repeated the motion, this time with more pressure, then again.

'Oh!' she cried out. 'That feels good.'

He thrust into her, again and again, building the tension inside her. Reaching back, she grasped at the back of his neck and pulled at his hair. This caused him to curse and increase his thrusts. His arm snaked around her, between her breasts, and grasped her shoulder, bringing her down as he moved upwards with ever increasing speed. Finally, she lost control of her body, and shattered into a million pieces as her orgasm ripped through her very being.

His movement slowed, then halted. She unclenched her fingers from his hair, then twisted her neck, so that she could look up at him, his handsome face scrunched up in concentration.

Reaching up, she brought his head down for a kiss. 'Thank you.'

He smiled against her mouth. 'You're welcome. But we aren't finished yet.'

She inhaled a quick breath when he left her, feeling oddly disappointed. But then he pushed her onto her back and climbed on top of her. Once again, the pressure of his body soothed her.

Nudging her knees apart, he began to enter her again, but this time it was only mildly uncomfortable, and once he was inside she found that she liked the sensation of fullness. When his pelvis came into contact with her swollen bud, the friction sent a delightful shiver through her. She repeated the motion, and both of them moaned aloud.

Ash braced his elbows on either side of her, his arms slipping under her before his mouth covered hers in a hungry kiss. Violet raked her fingers down the strong muscles of his back, gasping and crying into his mouth as he moved inside her, their bodies dancing in perfect rhythm as they both raced to the peak. She was just over that crest when he let out a deep, rough growl and he thrust into her one more time, convulsing as he flooded her with his seed. With one last grunt he collapsed against her, burying his face in her neck.

'No, don't go,' she pleaded, when he attempted to roll away from her.

'But I'm heavy.'

'I know,' she said with a sigh, tightening her arms around him. 'And I love it. You're like a heavy blanket. A really heavy one.' There was something about the weight and pressure of him that was soothing. 'Please? Just stay?'

'For a little bit.'

'All right.'

Violet relaxed under him, allowing his weight to settle over her. She remained there, blissful.

'May I move now?' he asked a few minutes later.

She supposed he couldn't remain there for ever. 'Yes.'

He shifted away. 'I can't be your blanket for the entire night. But I can offer you the next best thing.'

'And what is that?'

He spread an arm out. 'Come. Lie here with me.'

She stared at him, unsure what to do.

'It's like a hug,' he explained. 'But lying down. And we can do it the whole night.'

'We'll be hugging for the entire night?'

'Well, at least until I lose the feeling in my arm,' he said with a chuckle. 'Give it a try.'

That didn't seem necessary. Perhaps she should send him back to his own rooms. Married people didn't sleep in the same bed, did they?

However, seeing Ash lying on the bed with that lazy smile on his beautiful face made something in her chest flutter in the most pleasant way.

Shrugging, she lay down beside him, placing her head

on his arm, her back to his front. When his other arm came around her she finally understood. And while it wasn't the same as having him on top of her, this was just as good.

Everything about tonight had been good.

No, it hadn't just been good. It had been...marvellous.

Violet couldn't even recall why she'd thought being touched was repulsive.

Well, she still thought it was, but not Ash's touch.

His hands...his clever mouth...every part of him was wonderful. And the pleasure he gave her was nothing like she'd ever felt before.

Being with him in this way didn't seem repulsive to her, not the way it had been described in Papa's medical books. There had been perhaps a brief mention of pleasure, but the authors had glossed over it, or intimated that it was only men who experienced it.

But with Ash...except for the pain, everything had been exquisite.

Was she cured of her aversion to touch now? Would any other man make her feel this way?

The thought of being touched by another man, however, still made her stomach churn.

There was no need to think of such thoughts now, she thought with a yawn, and then she settled into his arms and closed her eyes.

When Violet awoke the next day, panic rose through her at the unfamiliar sensation of a warm body pressed behind her. But it quickly receded once memories from the night before flooded back.

She breathed a sigh of relief and relaxed against Ash.

Her husband.

They had remained entwined the entire night, their bodies touching.

And because it was Ash, she didn't mind at all.

'Awake already?'

The rough, raspy quality of his voice caught her off guard. But she found that she quite liked it.

'Is your arm asleep?'

'It's dead,' he said with a chuckle, then yawned. 'But do not fret. I have another one.'

'You're jesting.'

'I am.' He shifted her around so that she faced him, then lowered his head and kissed her. 'Good morning.'

'Good morning. Do you think…? Do you think we conceived last night?'

It was the question niggling at the back of her mind and she just couldn't stop herself from asking it.

The corners of his mouth turned up. 'We can't be certain. We must wait for your monthly flow. If it doesn't arrive, then you may be pregnant.'

'That's at least three weeks away,' she stated. 'Is there anything we can do to ensure our success?'

'Of course we can. We must continue our efforts until we can confirm you are with child,' he said in a most serious tone.

'Continue? How many times? For how long?'

'As many times as it takes. And for however long it takes.'

Chapter Ten

Ash had been so focused on his plan to woo Violet, and then the wedding, he hadn't thought much about what would happen after the ceremony. While Sebastian and Kate were happy to host them at Highfield Park, they couldn't stay there for ever. And so, two days after their wedding, Ash took Violet, along with Lady Avery, to his home in Hertfordshire, Chatsworth Manor.

'Oh, your home is beautiful, my lord,' Lady Avery exclaimed as they alighted from his carriage, which had stopped just outside the manor.

'Thank you, Lady Avery. It's been in my family since the First Marquess.'

Slowly, he glanced up at the house. The outside was made of yellow Bath stone and built in the Palladian style, as indicated by the portico. There was one main block, or *corps de logis*, which had three storeys and contained all the bedrooms and living areas. The two pavilions on either side each had two storeys, and consisted of the kitchens, the scullery, and servants's areas.

It was indeed, a very grand manor, part of his heritage. Something real and solid he could be proud of.

Yet, a knot grew in his stomach as the memories flooded back into his mind, reminding him of why he didn't come here often.

Maybe it wasn't worth saving and he should just let the Canfields have it. Then perhaps the memories of the past would disappear.

'Ash, it's lovely. Thank you for bringing us here.'

He glanced down at Violet as she too, stood gawking up at the house. He couldn't help but drop his gaze to her belly, wondering if she was with child at this very moment.

For some reason the thought both thrilled him and filled him with dread.

Which was preposterous. The sooner they confirmed she was carrying his child, the better. Then they would be much closer to securing his lands and his wealth, as well as her Oakwood Cottage.

It would also mean he no longer needed to sleep with her.

'Come, let's go inside.'

Placing a hand on her lower back, he guided Violet towards the front door. The servants were lined up in a row to welcome them, with his butler and housekeeper at the head.

'Thank you, everyone, for welcoming us. May I present Violet, Marchioness of Ashbrooke, and her mother, Lady Avery.'

'Lady Ashbrooke. Lady Avery,' the butler greeted with a low bow. 'Welcome to Chatsworth Manor. My name is Bennet, I am the butler, and this—' he gestured to the white-haired woman in a black uniform '—is Mrs Hogsworth, the housekeeper.'

'My lady.' She bowed her head.

'How do you do?' Violet replied.

Bennet continued, 'Please, if there is anything you need, do not hesitate to ask.' The butler led them inside, into the richly appointed hall. 'Would Her Ladyship like a tour? Perhaps she'll want to go over the accounts with Mrs Hogsworth?'

Ash shook his head. 'I'm afraid we are tired from our long journey here, Bennet.'

'My sincere apologies, my lord, my lady. That can wait. All your rooms are ready, and Her Ladyship's and Lady Avery's things were unpacked by their maids when they arrived yesterday.'

'Thank you, Bennet. Could you kindly show Lady Avery to her room?'

'Of course. I've put her in the Queen Anne room, as you requested.'

'The Queen Anne room?' Lady Avery said.

'It's our best guest room, Lady Avery,' Ash said. 'The Second Marquess had Her Majesty's bedroom recreated there. It is said the chest of drawers inside belonged to her.'

It also happened to be at the other end of the manor—the farthest from the master bedchamber.

'I do hope you like it.'

'It sounds wonderful. Thank you, my lord.'

As Bennet led Ash's mother-in-law away, Violet took his hand and squeezed it. 'Thank you for inviting her to live with us, Ash.'

'Of course.'

Despite Violet's exasperation with her mother, he knew she was the one constant in her life, and with the upheavals coming her way his wife would need all the stability she could get. 'Now come along, we need to rest.'

She lifted a dark brow at him. 'Are we really resting?'

He grinned. 'You know me so well, wife.'

Taking her hand, he led her up the stairs and down the hall to the east wing of the manor where his bedchamber was located. Pushing the door open, he ushered her inside. The massive room was decorated in dark colours and woods, plush carpets and thick velvet drapes. A large bed stood in the middle, atop a dais.

Violet glanced around. 'And where is my bedchamber?'

'Your bedchamber?'

'The Marchioness's room,' she stated, glancing around. 'Bennet said Gertrude had already unpacked my things. Is there a doorway to connect with it from here?'

Ash paused. It hadn't occurred to him that Violet would want her own bedchamber.

Of course she does, idiot. That's how married people live.

'Is it through here?' Violet walked over to a door on the left side of the room. 'It's the only door here.'

Ash blinked.

The Marchioness's room.

His *mother's* room.

He swallowed hard, forcing the lump down his throat. 'Yes. That's it.'

Turning the knob, she pushed the door open. Once she'd disappeared through the door Ash gripped the doorjamb as a dizzying feeling came over him.

How could he have forgotten about that room? When his mother had left, Father had forbidden anyone from mentioning her ever again. Then he'd had all her things taken out and burned, and the room sealed. As far as he knew, no one went in there. It was as if the entire bedchamber hads simply disappeared, vanished into thin air.

Like his mother.

'Ash?' Violet's head poked through the door.

Pushing those intrusive thoughts aside, he said, 'Is—is the bedchamber to your liking?' He hoped she wouldn't ask him to go inside.

'Yes. Gertrude has arranged all my things.' She hesitated. 'I…I suppose I'm expected to sleep in there?'

'If that is your preference.' His stomach knotted. 'Is it?'

Slowly, she lifted her head. 'I have not… We have never slept apart since the wedding. It would feel much too…new to me. Do you think, just until I've acclimatised myself a little, that I could stay—'

'Yes.'

He closed the distance between them in a heartbeat before pulling her back inside his room and into his arms. The thought that she wanted to be with him—even though it was because of her aversion to novel experiences—made his heart leap out of his chest.

'You should sleep here with me. For now. Until you've acclimatised yourself.'

She melted against him. 'I'd like that very much.'

'Shall we finally leave the manor today, darling?' Ash asked as he rolled away from her, his body boneless from another intense lovemaking session.

'Perhaps once my soul has returned to my body,' Violet replied with a long, drawn-out breath. 'Not that you give me any time to recover.'

Ash propped himself on an elbow and smirked at her. 'Are you complaining, wife? You seemed to have thoroughly enjoyed yourself this morning. After all I made you climax three times.'

'No complaints,' she replied. 'None at all.'

It had been two days since they'd arrived at Chatsworth Manor, and most of the time had been spent in their bedchamber. Thankfully, nobody in the household—not the servants nor Lady Avery—had remarked on their preference for indoor activities.

Ash supposed that was to be expected from newly wedded couples, and he didn't want to disappoint anyone. Besides, he was taking his duties as Marquess of Ashbrooke seriously. Making an heir and securing his lands was serious work, and he was focused on the task.

Ash glanced out of the window. 'We could go for a short walk outside. We could go exploring.' It had been one of his favourite activities as a child. 'It doesn't seem too cold. We could bundle up, take a quick gander, then come back for tea?'

She rolled over onto her stomach, her pert, adorable buttocks on display for him. 'I don't really like the outside. But I suppose we will have to see other people at some point.'

'It's settled, then.' He slid out of bed and put his robe on. 'I'll ring for Gertrude and then I'll get ready.'

'All right,' Violet said, as she stretched like a cat in her naked glory, making his mouth water.

He almost changed his mind about leaving the bed.

One hour later, Ash had finished dressing and Violet emerged from her bedroom, bundled up in her coat, hat, scarf and gloves, and they headed out.

Truly, he didn't want to leave; he could stay in bed with Violet all day and all night. However, his body and his lungs craved fresh air, and he wanted Violet to see the gardens and the woods around the manor. Besides, he and Violet had made love so many times in the last two days it seemed impossible that she wasn't yet with child.

A strange dread swirled in his gut. His mind told him that he wanted—no, *needed* her to become pregnant as soon as possible. It was the only way he could stop the Canfields from taking the lands. Perhaps that was why—despite his own reservations—he'd brought her here. To remind himself of what he could lose. Not just the house and the lands, but the income and the well-being of his tenants and servants.

But despite all that a small, selfish part of him didn't want her to be pregnant yet—not when it meant he would no longer have any reason to be in her bed.

Ash brushed off those thoughts. This was why he'd married Violet, after all. To produce an heir. And once that goal was met they could start leading separate lives. He had promised her that, and he was eager to have things back the way they'd been before he'd met her.

'Brr...it's still cold,' Violet complained as they stepped out into the back gardens. 'I hate winter.'

Ash tipped his head back and breathed in the cool air. 'Really? Believe it or not, I love it, especially out here.' It had been too long since he'd last visited Chatsworth at this time of year. He mostly stayed in London, where amusements were plentiful for a bachelor like him. Well, a former bachelor anyway.

'You love winter? But why? It's so cold and wet and slushy.' She shuddered. 'The only thing I'm glad for is that it's a good excuse to stay inside with a cup of tea and a book.'

'Shouldn't winter be your favourite time of the year, then? Since you're excused from outdoor activities?'

She shrugged. 'I stay inside most of the year anyway. Nevertheless, I'm allowed to hate or love whatever season I choose.'

'So, you like spring, then?'

She made a face. 'Ugh...it makes me sneeze.'

'Summer?'

'Too hot and sticky.'

'Autumn?'

She shook her head. 'I don't like the crunchy leaves.'

Stopping, he turned to her. 'You don't like *any* season?'

'I told you. I stay inside most of the time.'

He laughed. 'Of course, my lovely logical Violet.' He took

her hand. 'Come, some fresh air will do you good. Then I promise we can go back inside.'

A lovely blush painted her cheeks. 'Back to our bed?'

Minx.

'Or perhaps I could show you the wonders of the library.'

'What kind of wonders? Do you have a rare book collection?'

'No, but there are other wonders. Like…' He proceeded to whisper to her what he planned to do to her against his grandfather's volumes of medieval writings.

The colour on her face heightened. 'I don't think Thomas Aquinas would approve of such things.'

'Aquinas is dead, darling. Although you may be right… Perhaps I should take you against Chaucer's works instead. He was quite the bawdy bard, that one.' He brushed a stray lock of hair off her cheek. 'Shall we continue?'

Chatsworth Manor had an extensive garden to the rear, though at this time of the year there wasn't much to see. In the spring, however, it was a magnificent sight, filled with blooming flowers and lush greenery.

'It's actually quite peaceful,' Violet remarked as they strolled down the main path leading away from the house. 'It seems like there's no one around for miles. We had a lot of neighbours, and Mama's relatives were always dropping by. It was hard to find peace and quiet.'

'Except in your papa's library.'

'Yes.' Her hand gripped his arm. 'Thank you, by the way. For checking into Papa's finances.'

The day after their wedding Ash had told her what he had found out about the debts and repayments.

'Of course.'

A look of strain crossed her face, and a wrinkle appeared between her eyebrows.

'Do not fret.' Leaning down, he pressed a kiss on the worry line. 'Come, let's keep walking.'

'But where shall we go?'

'Hmm…' He tapped a finger to his chin. 'Why don't you lead us? And no, we are not going back to the house, not yet.'

Her lips turned down into the most adorable pout. 'But I've never been here before, Ash. How do I know where to go?'

'You don't.'

'But—'

He held up a hand. 'I told you—we are exploring. That means going forth into the unknown.'

'You know I hate surprises.'

'This isn't a surprise, darling. It's just…something you don't yet know.'

'By definition, that is the nature of a surprise.'

'Yes.' He kissed her cold nose. 'But you know what isn't a surprise?' He threaded his fingers through hers. 'This. Me. I'm here. And I promise everything will be all right. Do you trust me?'

Her hand squeezed his. 'I do.'

'So, lead on, dauntless explorer.'

Ash wasn't quite sure why he urged her to expand her boundaries, but he had a feeling it would be good for her. In the last few days Violet had opened up so marvellously, exploring her sensual side. She was so eager and uninhibited, he thought, why couldn't she apply the same enthusiasm outside the bedroom?

She led him through the gardens, mostly staying on the paths. When they reached the last of the tiled walkways, she stopped.

'It's the end,' she declared.

'Is it?' Raising his booted foot, he stepped off the path.

He grinned at her, and to his surprise she followed suit.

He was quite happy to let her meander about, allowing her to set their route. They moved deeper into the forested area, but thankfully since the trees were bare it wasn't too dark.

As they proceeded, Ash couldn't put his finger on why this particular area looked familiar. There was something about the way the land rose uphill and the line of trees on the east side that he recognised, but for some reason he couldn't place where they were, exactly.

A shiver ran down his spine.

Silly.

Of course this place was familiar. He'd spent a lot of time here as a child. As he'd grown older, he'd spent more time in the schoolroom, and less and less time in the woods. Perhaps his memory of this place had faded from being away for so long.

'Look over there.' Violet pointed to something in the distance.

'What is it?'

'Water. I think it's a lake.' She dragged him down the hill. 'I want to take a closer look.'

'Lake? We don't have a lake. But we do have a—'

The pond.

He halted as a tightness wrapped around his throat like a garrotte. His stomach tied up in knots and sweat built on his brow.

'Ash? Come, let's go and see what it is.'

She tugged at his arm, but he couldn't move his feet, his boots seemingly stuck to the ground.

'What's wrong?' She cocked her head to one side.

He swallowed the lump in his throat. 'Nothing.'

'It's not nothing,' she retorted. 'Ash, I'm not a child or a fool. Your complexion has turned grey and despite the chill in the air you're sweating profusely. Is it because of that pond?'

He nodded. 'It was *the* pond.'

'*The* pond?'

'Where my father drowned.'

His guts churned. Fearing he might lose the contents of his stomach, he pulled his hand away from her and spun around.

The climb back up the hill was gruelling—and exactly what he needed. With his lungs burning and calves aching, he could ignore the dull pain in his chest. When he reached the top, exhaustion took over, so he collapsed to his knees.

'Ash! Ash, please!' Violet scrambled to catch up with him 'I—I know I've made a terrible mistake, leading us here. Please, forgive me.' Her voice trembled. 'Th-this is all my fault. I'm sorry.'

'No, no, darling.' He pulled her into his embrace and her arms wrapped around him. The soft body melting into his soothed the ache in him. 'It's not your fault. You didn't know. Hell, I didn't know either.'

It was as if his mind had erased this place from his memory.

'I'd forgotten where we were.'

She inhaled as her arms tightened around him. 'I'm so sorry for your loss.'

'It was a long time ago.'

'What happened? How did he drown? Why did no one rescue him?'

'He died alone.'

'Alone? Why would he swim out here alone?'

'He wasn't swimming. He'd been drinking then stumbled out into the pond. They found his body floating in the middle of the water.'

She stiffened in his arms. 'Was it an accident or did he take his own life?'

'I don't know, exactly. Could be both.' An acrid burn rose up in his throat. 'He drank a lot, even before...'

'Before what?'

'Before Mama left us.'

Violet whimpered, burrowed deeper into his arms and pressed her face to his neck.

Ash wasn't sure why he was telling her this, but it was as if a dam had broken inside him and he couldn't stop the flood of emotions from rushing out.

'When I was a child, I didn't see my parents very much, but when I did they were always arguing. Mama was a beauty, and many men sought her out, even though she was married. My father was a jealous man, despite the fact that he had just as many lovers as she did. There was this one night, when I was nine years old, my parents hosted a ball, and my mother invited her current lover, an Italian count, to spite Father.'

Violet tightened her embrace.

'Father was livid. He cornered the Count, there was a fight, and Father nearly killed him.'

Ash only knew this because his father had confessed it to him one night while in a drunken stupor.

'That was the final straw for Mama and she left us the next day. I never saw her again.'

He paused as the ache in his throat made it difficult to speak.

'My father hung on for another year, drinking himself into oblivion each day.'

His father had spent most of his days passed out or screaming and crying at anyone who dared to get close enough.

'Then one night he disappeared. He was missing for three days. One of the groundskeepers found in him the pond.'

Ash had never ventured out to the pond ever again.

Violet said nothing, nor did she ask any questions. She just held on to him tightly, never wavering, never letting go.

After what seemed like an eternity, Ash gently prised her arms off his body. 'I'm cold,' he said.

Brushing her hands on her thighs, she rose to her feet and offered him a hand. 'Then let's go home.'

Ash allowed her to lead him back, and by some miracle they made it without getting lost. But then again, this was Violet, so he had no doubt her keen mind would find a way to navigate them safely back.

'We were out much too long in the cold,' she explained to Bennet when they entered the manor. 'Please have some hot tea sent up.'

He followed her up the stairs to their bedchamber, where she proceeded to strip off all his damp, cold clothes. She pulled back the covers and nudged him to slip between them. There was a knock at the door, then a maid came in with a tray.

'By the bed, please. Thank you.' When the maid slipped out, she said to him, 'How about a cup, Ash?'

He shook his head. 'No, thank you.'

'Then what would you like?' She inched closer to him, placing a hand on his forehead. 'Do you need anything else?'

'Just you.' He snaked a hand around her wrist and pulled her down, melding his lips to hers.

Without a word, she crawled between the covers. Her clothes came off quickly, and he rolled her underneath him. Spreading her thighs he entered her in one stroke, filling her to the hilt. She cried out into his mouth, wrapping her legs around his waist.

Ash lost himself in her, fusing their bodies together tightly, bringing them both to the peak of ecstasy. Her cries and purrs were like sweet music to his ears, drowning out the haunted past. When she clasped him, he surged into her, flooding her with his seed.

Ash couldn't bring himself to let go of her.

Not yet, he pleaded to some unknown entity.

Violet was real. She was here. She was not a memory from the past that threatened to consume him until nothing was left.

Violet sighed, not saying a word, her arms still grappled around him. She wouldn't release him—she never did. She had told him that for some reason she found the weight of his body soothing. When he tried to move, she would always protest, begging for another minute. He usually indulged her until she fell asleep.

It was a mistake to come here. To bring her here.

He gently pulled her arms away and rolled off her. Thankfully, Violet didn't object. Instead she let out long sigh and moved onto her side. She let out a small yawn, but nothing else as she curled herself around a pillow.

Ash stared up at the ceiling, unable to move. He longed to curl up with Violet, but he could not bring himself to touch her again.

Being here...the memories...his parents...it was too much.

They had to leave.

Some time must have passed before Violet woke up, because the room was dark as pitch.

'Ash?'

'You're awake.'

'Mmm-hmm.'

Her hand reached for him, and upon finding him across the bed from her, she cuddled up to him. Pressing her nose to his chest, she breathed in his wonderful, unique scent. She could find him in the dark just by that amazing smell alone. Indeed, some days it was all she could think of.

Correction: *he* was all she could think of, all the time.

And that thought, which was illogical, scared her.

It had been less than a week since their wedding, and yet Violet had many questions in her mind.

Did Ash enjoy their lovemaking?

Was she doing the right things?

Was she pregnant yet?

How long would it take?

And how soon would Ash leave her bed once they confirmed it?

It was that last question that made her mind lock up and cease functioning.

'I was thinking of something.'

Ash's voice in the dark shook her out of her thoughts. 'And that is?'

'We should go on a honeymoon. There wasn't time to plan one, with the wedding and all, but it's only proper that as newlyweds, we should go abroad and travel. Would you like that?'

That idea had her mind—and limbs—locking up. Outside England everything would be new to her. It would be like the proposal debacle in the ballroom, only a thousand times worse.

But then she remembered his face as he'd told her about his father. The way his skin had turned pale at the sight of the pond. And how his lower lip had trembled as he'd struggled to breathe.

That expression had been marked—no, it had been burned—into her consciousness permanently.

The look of distress.

And she decided she never wanted to see that expression on his face ever again.

Moving deeper into his arms, she placed a kiss on his chest. 'Yes, Ash, I would like that.'

Chapter Eleven

When Ash had told her they were going to Paris, Violet had been overcome with panic.

She'd never been before—never been abroad at all—and the idea of going to a place where everything was unknown to her had made her want to run into a closet and hide.

However, she understood why he wanted to leave. He might not have said it aloud, but she knew. Just as Oakwood Cottage would always remind her of her Papa, staying at Chatsworth Manor brought back memories of his father.

And she didn't want him to suffer.

It didn't make logical sense. Their marriage was a mutually beneficial agreement. Whether he suffered or not should not be any of her concern. But seeing the look of distress on his face had her pushing logic—and her own fear—aside.

And so she would endure Paris for him.

On the day of their arrival, the concierge at the hotel had informed them that the owners, upon hearing they were on their honeymoon, had given them a gift—a special meal at the hotel's restaurant.

'Must we go?' Violet asked as they prepared to leave. 'Can't we eat in our suite?'

The very idea of dining in a crowded restaurant—her first time ever—sounded daunting.

'I'm sorry, darling, but it would be rude to refuse a gift. We won't be long, I promise.'

'All right.'

They headed downstairs to the restaurant, where the staff showed them to their 'best' table, which Violet hoped would be one tucked away in the corner, away from everyone and everything. To her horror, they were seated in the centre of the room, right in the middle of the din, with staff rushing about, the clinks and clanks of cutlery echoing off the domed ceiling, and too-loud conversations booming across the room.

'The chef has prepared a special menu just for you, and I shall serve the first course soon,' the waiter informed them in heavily accented English. He then poured them each a flute of champagne from the bottle inside an ice bucket by the table. 'But for now, enjoy your champagne.'

Violet sipped at her drink nervously, looking at Ash as he glanced around. He seemed to be enjoying himself, marvelling at the sights around them.

'Do you dine at restaurants frequently in London?' she asked.

'I do,' he said. 'Often I'm at my club, which does have a restaurant, or I go to the West End. Once in a while I'll even dip into a public house. I have an excellent cook at home, but I hate dining alone.'

Eating in a quiet room by herself sounded wonderful to Violet, especially now as the cacophony of sounds around them swelled.

'Hey, what are you two celebrating?'

Violet started as the lanky, bespectacled man at the table beside them turned in his chair to face them. The grating sound the feet of his chair from scraping on the wooden floor made her teeth hurt.

'We're on our honeymoon,' Ash replied, lifting his champagne flute.

'Honeymoon? Congratulations to you, then. Hey, guys!' He turned back to his companions. 'These two here are on their honeymoon!'

The rest of the group cheered, shouting and hooting as they offered their congratulations. The throb in Violet's temple pulsed.

'Thank you,' Ash said. 'Are you by any chance American?'

'We sure are.' The man extended his hand. 'Thornton Owens, from Boston, Massachusetts.' He then proceeded to introduce the rest of his group. 'This is Christopher Davies, that lovely young woman in the green dress is Julie Wright, and the stunning blonde over there is Sophie Watson.'

'I'm pleased to meet you,' said Ash. 'I am Devon St James, Marquess of Ashbrooke. This is my wife, Lady Ashbrooke. We're from London.'

'I was just there last year, Your Lordship,' Mr Davies shouted as he attempted to be heard over the hubbub. 'Nice city.'

'Great meeting you, my lord, Lady Ashbrooke.' Mr Owens lifted his glass to them. 'We should let you get on with your dinner.'

Violet breathed a sigh of relief once Mr Owens turned his chair back to his companions and their first course arrived. However, her reprieve was only temporary as every once in a while, Mr Owens would turn his chair again to ask Ash something about London or his opinion on trivial matters, like the weather or Parisian food. By the time they were on their dessert course, Mr Owens suggested they joined their tables together.

'You don't mind, do you, Violet?' Ash asked.

Mind? Of course she did. But how could she say no,

when Ash flashed her that handsome smile that made her lose all thought. 'N-no, I suppose it's all right.'

His smiled turned brighter as he stood up and helped Mr Owens push their tables together.

'Tell me,' Ash began, 'what is a group of Americans doing in Paris?'

'We've come here for inspiration.' Mr Owens waved around them. 'We're starving artists, seeking to create our masterpieces. I'm a writer, by the way.'

'What have you written? Can I purchase it in a bookshop?' Violet couldn't help but ask; she'd never met a real writer in the flesh. Was he a philosopher? Or perhaps a playwright? Or maybe he was a novelist?

'Nothing yet, Lady Ashbrooke,' he said. 'I'm still waiting to be inspired by Paris.'

'And how long have you been here?'

'Three years.'

'Oh.'

'I'm a dancer,' Miss Wright interjected. 'At the ballet.'

'I saw *Swan Lake* a few weeks ago,' Violet offered. 'Have you performed in that?'

Miss Wright inhaled from the cigarette between her fingers, then blew out a plume of smoke. 'It's not that kind of ballet, honey.'

As Violet choked on the harsh air, the rest of the table broke out into peals of laughter. She looked at her husband, confused, but he only said, 'I'll explain later, darling.'

'And I'm a painter,' Mr Davies announced proudly. 'And, yes, I've had my paintings exhibited, and that's all thanks to my muse, Sophie.' He nodded to the stunning blonde woman in the red dress.

'That means she don't work,' Miss Wright scoffed.

'You're just jealous,' Miss Watson retorted.

'Now ladies, put the claws away,' Mr Owens said. 'We have guests and we don't want to scare them away. My lord, you're a delight and so is your beautiful wife. It's great to meet you.'

'And you are a lively, interesting bunch. Isn't that right, Violet?'

She could only swallow a gulp and nod.

No one seemed to notice how uncomfortable she was— or no one cared. The spirited conversation continued with a lively and energetic dynamic that Ash seemed to enjoy. He had a clever comeback for every question or thought thrown his way, and he volleyed back with witty remarks of his own.

He fit in perfectly.

Violet, on the other hand, couldn't help but be reminded of the moral philosopher Sydney Smith, who had written about a square person trying to squeeze himself into a round hole.

She simply did not fit in.

'So, Devon,' Miss Watson began as she scooted closer to Ash. She had placed her chair on his left side once they had joined their tables together. 'What does being a marquess mean, aside from people having to call you "my lord".'

Violet's stomach knotted at the woman's audacious use of Ash's Christian name. Had she not been taught proper etiquette as a child? She also seemed to be missing key pieces of her gown, as her décolletage was thoroughly exposed whenever she leaned forward.

'It means I don't work either,' Ash joked.

Miss Watson threw her head back and laughed. 'Devon, you are utterly hilarious.'

Her hand landed on Ash's arm. The touch was brief, but Violet did not miss it.

It had been years since Violet had had a proper fit of anger, but at this moment she was coming very close. A white-hot fury rose inside her, and she grabbed a fork, her knuckles going white with her grip. The urge to stab the woman's hand grew with each passing moment.

A warm, firm hand landed on her arm—Ash. He was peering at her with an expression she hadn't yet catalogued, trying to catch her gaze. Ashamed of her violent thoughts, she couldn't bear to look him in the eye, but she did release her grip on the fork.

'Ladies, Gentlemen,' he announced in a calm tone. 'I'm afraid the hour is growing late. Lady Ashbrooke and I must retire.'

'Aw, you can't go.' Miss Watson pouted. 'We were just getting to know each other.'

Violet was sorely tempted to retrieve the fork.

'It's not even that late,' Mr Davies protested. 'We should go check out some restaurants on the Seine.'

'I'm afraid you will have to make do with your own company for the rest of the evening. Shall we, Violet? Goodnight, everyone.'

Gently, he tugged her to her feet.

'I'm sorry, darling,' he said once they were safely behind the doors of their suite. 'I should have realised that might have been too much for you.'

She still couldn't speak, as the vision of the American woman touching Ash permeated her mind. She wished she could wash it away like dirt on a window.

'Come. Let's get to bed.'

His voice was soft and soothing as he guided her towards their bedroom and then proceeded to make her forget about the terrible dinner and that horrid woman.

* * *

Despite the rough beginning, for the rest of their time, Violet thoroughly enjoyed Paris.

Yes, the city itself was a twisting, gloomy, maze of cramped streets and the buildings of all shapes and sizes and styles were all smashed together with no sense of rhyme or reason, and yet Violet thought it was quite charming once she got used to it.

Their hotel on the Seine, La Neuville de Paris, was a marvel, but it wasn't its grand facade or luxurious decor and furnishings that had impressed her. At first, the idea that they would be living and sleeping in a place where there were people all around, above and below them had made her skin crawl, but Ash had reserved the top corner suite just for them. It was quiet up there, and their suite of rooms was expansive, not to mention, the bed spacious and the sheets were made of the softest silk. They felt marvellous on her naked skin, especially when Ash made love to her on top of them.

Then there were the various activities and amusements, like museums, pleasure gardens, restaurants and cafés. Normally they would have set her nerves on edge, but Ash scheduled their daily jaunts for very early in the morning or in the late afternoon, so there were fewer people around. Sometimes, instead of dining out, they would sit in parks, tucked away in cosy corners on benches around the city, and eat from a basket full of goodies prepared by the hotel staff. Or they would have cold sandwiches, cheese and bottles of wine bought from local shops, as they sat wrapped in winter coats. In fact, he seemed to have a knack of finding quiet, serene places in the middle of this noisy, crowded city.

Of course, the rest of their time was spent in bed, and

Violet found she really didn't mind it at all. She had never known there could be so much more to lovemaking than the marital act itself, and she found she enjoyed most if not all of it. Her body was so attuned to Ash that he only had to send her one look—an expression she had catalogued as lust—and she practically vibrated with need when she recognised it. She craved him, obsessed over him, wanted to know all the ways to please him and record them in a mental list she could access at any time.

It was illogical, and no matter how many times she ran through the possibilities in her head, she couldn't find a good reason why she was so obsessed with him. The chaos made her head hurt whenever she tried to define it or find reason for it.

Surely this will pass.

Once she was with child, and had given birth to said child and heir, she could go back to an orderly life, one with a predictable routine. No more passionate encounters, surprises, or the unpredictable ball of chaos that was Ash.

In other words, no more Ash.

The idea hollowed a pit in her stomach.

Preposterous.

Yes, these emotions had to pass.

Once they were back in England, back to what was familiar, her obsession for him would wither away.

At the moment, however, she was still in France, lying in bed alone. It was their last day and it had been particularly busy, leaving her drained. All the sights and sounds had been too much, and she had begged Ash to take her back to the hotel and leave her be. So he'd left her alone in their bedroom, where she'd lain down for an hour.

Now she was finally feeling refreshed, she padded out

into the living area, where he was sitting in an armchair, feet up on the coffee table, reading a book.

'Ash?' she called.

He glanced up from behind the book, concern marring his handsome face. 'Are you feeling better, darling?'

She nodded, then walked over to him. He tugged at her hand and planted her on his lap. 'I was just feeling drained.'

'I was afraid you were sick, or that you were cross with me.' He looked like a young boy being scolded by mother.

'I'm fine.' She cupped his cheek. 'And I'm not cross with you. Sometimes when I'm overwhelmed and surrounded by too many people I need some time by myself. So please do not think that just because I do not want to be near you I'm angry with you.'

'I shall remember that.' His face relaxed. 'Do you feel refreshed enough to go on one last walk with me?'

'I would very much like that.'

After bundling up, they left the hotel and took their usual path along the Seine, in a quiet section away from the markets and cafés and the noise from the restoration work being done on the Notre-Dame cathedral.

'Have you enjoyed our honeymoon, darling?' Ash asked as they made their way along the serene waterside.

'Oh, yes. Very much so.'

'I'm glad.' His hand tightened around hers. 'What was your favourite part?'

A blush tinged her cheeks, making him throw his head back and laugh aloud.

'Aside from *that*.'

He winked at her, obviously guessing she'd been thinking of their time spent in bed.

'The churches,' she said. 'And the library.' They had been

a godsend, as they had been quiet and peaceful, an oasis in a messy, crowded and frenetic city.

The corner of his mouth tugged up. 'Of course you enjoyed those the most. What about your least favourite part?'

She thought about Miss Watson, but decided there was, indeed, something much worse than that odious woman.

'The stinky cheese.'

They continued their walk in silence, reaching the end of the path, then turned back. As they made their way to the hotel a flower seller stopped them, offering her wares, speaking in soft, rapid French.

Ash looked to Violet.

'She says you should buy some pretty flowers for your pretty wife.'

Violet had been their translator for most of their trip, as Ash could only manage a few words of French on his own.

The woman's head bobbed up and down then pushed her basket at him.

'How could I say no to a woman who obviously has good taste?' Winking at the woman, he produced a coin from his pocket and offered it to her.

She, in turn, handed him a bundle of pink camellias. '*Merci, monsieur.*'

'*Merci, madame,*' he replied. 'Well, I'm afraid I've exhausted all my French. I'm sure my tutors would be terribly proud of me.'

Violet said a few more words of thanks to the woman before she hurried off. 'Thank you,' she said when he handed her the flowers.

'You must have had excellent tutors when you were growing up,' he remarked. 'Being that this is your first time in France and yet you know so much of the language.'

'I didn't have any tutors,' she explained. 'I taught myself.'

'You taught yourself how to speak French?' His jaw looked as if it might become unhinged at any moment. 'How? And why?'

'I didn't exactly teach myself to speak French,' she began. 'I taught myself to *read* in French.'

Her pronunciation was horrible, if the number of times the people she'd spoken to had asked her to repeat things was any indication.

'Papa had a paper that I wanted to read, but it was in French. He was far too busy to read and translate for me, so I took it upon myself to obtain language books and teach myself.'

'And what was this paper?'

'It was written by a mathematician,' she stated. 'A female mathematician. Madame Lenoire. And the paper was the Mathematical Theory of Elastic Surfaces.'

'And it was worth it? Learning an entire language to read one paper?'

She crossed her arms over her chest. 'It won the Grand Prize at the Paris Academy of Sciences.'

He tsked. 'You truly love numbers, don't you?'

'What isn't there to love about mathematics? It is truth, because numbers cannot lie, and nor is it vague. Yes means yes and no means no. It's precise and concise. Mathematics can explain anything and everything. It is, at its core, the very universe itself.'

He seemed to ponder her words. 'I'd never thought of it that way before. My logical, lovely Violet.' Taking her hand once more, he tucked it into his arm. 'Let's enjoy our last evening in Paris.'

Thankfully that evening, Ash had once again arranged for dinner in their suite, consisting of Violet's favourite dishes she had tasted in Paris. They dined on crispy duck confit, rich beef cooked in red wine, and an assortment of sweet baked desserts. Violet was eating a delicious pastry in the shape of a cone when some of the sweet cream inside oozed out, spilling onto her fingers. Putting the pastry on a plate, she licked her fingers, then unexpectedly locked gazes with her husband. Instantly, she saw it—the look of lust on his face, plain as day. Heat pooled in her belly.

He cleared his throat, dismissing the lone waiter standing in the corner. Once they were alone, Ash leapt out of his seat, then dragged her to the settee, their mouths crushing together in a desperate kiss.

Ash clawed frantically at her clothes. 'Damn buttons.'

The ripping of fabric told Violet that he'd torn the back of her dress. Her skirt, petticoats and hoops thankfully easily came off and pooled around her feet. When his fingers came upon her corset, he let out a string of curses. Then, 'Wait.'

'Wait?'

Reaching over to the dining table, he grabbed something shiny—a knife.

'I'll buy you a new one,' he growled as he twisted her around.

The compression around her torso loosened as he cut through the strings, then ripped the offending corset from her body and tossed it aside along with the knife.

'You're beautiful.'

He pulled off her drawers, then whipped off her chemise, exposing her breasts to his hot gaze. Pushing her down on the settee, he covered her body then fixed his mouth over a nipple.

Violet threw her head back, enjoying the sensations of his wet tongue lashing at her nipple. He switched his attention to the other one, torturing it equally. When he made a motion to rise to take off his clothes, she stopped him.

'Violet?'

She rubbed her cheek against his wool coat. 'This feels nice. You feel nice.' The scratchy fabric abraded her nipples deliciously, and she spread her legs and wrapped them around his hips, the velvet of his trousers rubbing against the insides of her thighs. 'Is it possible…for you to keep your clothes on?'

Without another word, he reached down between them to unbutton his falls. 'I need you, Violet,' he groaned, then thrust into her in one stroke. 'Want you. Only you.'

Violet clung to him, the sensation of his clothes rubbing against her naked body brought her pleasure to new heights. She quickly orgasmed, shuddering violently beneath him as he continued to pummel into her. Once she was done, he slowed down to a stop.

'That was…amazing.' She buried her face in his neck to breathe in his scent. 'Did you…?'

'No, darling. But it's early and I'm not done with you yet.'

Rising to his feet, he slipped his clothes off, tossing them onto the floor along with her destroyed shirt and corset. 'Since we're trying new things, do you think you'd like to try something else?'

She was too mindless deny him. 'All right.'

'Excellent.' Taking her hand, he pulled her up to stand, then sat down on the settee. Reaching between his legs, he wrapped a hand around his member and stroked it up and down. 'I love looking at your naked body,' he groaned. 'Violet, do you want to make love to me?'

'Me? What do you mean?'

His gaze moved from her to his stiff shaft. 'I want you on

top of me, Violet. I want to watch you move and bounce and writhe as you take your pleasure. Can you do that for me?'

Violet hesitated, though the sight of him bare and naked before her excited her. 'I want to, but I don't know how.'

'I'll help you. Come.'

With his help, she straddled his lap, the tip of his erection brushing against her curls. 'Hold the tip…guide it into… ah yes, Violet.' His head rolled back.

Slowly, she sank down, taking him inside her inch by inch. The feeling was the same as when he was on top, but somehow it was different. When he filled her to the hilt, she braced herself on his shoulders. 'Now what?'

'Move, darling.'

'How?'

'Any way you want to.'

Violet paused, unsure what to do. Then she wiggled her hips. 'Does that feel good?'

'You feel good,' he said. 'But see if you can move more.'

Lifting her hips, she slid up his length, then pushed down. The friction sent a jolt of pleasure through her. 'Oh.'

'There.' His hands cupped her buttocks. 'Let me help you.'

He helped her set a slow, steady rhythm. Once she found her stride, he let go, allowing her to do the work. She set a slow pace, but eventually began to move faster and faster. Each downward stroke of her hips sent shocks of delight up her spine.

'Violet… Violet…' Ash gripped her buttocks, kneaded at her soft flesh.

Raking her fingers into his hair, she pulled his head back and brought her lips down for a kiss. He groaned into her mouth, his hips thrusting up to meet hers.

Violet shifted her knees, pushing forward. 'Oh!' Her

pleasure increased with each movement, building up inside her.

'Come, Violet,' he said through gritted teeth. 'Please. I need you to— Oh!'

She shuddered above him, her breasts bouncing as she rode him hard. He captured a nipple in his mouth, biting down just as her body exploded. He let out a throaty cry, his hips rocking erratically as he pulsed inside her. Her release wrung every ounce of pleasure from her body, leaving her limp as she collapsed against him.

'You were magnificent.' He crushed her against him. 'As I knew you would be.'

That had only the beginning, and for the rest of the evening Ash took his time with her, teased her, gave her endless pleasure, all the while telling her again and again that he wanted her.

Afterwards, as she lay in his arms, she slipped a hand down to her belly, as she had done every night since their wedding, wondering if there was a child inside her at that very moment.

Ash had said he wanted her—but perhaps only until she'd had his heir. What he really, truly wanted was his lands and his income. This was the reason they'd married after all.

And once she'd given birth to the future Marquess of Ashbrooke, she too would have what she wanted—Oakwood Cottage and Papa's library.

They would be back in England soon, and things would go back to normal.

That idea, however, caused a different thought to take root in her mind.

What was normal?

And what about after she gave birth? What would normal be like then?

Violet urged herself to think of Papa's library and Oak-wood Cottage. Of Papa and how he had been the only person in the world who'd loved and understood her. She would never have her father back, nor the same life she'd had before he'd passed away, but she would at the very least have the memory of him.

That was the 'normal' she should be thinking about. Of her routines, of curling up on a chair, surrounded by the warmth and reminder that her father had understood and loved her.

She closed her eyes and nestled deeper against Ash, allowing his scent to envelop her senses as she fell asleep.

Chapter Twelve

The smells and sights of London felt like a welcome balm to Ash. Everything here was familiar, the soul of the city so attuned to his own.

Paris had been much too frenzied and dizzying, even for him. He'd enjoyed the city, but their time there hadn't been real—it was like a pleasurable dream, but one he ultimately had to wake from. No, London was where he belonged.

'Thank you for agreeing to stay here,' he said to Violet as they pulled up at his townhouse.

'We had to come back sometime.'

On her lap, her fingers did that little dance where the thumbs touched her fingers one by one. Ash had noticed she did that whenever she was nervous or anxious.

'We'll visit Chatsworth Manor again one day, won't we?'

'Of course.'

Though the reason for leaving Chatsworth remained unspoken between them, it was obvious to Ash that Violet knew exactly why they had to leave. Besides, it wasn't as if they would never ever go back there.

Unless he lost the lands due to that damned clause.

But only time would tell, though if he remembered correctly, Violet had said she should have her monthly flow any day now, which would at least tell them if their efforts during the last month had been successful. If so, she would soon start growing large with his child, and eventually give birth to the heir who would save his legacy and her home.

That would also mean they would no longer need to share a bed.

That dreaded feeling pooled in his gut once more at the thought of never touching Violet again. Of never feeling her sweet body under his or hearing her cries of pleasure. Of possibly never seeing her.

Which was a ridiculous thought because that was their bargain. And he couldn't come up with any logical reason why they should continue sleeping together once she was pregnant.

In fact, Ash realised, after his thirty-first birthday, whether or not she gave birth to his heir, there would be no reason for him to be with Violet.

'Welcome, my lord.' Bennet greeted him as they entered the house. 'I hope you had a wonderful honeymoon.'

'We did, thank you.'

'My lord. Violet.' Lady Avery descended the stairs and headed straight for them. 'Welcome back.' When she opened her arms to embrace Violet, Ash stepped into them instead. 'Oh. Oh, my...'

'I've missed you, Lady Avery.' He released her, then gripped her shoulders to prevent her from reaching for Violet, who audibly sighed with relief. 'And, please, what is this "my lord" business? It's Ash. We are family now.'

Lady Avery looked positively giddy. 'Yes, my lor— Ash. And you must call me Mama.'

'I would be honoured.' He wrapped an arm around her shoulders. 'How about some tea in the parlour, Mama? Have you been enjoying London while we were away? Violet, why don't you go and refresh yourself for now, and join us when you can?'

Once he had finished his tea with Lady Avery, he crept upstairs to their bedchamber. The curtains had been drawn to keep out the sun, save for a sliver of light. Violet lay in bed, curled up on her side.

Her eyes opened the moment he walked in.

'Your mother does love to talk.'

Sitting beside her, he brushed a lock of hair from her forehead. He soaked in the image of her sleeping, saving it in his mind that when the time came they would no longer need to be together.

'I know. I have lived with her all my life.' Violet sat up. 'Thankfully, she will be leaving tomorrow to visit friends in Bath.' She rubbed at her eyes. 'Thank you for distracting my mother so I could have some time alone. She would have had a million questions about Paris, and I wasn't ready to be bombarded with them.'

'So I had to answer them all,' he said with a chuckle. 'Feeling better? I know the journey was long and difficult.'

'It was, but I'm glad to be back on English soil where most things are familiar.' She grimaced.

'Then why the frown?'

'Because we are also back in *London*.'

'Ah, you mean, society.' He clucked his tongue. 'There is nothing to worry about, darling. I'm certain the gossip about our hasty wedding has died down.'

Everyone in town would be guessing that their expeditious marriage was due to the fact that Violet had either been compromised or was already with child—which was precisely what he wanted the Canfields to think.

'No one will dare disparage you. You are now the Marchioness of Ashbrooke.'

Groaning, she fell back onto the pillows. 'That's precisely why I'm dreading being back. Being your marchioness means we must attend all sorts of events. Balls and soirees and dinners. I've already seen the pile of envelopes on Bennet's tray.'

'You poor girl.' Cupping her cheek, he kissed her temple. 'Do not worry about accepting every invitation.'

'But you still have to accept some, right?'

'I do.'

'And now we are married, so must I?'

'Unfortunately, yes.' He took her hand. 'But I promise I will do everything in my power to ensure you're comfortable wherever we go. Why don't we look at the invitations together and we can choose which ones to accept?'

Wide, luminous blue eyes looked up at him. 'All right.'

Ash wanted nothing more than to allay Violet's fears, so he did not accept any invitations for the next three days. They still came pouring in, of course, especially now word had spread that they had returned from their honeymoon.

Eventually though, they had to accept some of them, but he allowed her to choose which ones. After sifting through them, Violet chose the Houghton Ball, as Kate, Sebastian, and the Dowager would be there as well.

'Have I told you how ravishing you look, darling?' he said as they rode to the Earl of Houghton's home in Hanover Square. 'That blue gown suits you so well.'

'Not yet.' She was doing that exercise with her fingers. 'But since we left you have called me beautiful, stunning, and graceful.'

He chuckled. 'Only you would keep track.'

Once they arrived at the ball, Ash held Violet's hand tight. He'd noticed that adding pressure to his touch seemed to soothe her, so he was mindful to do it whenever she seemed fraught.

'The Marquess and Marchioness of Ashbrooke!' the butler announced as they arrived.

A hush fell over the crowd, followed by a low buzz as all eyes in the room fixed on them. Despite his grip, Ash felt Violet falter.

'Don't look at them,' he instructed. 'Not if it makes you ill at ease.'

'Where am I supposed to look?'

'Anywhere, as long as you are comfortable. Haven't you noticed that when haughty titled ladies are announced, they don't look anyone in the eye? That's because they don't think of anyone as their equal, and therefore believe they do not deserve a second glance.'

'I see.' She tilted her head. 'All right, I shall try it.'

Jutting her chin forward, Violet kept her gaze above most people's heads. They glided across the room and she seemed to him to be a queen among her subjects.

Spotting Sebastian and Kate, he guided her to them, and she visibly relaxed once in their company.

'You did well, darling,' he said, leaning down to whisper in her ear. 'I'm proud of you.'

Perhaps making a successful entrance had taken the pressure off Violet, for she was more at ease for the rest of the ball. Many of the guests clamoured for an introduction, and she was polite and gracious to all of them. However, as more and more people descended on them, he could see her patience was wearing thin.

'If you would excuse us?' he said to a group of ladies who had surrounded Violet. 'I would like to dance with my wife.'

He led her towards the dance floor, where they took their place as the waltz was announced.

'If you'd prefer to have some peace and quiet we could go out to the gardens instead,' he said. 'We can leave before the music starts.'

She shook her head. 'I actually don't mind dancing at all.'

'You don't? You actually like it?'

'I don't like the social aspect of it or having a stranger touch me.' She placed her hand on his shoulder while he took the other one in his. 'But everything about dancing is beautiful. The symmetry, the rotations, the repetition. Dancing uses all kinds of mathematics, like counting, shape-making, mapping, patterns, formations. No two dances are ever the same, but that's the beauty of it.'

The music began, and Ash whirled her across the floor.

She continued. 'All the dancers must stay in rhythm, counting the same pattern, so as not to bump into each other and stay in time with the music. And as you're leading the dance you're mapping out the size of the dance floor, so we don't go out of bounds, as well as—' Her lips clamped shut. 'I'm boring you, aren't I? I do tend to ramble on and on, my apologies.'

'You're not boring me, Violet.' He tamped down the urge to stop in the middle of the dance floor and kiss her. 'It's fascinating, what you're saying.' Only his lovely, logical Violet would equate something frivolous like dancing with mathematical concepts. 'I want to hear more. Please, do go on.'

And so she did, explaining further how mathematics and dance were closely related. Truly, it was perhaps the most enjoyable dance he'd ever had in his life, and he was almost sad when it came to an end.

Almost, but not really, because they'd stayed at the ball long enough.

Now he needed to be alone with his wife.

And the only reason for that, he reminded himself, was that she was not yet with child. There was still the danger of losing his lands and income. He had a duty to his name, title, and his servants and tenants to do what he could to save his legacy.

'Would you like to go home, Violet?' He lifted her hand to his lips and kissed the inside of her palm, not caring if anyone saw them.

Her lashes lowered and her cheeks pinkened. 'I would.'

One benefit of married life, Violet realised, was that it was much easier to establish routines. When she'd lived at Oakwood Cottage, she'd observed the same ones every day since the age of eight: upon waking, she washed, dressed, had breakfast. Whenever she entered her father's library she sat in her chair, placed her teacup on the table to her left, picked up whatever book she was reading with her right hand, and curled her feet underneath her. At night, she did the reverse of her morning routine. Dinner, undress, wash, then bed.

When she had been under the Dowager's sponsorship for her Season, it had been difficult to stay within the confines of a predictable routine. She'd constantly been dragged from country to Town, from early-morning dress fittings to afternoon tea, from balls to the ballet. Additionally, every day had been like a bombardment of information to process—where were they going? What would they do there? Who would they meet? What were they going to eat? It had been exhausting, to say the least, and she hadn't been able to count on any day being the same.

Now that her days were predictable, she gravitated towards those routines she craved. Her morning and evening routines were mostly the same as in Oakwood Cottage, save for the addition of her husband's presence during breakfast and dinner, as well as their making love at the beginning and ending of the day.

Her afternoon routine, on the other hand, was devoted to her work and duties as Marchioness of Ashbrooke. She had transformed the sitting room into her own office, where she worked on calculations for Kate, read through the latest scientific journals, sifted through invitations and letters, and met with either Bennet or Mrs Hogsworth to discuss any household concerns. Of course, Ash almost always introduced chaos to her day, coming in at all times and coaxing her to do something with him—usually in the bedroom. Although at other times he'd taken her to a museum, a sweet shop, and even Hyde Park one unusually warm afternoon.

Of course, now that she had found peace and serenity in the steady, predictable pattern of her daily life, she feared it would all come crashing to an end. And one day, in the middle of her morning routine, she saw the spot of red on her wash cloth.

No.

She checked once more and sure enough, blood had stained the white cloth like crimson ink.

'Gertrude!' she shouted. 'Gertrude, help!'

After helping her clean up and dress, the maid was dismissed, then Violet sat down on the bed, her hands gripping the edge of the mattress, the dull ache in her lower back like a portend of doom.

She was not pregnant.

What am I going to do?

Ash had left early today, as he had to attend to some business with his solicitor, so she would be alone at least until dinner time.

I should just go on with my day.

And she did just that—or at least she tried. She had taken too long to come downstairs, so her breakfast had gone cold. The eggs were congealed and the sausages tough as leather, so she pushed them away and headed to her office. But with her current state occupying her mind, she couldn't concentrate on the figures she was supposed to be working on for Kate's prototype test, and when Mrs Hogsworth came to discuss tonight's menu, she didn't even answer the door.

By the time she had to dress for dinner, Violet had turned into a disorderly mess.

Leaving her office, she rushed upstairs towards the master bedchamber, but stopped just outside the door.

Ash would be home any moment.

He can't see me like this.

But where would she hide?

Glancing over to her left, she found just the place.

The Marchioness's—*her*—bedchamber.

While all her clothes were neatly stored there, the only time she ever entered the room was to dress and undress, as she still slept in the master bedchamber with Ash. The covers and sheets on the bed remained untouched and perfectly stretched out over the mattress, as if they'd been preserved. Ash had never been in here either, preferring to wait for her in the other room, so it was the perfect hiding place.

Flinging the door open, she rushed inside, slammed the door shut, and locked it for good measure.

Then she waited, sitting at the edge of the bed, looking out of the window as the sun waned in the distance.

'Violet, are you in there?'

Ash.

'I've been going mad, looking for you. Bennet says no one has seen you for hours. What are you doing in there?'

'Go away.'

'Darling?' The knob jiggled. 'Did you lock yourself in there by accident?'

Flinging herself off the bed, she marched towards the door. 'I said, go away.'

'Violet, what's wrong? Are you sick? Hurt?'

Yes. And yes.

'Leave me alone.'

The jiggling of the knob intensified. 'Please, I'm worried about you. Tell me what's wrong.'

'No! I don't want to see you.'

'Don't want to see me—why not?' he asked, outraged.

'I just don't.'

'What have I done wrong, darling? Have I done or said something to offend you?'

She bit her lip, feeling her eyes well up with tears. Lord, he was going to be so disappointed in her.

'Please…' she hiccupped. 'Leave me alone, Ash. I don't want to see you.'

'Violet, open this door now!'

'Go away!'

'Violet!'

Bang-bang-bang.

The violent crack of his palm against the door made her jump back.

'I demand you open this door!' he shouted. 'Or I will break it down.'

'You wouldn't.'

There was a pause. 'No, I won't. But Bennet has the key, and I can easily retrieve it from him. It would take me all of five minutes to have this door opened. So I'm afraid that if your idea was to hide in there for all eternity, you might have to change your plans.'

His words sank in, and she conceded to his line of reasoning. Her plan to hide was irrational. She unlocked the door and took a step back. The knob turned and the hinges creaked with an ear-splitting noise that frayed her nerves.

Ash stood in the doorway, expression grave. 'What's the matter, Violet?'

Her lips parted, but no sound came out. Her thumbs began to touch her fingers in a rapid, frenzied movement. 'I have terrible news.'

'What is it?'

'I…I am… My monthly flow has arrived.' His expression remained impassive. 'So… I am currently indisposed, my lord.'

'I see.'

She spun away from him, not wanting him to see the tears ready to spill down her cheeks. 'I—I will sleep here for the week, u-until—' A gasp escaped her as strong, muscled arms wrapped around her.

She burst into tears.

'Violet, oh, Violet…' he soothed, kissing her temple and trailing his mouth down the side of her cheek. 'It's all right, darling. Shh…'

Bending down, he slipped an arm under her knees and lifted her up, then carried her all the way into the master bedchamber. He laid her down on top of the mattress with a gentleness that made her heart ache.

Then he turned and left.

Violet curled up on her side into a tight ball, as if doing so would protect her from the outside world. She had let Ash down. There would be no heir and he would lose everything. All because of her. The very thought made her sob harder into the pillows.

'Violet, please don't cry.'

Ash?

Turning to face the other way, she saw his shadowy figure in the doorway.

'You'll make yourself sick.' He carried a tray in his hands. 'I have tea for you,' he began as he strode inside. 'Also some sweets, biscuits, scones, lemon tea cakes that Gertrude says you crave at this time of the month, those chocolates from Paris that you like, and a poultice for your, er, condition.'

She sat up, marvelling at the heavily laden tray he set down on the bed next to her. 'A poultice?'

'Yes.' He scratched at his neck. 'I asked Mrs Hogsworth what women…who are indisposed need during this time to help them. I've heard that, well, it's not the most pleasant time, but having no experience in such matters, I sought out assistance. Gertrude helped as well, and Mrs Hogsworth made a poultice to place on your stomach to ease the pain.' He took a linen-wrapped pouch from the edge of the tray and offered it to her.

Leaning forward, she sniffed, then wrinkled her nose. 'Ugh, take it away. It smells horrible.'

He looked visibly relieved. 'Thank goodness. I was dreading having to smell it the entire night.'

'Entire night?' Did he mean to still sleep in here with her, even though she couldn't make love?

'It would have been dreadful. I am certain she put something ghastly in there, like chicken hearts or rat tails.' He shivered. 'Are the pains too much? Shall I have Bennet call for a doctor?'

'There's no need for a doctor,' she said. 'And no, the

pains aren't debilitating for me. But I do get a sore ache in my lower back for the first few days.'

'Ah, I see. We must keep you comfortable, then. Let's get you undressed. Can you stand? Or would you prefer to sit up?'

'You must call for Gertrude,' she instructed. 'She'll assist me.'

'Nonsense.' He waved a hand at her. 'I've been removing your clothing by myself for the last month, I think I can manage.'

Tugging at her hand, he helped her to her feet, then proceeded to remove her dress and all the outer layers of her clothing until she was down to her shift, drawers, and of course, the usual undergarments for her menses.

Once she'd settled back under the covers, he handed her a cup of tea. 'Are you hungry? I had forgotten it's dinner time. Shall I have a tray sent up?'

'I cannot have a full meal when I'm indisposed. But please do not miss out on your dinner because of me,' she urged.

'What, and have you gobble up all these treats without me?' he asked, seemingly offended. 'I've brought enough to feed an army.' Dragging a chair over from the corner of the room, he set it beside the bed. 'Hmmm…perhaps it's not so bad to be a woman, after all, if it means having an excuse to eat like a spoiled child once a month.'

A giggle escaped her mouth as he winked at her. 'It's usually only those tea cakes that I indulge in when I'm in this condition. You did not have to bring half of Cook's pantry up here.'

'Oh, really?' He plucked the box of chocolates from the tray. 'I can finish these off, then?'

She scowled at him. 'Not if you value your life.'

Chuckling, he took a piece of chocolate from the box, then leaned over to pop it into her mouth.

Together, they feasted on the treats while Ash entertained her, telling her amusing stories from his childhood and university days, as if his sole purpose in life was to make her laugh. When there was nothing but empty plates and crumbs on the tray, he left to take it—and the putrid poultice—outside, then came back to the bedchamber and proceeded to remove his clothing.

'Ash,' she began. 'I cannot…in my state…'

'What? Oh, no, darling, I just wish to be more comfortable for bed.' He discarded the rest of his clothes until the was down to his shirt and drawers. 'We don't have to do anything.'

'It's a bit early to sleep, don't you think?'

'Then why don't I read to you?'

As he climbed into bed he glanced at the book on her bedside table. Picking it up, he read the title aloud.

'*Algebra, with Arithmetic and Mensuration, from the Sanscrit of Brahmegupta and Bhascara.* Sounds riveting.'

Violet did not need to rifle through her catalogue of expressions to know he was being sarcastic.

'It is,' she replied, moving to his side so that she could lean against him and lay her head on his chest like a pillow. She sighed and breathed in his comforting scent. 'You can start at Chapter Twelve, page one hundred and fifteen, section two hundred and forty-nine to two hundred and fifty-one.'

He cocked an eyebrow at her, but said nothing as he rifled through the pages to the correct section. '"The last remainder, when the dividend and divisor…"'

Violet wasn't really paying attention to Ash—at least not to the words he was saying. No, she just loved hearing the sound of his voice, the low dips of his tone and the vibrations of his chest as he spoke. She didn't even mind when he tripped on the words in Sanskrit or skimmed over the tricky symbols and formulas. In fact, some of the sentences he read out weren't even coherent, but she didn't notice as his hand had found its way to her lower back, moving around in soothing circles, easing the ache away.

At some point, Ash's hand simply dropped to his side and when she glanced up, she saw that her husband was fast asleep. She reached over and put the book aside, then pulled the covers over them, then breathed out a sigh.

Ash had been so good to her these last weeks, which was why she was so afraid of disappointing him. He'd helped her so much while they were in Paris, and at the Houghton ball, making sure she was comfortable in all kinds of situations. She wanted to do the same for him, to be a good wife, a good marchioness, since she'd already failed in the one thing she was supposed to do.

And now he was saddled with a wife who abhorred meeting new people and attending loud parties.

It was obvious that from the few occasions they did go out, Ash was in his element when surrounded by people. He charmed others so effortlessly, but more than that, he just naturally drew them to him, like a sun in the centre of the universe, surrounded by planets.

He probably missed going out and socialising. He must find it boring to stay at home or go to the same few places with her. He was probably itching to attend raucous parties and stay out dancing until dawn, but held back because of her.

Maybe if she could find her place next to him, among those other planets, she could at least make him forgive her for not getting pregnant. She would try to fit in his world, to somehow change into a round peg. This was something she could do for him, seeing as he had been so considerate to her all this time.

I can do that for him, she thought as she snuggled deeper into his arms.

Chapter Thirteen

'Tell me, darling,' Ash said as he guided Violet to her seat. 'How does mathematics play into the world of opera?'

This evening they were attending a performance of Rossini's *Otello* at the opera. He had been surprised by her choice, as he knew that the loud music and crowds would certainly fray her nerves by the end of the evening.

But then again, he was astonished that she'd planned this outing at all and she had accepted a few other invitations too. In the past week they had gone to some ball or soiree nearly every night. The strain on her face at the end of the evening was evident, but she didn't complain or beg him to go home. No, she soldiered on, allowing herself to be surrounded by well-wishers and curious onlookers who wanted to see the new Marchioness of Ashbrooke. There had even been one evening when they hadn't gone home until dawn, and though she'd looked ready to fall over, she had nonetheless stayed by his side.

Violet sat down and smoothed her gloved hands down the skirts of her gown. 'Aside from the composition of music, the patterns, the structure, transpositions and inversions?'

'Oh, please, give me the more difficult answer,' he said, grinning at her.

The corner of her lips next to her beauty mark quirked up. 'You're jesting again.'

'Me?' He placed a hand over his heart, but when she scowled he took her hand and squeezed it. 'I was merely wondering if you truly wanted to be here. While it's quite nice that we have Sebastian's private box to ourselves to-night—' he gestured to the empty seats beside them '—I'm worried the music might be too much for you.'

'Not at all. I mean, I've only been to the opera once, and I quite liked it. Anything music-related—assuming the musicians are well trained—I enjoy.' She focused on her fingers where she fiddled with the lace edge of her gown. 'Papa loved music. He played the violin, was quite good at it. He could have been a professional if he hadn't gone into academics.'

'Really?'

She nodded, but kept her gaze cast downwards. 'He would play for me once in a while. I remember just watch-ing him, listening to him, and the rest of the world seemed to disappear.'

''There is geometry in the humming of the strings, there is music in the spacing of the spheres.'

Her head snapped up to meet his eyes. 'Pythagoras.'

'You must be rubbing off on me,' he said with a wink. 'I'm very glad you're feeling much better now.'

The light drained from her face. 'As am I,' she replied flatly.

He cursed inwardly at his thoughtlessness. 'Violet, I—'

The lights dimmed before he could even finish his sen-tence, so he settled back as the orchestra began to play.

Ash hadn't meant to bring up her condition, but he was truly concerned for her. In the last week she'd seemed like her usual self, going through her routines, acting as she usually did. However once in a while, he would observe the brief flashes of melancholy on her face.

He hated seeing her like this, but then again, he couldn't sulk and give up. There was still time, his birthday was months away. Besides, just because she hadn't conceived this month, it didn't mean she wouldn't in the next.

And if he were truly honest, he was looking forward to continue trying with her.

'Violet, what's wrong?' he whispered.

The overture was barely halfway done and she was fidgeting in her seat.

'It's my glove.' She scratched at the back of her left hand. 'There's a loose seam.'

'Just ignore it. Mrs Hogsworth can mend it when we get back.'

'I can't.' Her fingers clawed at the fabric. 'Help me, please.'

'Fine.' Seizing her left hand, he began to pull at the fingers of the glove.

'Ash!' she hissed. 'What are you doing?'

'Helping you.' When he reached the little finger, he tugged the entire thing off.

'You can't do that— Oh.' She sighed when he rubbed her hand soothingly.

'There, is that better?'

'Yes, but you can't do that in public.'

'Do what?'

Her mouth parted as her eyelashes fluttered and a small moan escaped her lips. 'U-undress me.'

He leaned down and whispered in her ear. 'But it helped, didn't it? Are there any other parts of you that are itchy?'

Before he could say anything else, the opera chorus welcoming the conquering general Othello reminded them where they were.

Violet settled back into her seat and focused on the stage, pulling her hand away.

Ash fixed his attention on her ungloved hand, so dainty and perfect with its long, slim fingers and the soft skin of her palm. And what talented hands they were too; he recalled how they'd explored his body, wrapping around his—

He groaned, blocking the vision of her sweet hands on him. It had been over a week since he'd made love to her, but it felt much longer than that. He was like a man dying of thirst and hunger in the desert. He longed to touch her and to be inside her again.

Ash, you randy dog, she's unwell, he berated himself silently.

Still, he couldn't help himself. After a month of having Violet whenever he pleased, having to abstain was like torture. And now apparently his loins were so full that even the sight of her un-gloved hand was ready to undo him.

Which was, as he seemingly had to constantly remind himself, preposterous. He'd been with many women in the past and eventually he'd become bored with all of them.

Surely this obsession with Violet had to burn itself out eventually?

Determined to control himself, he straightened his shoulders and turned back to the stage, focusing his attention on Rodrigo and Iago as they plotted to bring down the titular main character. Everything was proceeding well enough, at least, until Desdemona made her entrance.

Who tonight, happened to be played by Alessandra Moretti, his former lover.

'Oh, hell.'

'Ash?' Violet's head snapped towards him. 'Are you all right?'

'Yes. Apologies, I was just…never mind.'

Shrugging, she turned back to the stage.

His affair with Alessandra Moretti seemed like a lifetime ago, though truly it had been only four or five years ago. She'd been a budding understudy back then, freshly arrived from Italy. As he was no opera enthusiast, he couldn't even remember how they'd been introduced—perhaps at a party held by some important foreign attaché, or a dinner hosted by some business magnate. But he did recall that she'd immediately set her sights on him—and he, of course, had been glad to be caught.

Their affair had lasted for weeks, but eventually he'd lost interest in her and ended things. Alessandra had been livid, proclaiming that she was in love with him, but a generous gift of jewellery had soothed her broken heart and he hadn't heard from her since.

Maybe she doesn't remember me, he thought.

However, at that moment Alessandra's head lifted towards Ash and their eyes met. She smiled at him before turning her attention to her scene partner.

Damn.

Ash sat through the rest of the opera, growing more and more impatient as the night drew on. Violet, thankfully, did not want to leave the box during the intermission, nor did she want to be crushed in the crowds as they filed out of the theatre when the opera had finished, so Ash suggested they wait inside until everyone was gone.

Once the theatre had emptied, he wrapped her cape around her, signalling that it was safe to leave. Before they could exit the box, however, the door opened and someone stepped in.

'Ash, I was told you haven't left— Oh.' Alessandra's full, pouting mouth rounded in a perfect O. 'I thought you were alone.'

The touch of a smirk on her face told Ash she had known very well that Violet was here. Alessandra had always been a vicious little thing. He wasn't surprised she'd made it up the ranks from understudy to lead soprano in such a short time.

'Good evening, Miss Moretti,' he greeted.

'Ash, I didn't know you knew the soprano,' Violet said. 'Hello. You were magnificent tonight. I truly enjoyed your performance. It was riveting.'

'And who is this, Ash?' Alessandra's eyes perused Violet from head to toe. 'Another one of the London beauties you run around with? How long will she stay with you?'

Ash was aware she knew damned well who Violet was, but Alessandra did enjoy toying with people's emotions, luring them into what they thought was a safe situation before striking like a viper. He would not allow her to hurt Violet.

'It's getting late. We should—'

'Ash, don't be rude,' Violet said. 'Please, introduce us.'

'Yes, please introduce us,' the soprano mocked as she mimicked Violet.

Ash looked at his wife incredulously. Alessandra's comments seemed to have completely gone over her head.

'Violet, this is Miss Alessandra Moretti. Miss Moretti, this is my wife Violet, Marchioness of Ashbrooke.'

'How do you do?' Violet said.

'How beautiful you are, my lady,' Alessandra said.

'So are you,' she replied. 'I liked your costume in Act One. It looked very uncomfortable, though. How do you manage to sing in it?'

Alessandra flashed him a look that seemed to say, *Is she joking?*

'We have some very talented seamstresses,' she said. 'And the costumes are not as tight as you may think, to allow me to breathe properly and hit the high notes.'

'Ah, yes, breath control is important for singers,' Violet remarked. 'Your lung capacity must indeed be superior.'

Alessandra laughed. 'Perhaps your husband can answer that. Ash, do you recall that time in the bathtub—'

'We really should be heading home.' Ash shot daggers at Alessandra.

'Oh, I do miss your home!' the soprano exclaimed. 'Does your cook still make those delicious crumpets? I love the way the butter melts over them when they're hot and gets into all the nooks and crannies.'

'Have you been a guest at the house?' Violet asked, and cocked her head to one side.

'Alessandra!' he warned. 'Don't—'

'Why, yes, my lady. Many, many times.' Her lips spread into a wide smile.

'Many times?' Violet's brows drew together. 'When?'

Alessandra's expression turned annoyed before she snapped, 'When he and I were lovers, of course. Are you bird-witted?'

The air was seemingly sucked out of the room and the tension grew thick. Violet blinked, then turned her head to look at Ash, a myriad of emotions visibly passing through her.

'Violet—'

She brushed past him and darted out through the door. He was about to run after her when Alessandra blocked his way.

'Ash,' she said in a low, sultry voice. 'I've missed you so much. I haven't forgotten about you even after all this time.'

'Go away, Alessandra!' he shouted, and he shoved her aside to dash out through the door.

He heard a faint string of Italian curses behind him, but he didn't care. He had to find Violet.

He ran down the corridor and spotted her just ahead, looking around, confused. 'Violet!'

She halted, then turned her head. Upon realising it was him, she scowled, then darted around the corner.

Oh, hell.

He pursued her, then spotted her going through a doorway at the end of the hallway. Following her, he realised the door led to the backstage area. It didn't take long to catch up with her, and as soon as he did, he hooked his arm into hers, then dragged her to the nearest room. Pushing her inside, he locked the door behind him.

Taking a deep breath, he turned around slowly. 'Violet...'

She stood there, her chest heaving deeply. 'You were lovers?'

'Yes.' He wouldn't lie to her. 'We were. It was a long time ago.'

'How long?'

'Four...maybe five years.'

'But not any more?'

'No, we parted ways after a few weeks.' He took a step towards her. 'Violet, I'm sorry.'

'Why?' Her eyebrows furrowed.

'You shouldn't have... I shouldn't have...' He raked his fingers through his hair. 'I didn't mean to hurt you.'

'You didn't,' she stated.

'But she did.' *Damn Alessandra.* 'She shouldn't have said that about you.'

'It's true, though,' she sniffed. 'I didn't understand what she was trying to say. Why won't people just state what they mean, instead of making insinuations and dropping hints? It's frustrating when I can't make sense of what people say. She's right. I am bird-witted—'

He quickly wrapped his arms around her. 'Don't say that.'

'But it's true,' she murmured against his chest. 'No matter what I do, or how hard I try, I can't read people. I wish I were smart and witty, like you, then it would make all this easier.'

He frowned. '"All this"?'

'Attending parties and balls. Socialising with your peers, meeting and making conversation with people, trying new things. I'm trying to be better for you.'

What the hell was she saying?

'You've been so wonderful to me these last weeks— making sure I'm comfortable, avoiding situations that could cause my anxiety to rise. You're probably bored to tears with me and miss going out to parties and soirees and being surrounded by people. I just want to be a good marchioness, since I have failed to conceive. I want to do this for you.'

'"Do this"? This is why you've been accepting so many invitations? As some kind of misguided attempt to placate me because you think you failed me?'

'It's true.'

Gripping her shoulders, he looked deep into her eyes. 'Violet, look at me, please?' When she lifted her gaze, he said, 'You have not failed.'

'The purpose of our marriage was for me to get pregnant, and that goal has not been met. That is the very definition of failure.'

He stifled a laugh. *My logical, lovely Violet.* 'It seems unfair to put the blame entirely on yourself when I'm half of the equation. One plus one equals two, correct?'

'I suppose.'

'We haven't failed—yet. We still have time. And many, many chances to try.' His hands slipped down to her waist. 'Darling, will you keep trying with me?'

Luminous blue eyes stared up at him. 'Yes.'

'Good.' Crushing her against him, he sealed his mouth over hers.

The tightness that had been building in his chest exploded, and his blood heated with desire. He hadn't kissed her in so long, only a few pecks here and there, and he'd forgotten how sweet she was. She opened up to him, tilting her head to one side so his tongue could fully invade her mouth, while her hands immediately dug into the nape of his neck to tug at his hair, making his desire spring to life.

A primitive sound erupted from his chest. His control, his reason and his wits dissipated as his hands slid down to her buttocks, then lifted her up.

'What are you doing?'

He planted her on the nearest surface he could reach— one of the dressing tables. 'Are you finished with your monthly flow?'

'Yes. Why— Ash!' she exclaimed when he lifted her skirts and slipped a hand underneath. 'You can't... Here? It's a public place. What if people hear us?'

'Who cares?' His fingers inched up her thighs. 'I've locked the door and everyone has gone home. And so what if they hear us?' Once he reached her sex, it didn't take him long to make her wet. 'Violet, I want you,' he whispered in her ear. 'I need you.'

'I need you too,' she whimpered, spreading her thighs. 'Please, Ash, come inside me.'

Needing no further invitation, he pushed her skirts up her thighs. He made quick work of his trousers, pushing them impatiently down his thighs. He surged into her, making her cry out. He drowned the sound by sealing his mouth over hers, their tongues tangling in a frenzied dance, feasting on each other as if they hadn't had a meal in days.

Lord, she was perfect, with her heat clasping around him so deliciously. He thrust rhythmically inside her, rough and wild, and she enjoyed every moment of it, urging him on by meeting his hips with every push. When her body began to shudder with her impending release he urged her on, riding it out with her until her glorious flesh gripped him tight. His release slammed into him like a wave, and he gritted his teeth as the force of it sent him into rapture.

Once his senses had returned, Ash withdrew from her and took a step back. Violet looked utterly delightful, her cheeks pink, hair mussed, panting hard. He pushed her skirts back down and helped her off the dressing table.

'Shall we go home?'

'Wait.' She wrinkled her nose at him. 'One plus one equals two?'

He burst out laughing. 'That was awful, wasn't it? I apologise for offending your sensibilities.' He kissed her square on the mouth. 'I shall leave the mathematical analogies to you from now on.'

'It is my speciality,' she replied.

'And when we reach home I'll show you *my* specialities,' he said, giving her a wink.

While Violet had seemingly forgiven him for the whole Alessandra debacle, Ash was still wrapped up in guilt. He'd had no idea that Violet blamed herself—and only herself— for failing to conceive. It was preposterous, of course. Not once had he ever thought she was solely to blame for their lack of success, nor did she have to compensate him by placing herself in unpleasant situations. While he did enjoy going to certain social events, it wasn't something that he needed in his life.

And so, the day after the opera, he sat down with her to sift through all their invitations and correspondence.

'Which shall we accept?' Violet asked as she eyed the stack of envelopes warily.

He shrugged. 'As long as we are present at the important events—weddings, funerals, parliamentary and royal functions and the like—you may turn down any or all of them.'

'Surely I can't decline all these invitations? You're the Marquess of Ashbrooke, you must accept them.'

'Says who?'

'The rules.'

'There are no written rules on accepting invitations.'

'Actually, there are,' she countered. 'Many of them.'

'Hang the rules, they're written by bored society matrons who have nothing better to do. Violet, I open only about half the invitations I receive and accept as few of them as possible.'

Mostly he went to events to socialise with other men or meet potential paramours—though perhaps he would keep that fact to himself.

'Musicales and teas bore me, and I can watch the symphony orchestra for better music and ring Bennet for a better brew. And don't even mention balls. I hardly ever go to balls—especially not in the midst of the Season, when the mamas are ready to fling their daughters at me.'

'Then what do you do to socialise?'

'Mostly I go to St James's with my friends.'

'Oh, to clubs like The Underworld?'

'Yes.'

There was also another type of establishment he frequented in St James, but he that was another thing he'd keep to himself.

'Anyway, Violet, as you are my wife, our socialising is

your responsibility now, and therefore I shall leave it entirely up to you to accept or decline these invitations on our behalf.'

Ash could not protect Violet from the Ton for ever, but he would do his utmost to make sure she never had to be in situations where she was anxious or uncomfortable or caught off guard.

Tonight, however, he was going to make an exception, because he'd been planning this particular outing ever since they'd arrived back from their honeymoon.

'I know you hate surprises, darling,' he said as they sat in his carriage on their way to their destination later that evening. 'But I hope you'll forgive me this once?'

Violet visibly paled. 'Oh, no.'

'I promise, it's a good surprise.'

'There is no such thing as a good surprise.'

He placed a hand over her hers. 'I aim to change your mind tonight. Ah,' he said as the carriage slowed. 'We're here.'

'And "here" is…?'

'Tut-tut, I told you it's a surprise.'

'I will see where we are once we leave this carriage, Ash,' she said wryly.

'Shall I blindfold you, then?' When she glared at him, he only chuckled. 'All right, come on.'

The carriage had driven into a wide driveway inside an enormous courtyard flanked by terraces on either side, with a bronze sculpture in the middle of what appeared to be King George III atop a pedestal and Neptune reclining on a platform below. They stood outside a large porticoed building with a large green dome on top.

'Welcome to Somerset House, home of the Royal Society,' Ash announced as he helped her alight. 'We're attending a reception here tonight.'

Violet's eyes grew large. 'This is your surprise? Why didn't you tell me?'

He blew out an exasperated breath. 'Because it's a surprise—and besides, this is not the real surprise.' He offered his arm. 'My actual surprise is inside.'

When they entered the building, they were led into a large exhibition room which was covered in oil paintings from floor to ceiling, which was already filling up with people.

'Who are all these people?' Violet asked. 'And what is this reception for?'

Ash shrugged. 'I don't know.'

'You don't know?' Her voice pitched unnaturally high. 'Then why are we here? How did you get an invitation?'

'I didn't get an invitation. But someone else did.' He nodded towards a group of people. One of them turned towards them, then smiled and strode over to them.

'Your Grace…' Violet curtseyed as the Dowager Duchess of Mabury approached them.

'Violet, it's been too long.' The Dowager looked at Ash slyly. 'Keeping her to yourself, Ash?'

'Of course,' he replied smugly. 'Any man with eyes and a brain would never let a woman like Violet out of his sight.'

'It is wonderful to see you, ma'am,' Violet continued. 'I have missed our time together.'

'As have I, Violet.'

'Thank you for bringing me here tonight, Ash,' Violet said warmly. 'You're right, there can be some good surprises.'

'You're welcome—but the Dowager isn't my surprise.'

She let out an impatient breath. 'Then what is it?'

Ash turned to the Dowager. 'Your Grace, is our guest here?'

'Yes, she's somewhere— Ah!' The Dowager waved at someone just behind Ash. 'There she is.'

Ash looked over his left shoulder and saw an older woman in a rust-coloured gown approach them.

'Madame Guilbert, *bonsoir.*' The Dowager accepted the woman's kisses on each cheek.

'*Bonsoir*, Your Grace, how lovely to see you after all this time,' Madame Guilbert greeted her in heavily accented English. 'I'm so glad you were able to attend.'

'I wouldn't miss it for the world, especially since you have come all the way to England. Now, these are the friends I was telling you about, who wanted to meet you.'

Madame Guilbert turned to them, *'Bonsoir.'*

'Ash, Violet…this is Madame Genevieve Guilbert. Madame Guilbert, this is Devon and Violet St James, Marquess and Marchioness of Ashbrooke.'

'How do you do, my lord, my lady?' Madame Guilbert greeted. *'Enchanté.'*

The Dowager continued. 'But perhaps you've heard of her work as Madame Lenoire?'

'*You* are Madame Lenoire?' Violet burst out.

Madame Guilbert's lips widened into a smile. *'Oui.'*

'Madame Lenoire…author of *The Mathematical Theory of Elastic Surfaces*?'

'Oui.'

Violet's eyes looked ready to pop out, and she inhaled a quick breath. 'Tell me how you derived your differential equation from your first paper? Why did you simplify your hypothesis when you made revisions? And can you explain—'

The Frenchwoman laughed. '*Pardon, madame*. My English it is…not so good.'

'*Je parle français, madame,*' Violet replied.

'Ah!' Madame Guilbert's face lit up, and then she began to speak in rapid French.

Violet listened intently, then responded with more questions.

'So, Ash,' the Dowager said, sidling up to him, moving away from the two women who were now deep in conversation. 'I can't quite believe I'm saying this, but marriage suits you.'

His eyes never left his wife's as he continued to watch her, enraptured by the way she spoke excitedly, her face lit up like a Yule log, her hands gesturing wildly in the air.

'You know, I think it docs.'

Chapter Fourteen

'What do you mean, you're not going to the ball?' Mama exclaimed.

Violet looked up from her tea, exasperated. Lady Avery had just arrived from Bath that morning and they were now sitting down to afternoon tea. She had asked Violet what she planned to wear to the Earl and Countess of Hereford's ball when Violet informed her she had not accepted their invitation.

Replacing her teacup on the saucer, she continued, 'I mean Ash and I will not be attending.'

Why did that need any further translation? How many other ways did she need to state it before Mama understood her?

'But it's the most prestigious ball of the Season. Mabury and the Duchess are attending, as well as Winford and his wife. You should come if only to see them. They are your friends, after all.'

'I can see Kate and Persephone any time at home,' she said. 'I don't want to go to the ball. Or any ball for that matter.'

And thank goodness she was now married and Mama would not be able to force her to go.

Mama tutted. 'Unfortunately, Violet, you'll have to show yourselves to society every now and then. It's expected.'

She shrugged. 'I haven't gone to any events, and I don't intend to.'

Her mother looked horrified. 'What do you mean?'

'Ash has given me free rein not to accept any invitations at all.'

'None at all?' Mama asked incredulously. 'You can't just never leave your home.'

'It's not never *ever*. We're still going to the important ones, like Henry's christening. But I don't plan to go to any balls or parties in the foreseeable future.'

'Oh, Violet.' Mama sighed. 'You are the wife of a peer, and though you may not realise it social connections can only be built when one is, well, *social*. These links and interconnections have to be maintained, not just for today, but for the future. Someday, your children might benefit from the relationships you cultivate now, ensuring they, too, are able to take their rightful place in society.'

Wait…*children*?

Her heart stopped at the thought.

Surely after she'd borne Ash's heir there would be no need for more children.

What about a spare?

She grimaced, the word tasting sour in her mouth. Though an only child herself, Violet thought it sounded crude and cruel to think of a second child as a 'spare', as if they existed as an extra cog for the machine, ready to be put in should the need arise.

'Violet? Are you listening to me?'

'Um…yes, Mama. I was just thinking…of the kitchen accounts.'

'Violet,' Mama pleaded. 'Think of your future. And your children's future.'

Violet let out a loud sigh. 'I'll think about it.'

'Thank you. It's in three days' time,' Mama said. 'You have plenty of time to respond.'

As they continued their tea, Violet couldn't help but ponder on her mother's words. They had buried themselves in her mind, and now she couldn't quite expel them.

Children.

When she'd first agreed to marry Ash and bear his heir the idea of a child had been an abstract concept for her. Something that didn't exist, a goal she had yet to achieve, like a mathematical formula that had yet to be completed.

But Mama's words had struck something in her, lighting up an area in her mind that reminded her that someday soon this 'abstract' being was going to be a real live person.

And fear seized her. True, abject terror at the thought that she would be a mother.

She would have to care for this being, nurture it, love it. What if she couldn't do it?

What if she made a mistake and something bad happened?

Maybe Mama was right.

Her future child was going to be Marquess of Ashbrooke. Ash's son. He would probably grow up to be just like his father—handsome, bright, and social.

And, as his mother, she would have to do the right thing to secure her son's future.

So three days later she found herself on her husband's arm, being announced at the Earl and Countess of Hereford's ball.

'Are you sure you want to stay?' Ash asked as they strode inside.

'Yes, I'm sure.'

For as long as she could, anyway.

'Oh, there they are.'

She nodded to the other side of the room, where Kate and Persephone stood with their respective husbands. As they made their way to their friends Violet could not help but feel as if everyone if the room was watching them—which they probably were.

'Violet!' Kate exclaimed. 'Thank goodness you decided to come after all.'

'Hello, Kate, and welcome back. Persephone... Your Grace,' Violet said. 'How was the honeymoon?'

'Wonderful,' Persephone said. 'How about you? It's too bad our time in Paris did not correspond. We could have gone to see the sights together, dined at the same restaurants, seen the same shows...'

'It was a last-minute trip,' Violet explained. 'But, yes, Ash and I had a grand time. I'm glad you enjoyed your honeymoon too.'

The three couples continued to chat and socialise with each other, and once in a while were joined by acquaintances and friends. At one point Ash claimed Violet for a waltz, which she had to concede was one of the best things about attending balls. In Ash's arms, she didn't feel so uncomfortable or awkward.

When they returned to their friends, Violet noticed a man she had never seen before speaking with Winford. The Duke introduced him as Viscount Luton.

'How do you do, my lady?'

Luton was dark-haired, and Violet supposed he was handsome, though his portly belly and bloated skin did not do him any favours.

'And of course I know Ash. We used to run around in our university days with Mabury, spending many a night carousing in St James's.'

'Hello, Luton.'

Usually when Ash greeted an old friend he was bright and cheery, which was why it was difficult for Violet to ignore his chilly demeanour towards the Viscount.

Luton didn't seem to notice the cold reception. 'Ashbrooke, when I read that you'd married I thought someone was playing a prank on me. What happened to your vow to never get shackled?'

'Haven't you heard the saying that people can change?' Ash replied curtly.

'But there's also another saying—a tiger cannot change its spots.'

'Stripes,' Violet blurted out. 'A tiger cannot change its stripes. Tigers have stripes. You may be thinking of another proverb from Ancient Greece which states that a leopard cannot change its spots.'

The Viscount narrowed his eyes at her. 'Ah, your wife is as intelligent as she is beautiful.'

Violet's skin crawled under the Viscount's scrutiny.

'Aren't you going to thank me for the compliment, Lady Ashbrooke?'

'She doesn't have to do anything.' Ash's voice was deadly serious.

Luton laughed nervously and punched him in the shoulder. 'Good God, old chap, you really have changed. Maybe you're getting old.' He waggled an eyebrow. 'And you, my lady, should smile more. It will make you look even more beautiful.'

Winford cleared this throat. 'Luton, I think I see Lord Talbot over there by the refreshment table. Would you mind making me an introduction?'

'Not at all, it would be my pleasure, Your Grace. I'll see you later Ash, Lady Ashbrooke.'

As soon as the two men had left, Ash visibly relaxed.

'Violet, I need you to listen to me,' he said. 'And listen very carefully.'

'What is it?'

'Do not, under any circumstances, find yourself in the company of that man. And definitely not alone.'

'But I though he was your friend?'

Her husband's jaw hardened. 'Not all my friends are good people,' he said cryptically. 'Promise me?'

'I—all right.' She shrugged. Besides, she really could not see how she would ever be alone with that man.

Just as she always did in these situations, Violet found herself continuously drained as the evening wore on. By eleven o'clock she'd definitely had enough interaction and needed to go home.

'I'll have the carriage brought round,' Ash said, giving her hand a squeeze. 'But first I need to say our goodbyes to our host and hostess. I see Kate and Sebastian over there, talking to Lord Huntington. Wait with them and I'll come and fetch you when I'm done.'

'I will. Thank you.'

Violet made her way over to Kate, who introduced her to Lord Huntington. However, a headache had begun to throb away at her temple, making it difficult to remain in conversation.

Kate noticed right away.

'You poor dear, are you all right?' her friend asked. 'Do you need to sit down?'

'I'll be fine,' she assured her friend. 'We're heading home soon.'

'Where has Ash gone?'

'He's saying goodbye to our hosts.' Violet glanced around, trying to see if she could spot Ash. 'He should be here at any moment.'

Kate tsked. 'Knowing Ash, "saying goodbye" could take much longer for him than most people—not to mention if he sees an old acquaintance along the way, and he might stop and chat. I think you should go to the retiring room and wait there, so you can be somewhere quiet.'

Violet hesitated, but the thought of an empty, peaceful room was much too tempting at the moment. 'Then I shall find my way there. If you see Ash, please tell him to come and fetch me from there.'

'Of course.'

As she made her way across the room the ache in her temple grew, but thankfully she was nearing her destination. She was but a few feet away from the ladies' retiring room when a strong hand grasped at her arm.

'I beg your pardon. Let me go.' She tugged it away, but to no avail. 'I said let— Viscount Luton?' Her nose wrinkled. What is that smell?

'Lady Ashbrooke.' The Viscount's grip tightened. 'You must come with me.'

'I beg your pardon?' She sniffed. The Viscount smelled an awful lot like brandy.

'Ash has asked me to fetch you.'

She froze, unsure how to process the Viscount's words. Ash had told her never to be in Luton's company under any circumstances, but now he had sent him to fetch her?

The throb in her temple became a full pounding.

'Please, you must hurry,' said the Viscount.

'Hurry? Why?'

'Ash needs you. He's been hurt, you see.' There was a slight slur to his words that made him extended all the *S*s in his speech.

'Hurt?' Fear and anxiety spiked in her, and she forgot

all about her headache. 'How? Why? He was supposed to fetch the carriage.'

'Wheel ran over his leg.' Luton tugged at her arm. 'Come, let's go outside now.'

Before she could protest, he began to drag her away. All the noise, the smells, the lights and colours around her combined with the fear for Ash, made Violet's head swim.

Please be all right, she pleaded.

However, when the cool night air hit her face, she sobered and realised they were not out in the street where all the carriages were parked.

'Lord Luton, where are we?'

'Why, we're in the garden, my lady.'

'The what?'

'The garden,' he repeated, licking his lips. 'Surely you've heard of them? They're perfect for trysts.'

He advanced towards her menacingly and Violet took a step back. 'My lord—'

'My, but you're beautiful.' His eyes roamed over her, stopping at her chest. 'No wonder Ash couldn't help himself, even though he never beds virgins. Or married women, though it's ironic that he's tupping one now.' He chortled. 'Get it? Because you're married and he's screwing you?'

Lord, he was confusing. What was he trying to say?

'My lord, please. Where is my husband? I need to see him, especially if he's hurt.'

Luton chortled. 'And I thought you were intelligent. Ash is not here, nor is he hurt.'

'He's not? Then why did you say he was.'

'To get you alone, of course.'

'Wh-what for?'

'What else?' His eyes darkened. 'For our tryst.'

'I don't recall agreeing to such a thing,' she said, indignant.

He took another step towards her. 'Don't be such a prig, Lady Ashbrooke. You can't possibly be married to Ash and act like a prude.'

'I'm not being a prude. Now, please, I want to go back inside. I want to go home with Ash.'

'What? Ash won't mind. We share women all the time.'

Violet's stomach churned. 'My husband wouldn't give me away like a party favour.'

'I don't always need his permission. We have an understanding, he and I.'

Her heart dropped.

Stupid Violet.

Her eyes darted around, trying to find a way out. Luton, however, was two steps ahead as he lunged at her.

She screamed, but it was too late. His arms came around her, trapping her in his vice-like grip. A hand covered her mouth, muffling the rest of her shouts.

'Shut up, you stupid— Ow! You bit me!'

Violet used the chance and scrambled away from his grasp, lifting her skirts so she could free her legs to run back into the house. Before she could reach the door, she bumped into something heavy and solid.

'No! Let me go! I—'

'Violet, darling. It's me.'

Her heard stopped. 'Ash?' She lifted her head and found the face of her husband. Relief made her go limp. 'Oh, Ash, it's you,' she sobbed. 'Thank God.'

'Darling, what's the matter? And why are you out here? I was looking for you. Thank goodness one of the footmen said he saw you go out here. I— Luton?' His expression turned grave, and his body grew taut. 'What are you doing out here with my wife?'

'Ash,' Luton said in a casual tone. 'I was just getting some fresh air…as was your wife.'

'He dragged me out here against my will.' Violet straightened up and turned around to face the blackguard. 'He said you were hurt and that I had to come with him'

Luton's expression shifted. 'Oh, please, Lady Ashbrooke. You were the one who started it. Ash, she persuaded me to come out here. She said she needed some fresh air, and then tried to kiss me.'

'I did not!' she protested.

'Who are you going to believe, Ash?' Luton said. 'We've been friends since we were in short pants. How long have you known this woman? Besides, all these married women are alike. Once they're no longer virginal debutantes, they start itching for more. For variety.'

'He's lying, Ash. I would never go with him.'

Ash's jaw clenched and unclenched. 'Did he hurt you? Touch you? Kiss you?'

'No. I bit him before he could try anything.'

Ash's eyes blazed and he pulled Violet behind him. 'You put your hands on my wife, you drunken sod!'

'Don't be a stick-in-the-mud. We've always shared women. Why is she any different— Bloody hell!'

Ash lunged at Luton, knocking him to the ground. Violet screamed as her husband pinned Luton down by straddling his torso, then pulled back a fist before smashing it into the Viscount's face. He repeated it with his other hand.

Luton let out a sickening, gurgling sound. The sound of breaking flesh and bone sickened her stomach.

'Stop! Please, Ash you're going to kill him.'

But her husband was like a madman as he pounded

at Luton's face. She was frozen, unable to move an inch, watching helplessly.

'Violet? Ash was search— Bloody hell!'

Violet whirled around.

Winford!

The Duke sped towards the two men, then pulled Ash off Luton. Squatting down, he leaned over the Viscount. 'For God's sake, Ash, you've made minced meat out of his face.'

'He…touched… Violet…' Ash gasped.

Winford's expression turned grave. 'Violet, are you—'

'I'm fine.' Her feet unfroze and she hurried towards them. 'Oh, Ash…'

He looked a fright, with his hair tousled, his eyes wild, shirt ripped and hands all bloody. She leapt at him, wrapping her arms around his torso, and buried her face in his chest.

'Ash…'

'He's still breathing, thank heavens.' Winford rose to his feet. 'Hell, Ash.' He raked a hand through his hair. 'You should go home. There's a side gate through the garden, use that to get out to the front. I'll get Luton cleaned up and walking again so you don't swing from the gallows for murder.'

'It would be worth it,' Ash muttered.

Violet clung to him tighter. 'Don't say that. Please, Your Grace, do what you can.'

While she hated Luton, she didn't want Ash to go to jail.

Winford nudged Luton with a boot, making him moan in pain. 'I'll take care of him. And don't worry, I'll make sure he won't talk either. He owes The Underworld and a few other places heaps of money. He'll keep his mouth shut. There won't be any scandal.'

'Thank you, Your Grace.' She pressed her cheek to her husband's chest. 'Please, Ash, let's go home.'

* * *

Ash winced as he dipped his hand into the washbasin, staining the water red with the blood from his knuckles. The pain felt good, however, as it distracted him from the thoughts swimming around in his head.

Luton had touched Violet.

She could have been hurt.

He'd nearly killed a man.

I never should have left her alone.

They should have left the ball the moment he saw Luton.

Ash couldn't believe they'd used to be friends. Indeed, they'd known each other since their days at Eton, and then continued their friendship through university. He'd spent many an evening with him, taking in all the delights St James's had to offer. Over the years, however, Luton had drunk more and more, and often lost control, getting into fights that usually ended up with both parties being kicked out of whatever establishment they were in.

One night, about six years ago, Luton had convinced Ash to visit his favourite brothel. Luton had been three sheets to the wind, but the madam of that particular establishment hadn't seemed to care. Ash had been enjoying the company of a delightful French girl when he'd heard screams from next door—Luton's room. Rushing out, he'd stormed in and seen the lady he had purchased for the evening cowering in the corner, holding her hand over her bloody eye as Luton screamed at her. Disgusted, Ash had dragged Luton out and vowed never to associate with such company ever again.

A terrible feeling had come over him the moment he'd seen his old 'friend' at the ball. Not only had it brought back bad memories, he hadn't missed that lecherous look in Luton's eyes when he'd looked at Violet. It was true, in the old days they had shared women, but never in a million years would he ever share Violet with him—or any-one for that matter.

That liar.

How dare Luton accuse Violet of trying to seduce him? The thought that Violet could be unfaithful had never even crossed his mind. She was not that kind of woman.

Gritting his teeth, he dried his hands and began wrapping them in clean bandages.

'Ash?'

He swung around and saw Violet peeking through the doorway. He said nothing and went back to binding his wounds.

'Ash, I… Can we talk about what happened?'

The pain in her voice made him ache, but he didn't answer her.

'Please, I'm just so confused. I don't understand.' Her voice cracked. 'I swear I didn't want to go with him. He said you were hurt and— *Mmm*!'

Wrapping his arms around her, Ash seized her and then slanted his mouth against hers. He couldn't bear to listen to her any more, to relive what happened to her and remember that he'd failed to protect her.

He led her back to the bed, undressed her, then kissed her all over, making her come over and over again with his tongue and his mouth. When he finally did surge into her he held off, determined to give her more mindless pleasure before he sought his own release. It was only when she begged him to finish, saying that she couldn't go on, that he finally allowed himself to spill inside her.

Afterwards he held her in his arms tightly, refusing to let her go, and he fought sleep so that he could watch her. His logical, lovely Violet looked like a sleeping angel.

He'd made her promise not to fall in love with him.

Somehow, in his arrogance, he'd forgotten to make that same vow to her.

He loosened his hold around Violet as panic gripped him. Gently, so as not to wake her, he eased his wife's slumbering form off him. The urge to flee grew strong as his stomach turned to ice.

Ash had seen first-hand how love could turn disastrous. He'd sworn off it his whole life, refusing to be destroyed like his father. He'd seen what could happen when one loved another person so much that it consumed them.

I can't fall in love with her.

He shouldn't.

He wouldn't.

Chapter Fifteen

When she first awoke, panic rose through Violet as she felt the unfamiliar sensation of being alone in bed.

'Ash?' she called softly as she rose.

Glancing around her, she realised the bed and the room were completely empty. She sat there as the minutes ticked by, unsure what to do. Her routine was thrown off without her husband to make love to her first thing in the morning.

Maybe he was still hurt and had had to see a doctor?

Fear gripped her as she hopped off the bed, jumped into her robe and slippers, then dashed out of the room.

'Where is my husband?' she asked a footman in the main hall.

'Y-Your Ladyship?' The young man's eyes bulged and his gaze dipped up and down. 'H-he's in the dining room.'

She thanked him, then hurried to the dining room. 'Ash? Are you—' She stopped short when she saw her husband sitting calmly at the table, coffee cup in hand, folded news-paper in the other. 'You're having breakfast.'

'Yes, darling,' was his only reply.

'Without me?'

Ash placed his paper on the table. 'Have a seat. There's still plenty to eat.'

She padded inside and took her place to his left. A footman immediately filled her plate with eggs and toast and her cup with tea. She was about to start eating when Ash stood up.

'Mr Bevis is coming today and he should be arriving at any moment.' He leaned down and kissed her on the temple, then smiled at her. 'Have a good day, Violet.'

A deep sense of foreboding swamped her chest as she noticed something strange about Ash. More specifically, his face. Though his lips were pulled up in the gesture of a smile, there were no crinkles at the corners of his eyes.

His smile wasn't genuine.

She stared after him as he left.

Was he still furious about last night?

After they'd come home from that disastrous ball and he'd made love to her Violet had assumed everything was once again right between them. He'd believed her when she'd said it was Luton who'd lured her out to the garden and not the other way around. After all, he wouldn't have thrashed the Viscount within an inch of his life if he'd thought Violet had been the instigator.

She shook her head.

Perhaps I read his smile wrong.

Yes, that was it. There had been many, many times in the past where she'd been wrong about the meaning of facial expressions.

However, try as she might, Violet could not put her doubts aside. She thought about it all day long, obsessing over that one smile. When Ash had not emerged from his study, nor sought her out in the middle of the day, the fixation only worsened.

By dinner time, when she found herself dining alone, it had grown to a level that had her on edge. 'Lord Ashbrooke did not tell you where was going?' she asked Bennet as he served her first course.

'I'm afraid not, my lady. He only asked me to tell you not to wait for him to eat.'

Violet pushed the plate away from her. 'I'm not hungry, Bennet. I think I shall retire for the evening.'

After dressing for bed, Violet tried to read her book as she waited for Ash. But none of it made sense to her, so she gave up and put the book away. She lay there until the candle burned out, but Ash still hadn't returned.

Exhausted, she eventually fell asleep.

The sound of a creaking hinge woke her up. 'Ash!' she called as she bolted upright. 'Ash?'

'Sorry, darling,' he murmured in the dark.

'Where were you?'

'In my study.'

He'd been here the entire time.

'Why didn't you come to dinner?'

'Got caught up with some paperwork for the estate.'

The rustling of clothes told her he was undressing.

A lump formed in her throat. 'Ash, are you still angry about Lut—?'

'I'm so very tired, darling.' He slipped into bed and remained on his own side of the bed. 'Goodnight.'

Violet lay back down on the pillows and stared into darkness.

He was just busy, she told herself. *That's all.*

'I baptise you, Henry Alexander Wakefield, in the name of the Father, the Son, and the Holy Spirit…'

Violet stood among the gathered guests who had come to watch the future Duke of Mabury's christening. Her husband, who was godfather, was at the front, next to a tall blonde woman who held Henry in her arms as the vicar poured holy water over the baby's head.

Once the ceremony was over, everyone crowded around the parents, godparents, and Henry to offer their congratulations. Violet elected to stay in the rear, until the sea of guests had receded.

'Congratulations, Kate, Your Grace,' she said when she finally approached them. 'I'm so happy for you.'

'Thank you, Violet, Ash,' Kate said. 'I'm so glad you made it.'

'Well, I'm the godfather, aren't I?' Ash quipped. 'You couldn't very well get this done without me.'

'Only because you pestered me until I gave in,' Mabury said drolly.

'As he usually does,' the towering, burly Scotsman beside him laughed.

Kate had earlier introduced him as Cameron MacGregor, Earl of Balfour, who happened to be Persephone's brother. The tall woman who had been appointed as Henry's godmother was Maddie, his wife, an American who had first arrived in England with Kate when they'd come in search of husbands. The MacGregors had travelled all the way from Scotland, and were the reason Kate had waited so long to have Henry baptised. She had wanted Maddie to be there as godmother, but the Countess had also just given birth to her first child, a daughter named Isla, so she'd had to wait until both mother and baby were strong enough to make the long journey.

'I'm hungry,' Ash declared.

'Then let us head back to Mabury House, where Chef Pierre has prepared a special feast,' Kate said.

Ash placed a hand on Violet's lower back. 'Shall we, darling?'

Violet turned away, avoiding his gaze. 'All right.'

They made their way outside the church to where a line of carriages awaited. When the familiar red and black coach arrived, a footman helped Violet inside, then Ash joined her. She kept her hands folded on her lap, resisting the urge to touch her thumbs to her fingers, all the while keeping her head lowered. However, she couldn't help but steal a glance at Ash's handsome profile as he stared out of the window.

When he turned to meet her gaze, her heart jumped in her chest.

'Is there anything the matter, darling?'

'N-no.'

He nodded, then smiled at her.

Another fake smile.

The foreboding returned—or rather, it had never left. It was like a pressure in her chest that had been there for the past two days.

Violet had tried to convince herself that everything was fine and right between them. She'd made excuses for him— he was tired, or preoccupied with the business of the lands, or perhaps Winford hadn't been able to make the troubles with Luton go away and Ash was facing charges, so he was having to speak to lawyers and prosecutors.

But when Ash's real smiles failed to make an appearance she knew there was something very wrong. While she found it difficult to read other people's expressions, with Ash it had been so easy. And then there was the fact that he hadn't made love to her in two days. Aside from when she'd had her monthly flow, it was the longest time they hadn't been intimate.

Her thoughts spiralled as she obsessed over his behaviour. Had he changed his mind and now believed Luton instead?

Had he gone back to his opera singer?

Or perhaps he just didn't want her any more.

That had to be the reason. After all, theirs was a marriage of convenience. He was a worldly man, a rake before they'd married, and so it was only logical that at some point he would become bored with her in bed. Or perhaps he was tired of her odd ways.

Her mind fixated on that thought.

Ash was tired of her peculiarities, her need to stay within her routines, her aversion to noise, being overwhelmed by crowds, her obsession with numbers and mathematics.

He wanted someone who wasn't so bizarre.

So broken.

'We're here,' Ash announced as the carriage drew to a stop.

Mabury House was filled with guests and well-wishers, but the usual dread Violet experienced in such situations did not surface—there was no space in her mind to process it as the tension between her and Ash hung over her like a dark cloud.

Unable to bear it any longer, she broke away from him and hurried over to where Kate and the other women were fussing over Henry.

'He's so beautiful,' Maddie cooed. 'I think he has your nose.'

'And Mabury's eyes,' Persephone added.

'And hopefully both our minds—Violet, there you are.'

'H-hello,' she greeted. 'How is the little one?'

'Recovered,' Kate chuckled. 'From the way he was screaming when the vicar poured the water on him, you'd think he was being murdered.'

Maddie lifted the bundle in her arms. 'Isla was the same way.' She kissed the baby's forehead.

'Violet, would you like to hold Henry?' Kate asked.

'M-me?'

'Yes. You haven't had a chance yet.'

'I've never held a baby. What if I drop him?'

'You won't,' Maddie interjected. 'Go on.'

Without waiting for her agreement, Kate transferred the bundle into Violet's arms. 'There…support his neck… Ah, that's it. See? Easy, isn't it?'

Violet stared down at the bundle in her arms. 'He's so… tiny.'

It was a silly thing to say because everyone in the world started out as a baby. But seeing one up close made her realise how small and fragile infants were.

'It's good practice,' Maddie said.

'Practice for— Oh.' She meant for when she had a child. Or rather *if* she had one.

Kate, being the only one who knew the real reason she and Ash married, quickly changed the subject. 'Violet, I know you absolutely hate balls, but do you think you could attend Lord and Lady Waverly's ball? I haven't been to one in ages. I've been working from sunup to sundown getting the engine ready, and Henry's keeping me up at all hours.' She sighed. 'I love him, I truly do, and my work, but I'm going mad. I just want to be somewhere that's not the factory or the nursery, and it would be nice if I could have my friends there too.'

'I shall be there.' Maddie clapped her hands. 'I haven't danced in a long while either. It would be truly lovely to see all of you there.'

'I'll come, of course,' Persephone said.

'What do you say, Violet?' Kate asked.

Violet worried at her lip. 'I suppose it's not too late to accept.'

'Wonderful,' Kate clapped her hands together. 'I can't wait.'

'I— Oh.' Henry was whimpering as he kicked his little feet and Violet froze, unsure what to do. 'Kate…?'

'Oh, dear… Hand him over, Violet.'

'Let her, Kate,' Maddie urged.

Violet blinked. 'Let me what?'

'Soothe him,' she continued. 'Like this, see?'

The Countess rocked Isla back and forth, then patted her bottom.

Violet paused, then copied Maddie. Soon enough the child calmed and closed its eyes once more.

'You're a natural,' Maddie remarked.

Violet caressed Henry's little face, marvelling at the soft, plump cheeks. As she continued to soothe him the most curious feeling washed over her. Lifting her head, she saw Ash across the room, staring at her. He quickly turned away.

A pit grew in her stomach, and she glanced back down at the bundle in her arms.

From Ash's reaction, she knew he *had* tired of her, and her brokenness.

Not just the brokenness of her mind, but of her body and its failure to produce his heir.

Violet stole a glance at the other women, thinking about their interaction with their husbands. Though the three men could not be more different from each other, she'd observed a commonality among them: whenever they were around their wives, they all had the same expression on their faces.

She saw it each time Mabury entered a room, his eyes lighting up when the first thing he saw was Kate or Henry.

Or the way Winford's gaze never left Persephone, whether she was six inches or six yards away.

And even though she'd only met Balfour this morning,

she could not ignore the way his mouth turned up and the corners of his eyes crinkled when he grinned at his wife.

How she longed to see the same expression on Ash's face when he looked upon her.

Because she was certain that if she were to study her own features whenever Ash was around she would find herself with that same expression.

Chapter Sixteen

'Thank you, Holmes, that will be all.' Ash dismissed his valet with a wave. 'Tell Bennet I shall be downstairs soon.'

'Of course, my lord.' With a deep bow, the valet left.

Ash observed his reflection in the mirror, smoothing his hands down his lapels, checking his coat for lint or stray threads Holmes might have missed. His valet, of course, would have been deeply insulted if he'd seen Ash, but he would never reveal the real reason he'd stayed behind.

He was stalling.

'Coward,' his reflection said, before it flashed a scowl at him.

Spinning away from the mirror, he strode over to the door. However, he still made no motion to leave, not even reaching for the doorknob.

Hell, he *was* a coward. A coward for hiding from his wife.

He knocked his forehead against the door.

He'd told himself this was for the best—that he was avoiding her to prevent his feelings for her from further deepening. It was much too dangerous. Whether or not he produced an heir and saved his lands, they'd made plans to part ways afterwards. He'd known that from the beginning, but his arrogance had got the best of him.

Now his emotions were muddling him, making it difficult to make rational decisions. Luton had been the proof of that—he'd nearly committed murder out of jealousy.

With a deep breath, he pushed himself away from the door and stepped out of his room, then made his way downstairs. He couldn't stall any more. They were already meant to be on their way to the ball.

Still, there was a problem with the clause and his need for an heir. Making love to Violet only confused him, which was why he'd stayed away from her these past few days. He'd planned to wait it out until they could confirm that her flow had not arrived that month.

If he was lucky, Violet would already be pregnant.

She would be a radiant mother-to-be. He could already picture her belly swelling with his child. And she'd be a good mother. He'd seen her holding Henry the other day. Watching her holding that bundle in her arms had awoken something in him, a longing he'd never felt before.

He pushed the thought away. Besides, there was also the possibility that they'd failed to conceive this month. If so, then he would have to try again. Until then, he had to find a way to distance himself from her in the next few weeks, so he could perform his marital duty without getting caught up in her.

Losing his lands seemed almost worth it.

When he reached the top of the stairs he saw Violet already waiting in the hall below. His heart crashed into his chest at the sight of her, looking breathtakingly lovely in a light blue tulle gown. He imagined taking all the pins out of her hair and watching those sable curls tumble down her creamy shoulders. He would make quick work of her gown, so he could bare those luscious nipples to his gaze. He'd kiss that plump mouth and the beauty mark—

Her head turned when she realised he'd been watching her. Quickly, she averted her gaze.

Guilt knotted in his gut at the hurt on her face she couldn't hide. In the last few days, as he'd pulled away from her, Violet had withdrawn from him too. After their wedding he'd watched her bloom like a flower as she'd learned to control her anxiety and fear. Now she had regressed to the nervous girl she'd once been.

'My apologies for keeping you waiting,' he said.

'My lord, the carriage is ready,' Bennet announced with a clearing of his throat.

'Thank you.' He descended the steps, then offered Violet his arm. 'Shall we?'

She took it wordlessly.

The journey to the Waverly ball was deathly quiet and agonisingly long. Though Ash had averted his gaze from her, he knew Violet was fidgeting with her thumbs and fingers. They should have declined the invitation, but he knew the reason she wanted to go—Kate, Maddie and Persephone would be in attendance. Thankfully, that meant his three best friends would be there tonight. He found it ironic that when they'd each fallen in love with their wives he'd secretly scoffed at them for allowing themselves to be shackled to women because of something trivial like love. And now he—

No, he was not in love with his wife, and if he kept a close guard on his heart, he never would be.

Though the carriage ride seemed to take all of eternity, thanks to their tardiness they were able to drive quickly up to the front gate of Lord and Lady Waverly's fashionable townhouse in Belgrave Square. Once they were announced, they immediately found their friends.

'Ash, I thought you'd never come. Did you get into any

fist fights on the way here?' Cam remarked. 'Lady Ash-brooke, how lovely to see you again. And forgive my jest—I only meant most of it.'

'Thank you, my lord,' Violet murmured.

'Violet, Kate tells me you're a mathematician,' Maddie said excitedly. 'I can't believe the Dowager has found another one like us.'

The women naturally gravitated towards each other, and at one point left to go the necessary together, leaving the men to converse amongst themselves.

'I never thought I'd see the day,' Cam said, poking his elbow in Ash's side. 'The Marquess of Ashbrooke, finally caught in the bonds of matrimony.'

He sent Ransom and Sebastian a pointed look. 'You didn't tell him?'

'Tell me what?'

'It's your story to tell,' Sebastian said.

Cam scratched at his head. 'What story?'

Ash told him all about the Canfields and the clause.

'Goodness.' Cam sucked in a breath through his teeth. 'I'm sorry, Ash. Is there anything I can do to help?'

'If you know a way to travel through time, so I can go back and knock some sense into my great-grandfather, now would be the time to tell me.'

'Nay, but if you drown yourself in enough whisky you'll wake up three days later, and that's similar to travelling through time.'

'Ha-ha.'

'It's not too bad, though, is it?' Cam nodded at Violet, who was coming back towards them along with the other women. 'Your wife is a pretty lass. Can't ask for more if you're looking to produce an heir.'

'Oh, Cam, they have just announced the waltz.' Maddie grabbed her husband's hands. 'Will you—?'

'Aye.' His face lit up like the sun as his gaze fixed on his wife. 'Anythin' for you.'

Ash watched Violet's face as she stared at the dance floor. She looked so achingly beautiful, and the longing on her face was evident.

I shouldn't—

'Will you dance with me, Violet?'

Damn.

His wife started, and her luminous eyes grew large. 'I b-beg your pardon, my lord?'

'I would like to dance with my wife.' He held out a hand. 'Please?'

It seemed an eternity before she finally placed her hand in his.

He led her out to the dance floor, his heart quickening with each step. As they got into position he realised his mistake. The waltz was an intimate dance, one that had the dancers' bodies perilously close. This was perhaps the first time in the last few days that he'd been near enough to smell Violet's sweet lavender and powder scent. Desire heated his blood and flooded his brain.

The waltz began, and the couples on the dance floor twirled about. Ash couldn't help but remember the first time they'd waltzed, and how Violet had so eloquently described the melding of mathematics and dance. He observed the dancers around them, searching for what she had been talking about, trying to find the beauty and symmetry there.

But he failed—because the only thing he found was Violet.

His heart stopped for a moment.

Then the dance ended.

Violet curtseyed, then lifted her head. 'Thank you, Ash.'

It was too late.

He was already in love with her.

The tightness began in his chest, like a vice wrapping around his torso. Then the world spun around him. His vision blurred.

Not sure what else to do, he turned around and fled.

Ash didn't care where he was going, nor even which way he was headed. All he knew was that he needed to be somewhere the walls weren't closing in on him, somewhere he could breathe without this massive pain in his chest.

Wading through the crowds, he found himself in the main hall, outside the ballroom. He entered the first room he could reach. Slamming the door behind him, he braced himself on the nearest surface—a pianoforte, signalling he was in a music room. In any case, it didn't matter where he was. As long as he was far away from Violet, so he could think and breathe.

Was this what love felt like?

If so, he didn't want any part of it.

'Ash.'

'Who the—' He spun around and saw the shadowy figure in the doorway. 'Violet?'

No, it wasn't her.

'Ash,' Emma Bancroft repeated. 'How wonderful to see you again.'

'What are you doing here, Emma?' She was the last person he wanted to see right at this moment. 'Leave me alone.'

'I'm a guest here, just like you.'

As if she hadn't heard him—or hadn't wanted to—she advanced towards him. 'I hear you're married now. To *her.*'

'Emma—'

'I was so disappointed. Not only did you leave me before we had a chance to make things interesting, but for *her*. The odd Avery chit.'

'Watch what you're saying,' he growled.

She took a few more steps towards him. 'The way I see it, we're in the same boat, now that we're both married.'

'No, we are not,' he said vociferously. '*I* did not deceive anyone into thinking I wasn't married and try to start an affair with them.'

'Grow up, Ash. Don't you know married people have affairs all the time?'

Oh, did he ever.

She guffawed. 'But does it really matter now? Can't we forgive and forget?' She was now toe to toe with him. 'I heard you speaking with your friends in the ballroom.'

'Heard—you mean you eavesdropped?'

'You can call it whatever you like.' A finger tapped at his chest with each word. 'She's but a broodmare for you, so you can keep your inheritance. It doesn't matter to me either way—all peers have to sire an heir eventually. But why should you limit your services to a single mare? Surely a stud with an appetite like yours needs more?'

Ash blinked. It dawned on him that Emma had him trapped between herself and the pianoforte. But why shouldn't he indulge? Maybe this was the distraction he needed to free himself of his feelings for Violet.

She caught his hand and brushed her cheek on his palm. 'Oh, Ash. You know this is inevitable. Don't fight it.'

Maybe he shouldn't fight it. If he did this, perhaps he could forget about Violet, and fall out of love with her. So it wouldn't hurt so badly when she left him.

But Violet wouldn't leave me.

The thought came from nowhere. His first instinct was to block it out.

He leaned his head closer to Emma's.

Violet isn't Mama.

Ash froze.

Of course Violet wasn't his mother. How could he have even thought she could be like his mother? At least, not after all this time, after he'd learned more about her.

Logical, lovely Violet. The quiet girl who loved numbers, who had learned French to read a mathematics paper, and who spoke truthfully with both her mind and her heart.

His Violet.

And then a different thought came to him.

He wondered if he'd been worried about the wrong thing all this time. Perhaps he shouldn't have been concerned that Violet would turn out to be like his mother, that she would leave him. Rather, he should have been worried that he might turn into his father and drive her away.

His poor tortured father, who'd spent the last year of his life in agony, in love with a woman who would never fully love him back. He'd watched him suffer, day after day. The pain had dug into him like hooks, and he'd been unable to release himself from the torment.

When he'd died, the only thing Ash had felt was relief that his father was free.

Oh, Violet. You'd never let that happen to me.

'Ash?'

Starting, he pushed Emma away. 'Violet?'

His wife stood on the threshold, gaping at them.

This time it really was her.

Unfortunately for him.

'Violet—'

'Lady Ashbrooke.' Emma remained cool and calm. 'I'm sorry you had to see that. But you didn't really think you could keep him to yourself, did you?'

Ash brushed past her and strode over to Violet. He wanted to hold her, but feared she would flinch away from. Or break into a million pieces.

'This isn't what you think. We haven't—'

Plink. Plink. Plink.

Annoyed, Ash turned his head.

'Does this bring back memories, Lady Ashbrooke?' Emma had opened the lid of the pianoforte, her fingers resting on the ivory keys. 'What was it they called you? I bet Lady Katherine Pearson remembers. Ah, yes—how could we forget? The Bizarre Beauty.'

'Emma!' Ash could have wrung her neck. 'Don't you—Violet!'

She was gone.

I have to go after her.

'Ash!'

Arms wound around him tightly, preventing him from leaving.

'Emma, let go!' He prised her arms away from him, then twisted her around. 'I don't want you—get that through your thick head.'

'But we've just got rid of her. Let's continue what we started.'

She lunged at Ash, but he evaded her this time.

Ash bolted out through the door and headed back to the main foyer.

But Violet was nowhere to be found.

He was nine years old all over again, watching the door slam as Mama left.

He shook himself out of his daze. She was not his mama and he was not his father. The only reason Violet had left was because he was an idiot who'd let Emma Bancroft corner him against a pianoforte.

He would fix all this. Get on his knees. Beg Violet to forgive him and confess his love for her.

Now if only he could find her.

Violet had never run so fast in her life.

When she'd left the music room she'd turned in the direction of the ballroom, then changed her mind. She didn't care where she was going, only knew that she'd had to leave that room. If it were possible, she would fly away and leave London for ever. Since that was not possible, she settled for leaving by the front door.

She ran as fast as she could through the streets, past towering white stucco houses and terraces. Despite the empty streets and the mansions looming over her like phantoms, fear did not even enter her mind as her tumultuous emotions wrapped around her like an impenetrable wall.

Once her lungs started to burn with exertion, she halted. Pressing a hand to her breast, she heaved in great big gulps of air, trying to ease the pain in her chest. She was unsure of where she was exactly, but surely she was far away enough from that place.

But it was not far away enough from *him*.

Not even if she were to fly to the moon would it put enough distance between her and the Marquess of Ashbrooke.

When Ash had run away from her after the waltz, she'd felt like a rag doll being thrown about by an errant child. One moment he'd acted so distant, then the next he'd asked her for a waltz. She almost preferred the cold Ash to the one who'd danced with her before running away. At least she'd developed her own shield against the former.

She had stood there like an idiot, watching Ash flee. People had moved about her, whispering, pointing, but she hadn't been able to move. It had only been when someone had gently guided her off the dance floor that she'd realised she hadn't moved at all, even as the next set of dancers had assembled around her.

I shouldn't have gone after him.

Though her first instinct had been to be angry with him, she just hadn't been able to bring herself to ignore what she'd seen. She'd recognised what was happening to him, because she'd experienced it many times before. The look of panic on his face, his difficulty in breathing, loss of balance. She just hadn't wanted to let him go through that alone. He might be hurt or worse.

So she'd decided to look for him.

And she had found him.

Violet bit the back of her hand, refusing to cry. No matter how much it hurt, she wouldn't cry, not for that rake.

How could I be so stupid?

Of course he'd sought out other lovers. That was why he'd turned cold against her. He had grown tired of her. He wanted a new woman in his bed, someone exciting and experienced.

Someone not broken like her.

Ash had tried to fix her. Whether or not he knew it, that was what he'd been doing. Trying to get her used to his touch, finding quiet places for her, letting her avoid exhausting social events. He'd thought to repair her, so that she could someday be normal. Normal enough to be his heir's mother.

If she ever bore him a child.

'Violet! Violet!'

She spun towards the sound of the voice.

'Violet!' Ash waved his hand maniacally as he raced towards her.

No!

Picking up her skirts, she bolted away from him. She was a good distance ahead, so she thought she could get away, but it was a futile endeavour. Ash was much taller and stronger, and he eventually caught up with her.

'Wait!'

He ran ahead of her, blocking her way. She sidestepped him, but he only continued to obstruct her.

'We could keep running all night or you can stop and listen to what I have to say.'

'You have nothing to say that I want to hear, my lord,' she huffed. 'I might be stupid when it comes to social situations, but I do have eyes. Leave me alone and go back to your Mrs Bancroft.'

'She's not my Mrs Bancroft.'

'I caught you in an intimate embrace.' She would never forget the sight that had greeted her in the music room. 'I just want to be left alone. I don't want to be married to you any more.'

Turning away from him, she wrapped her arms around herself.

He spun her to face him. 'You seem to forget we have an agreement.'

'We can get an annulment. And there's still time for you to find another wife and produce an heir. Lady Helen or any other debutante would be happy to sign a betrothal contract even before the ink has dried on our annulment papers.'

'True, but unfortunately we would never get an annulment. No one would believe that a notorious rake like me would have left our marriage unconsummated. And it would take too long.'

'How about a divorce?'

Ash crossed his arms over his chest. 'Even longer.'

'Then I will run away to the continent or America.'

'Absolutely not.'

He doesn't want me to leave.

'It would take too long to get you declared dead.'

Oh.

'So you see, Violet, we have no other alternative.'

She sniffed. 'And I'm supposed to stay true to our marriage vows while you frolic with other women?'

What a fool she was. Had she honestly believed he would be faithful to her?

'Violet, I don't want her. She cornered me in there, and I'm afraid you caught us at the worst possible moment. Yes, I was tempted, but it's not what you think.'

'I'm not pea-brained, Ash. I know why you ran away from me after our dance and why you've been so cold to me.' Tears sprang at the corner of her eyes. 'I'm too odd, too broken. I can't even give you the one thing you need.'

'Do not speak like that.'

'It's true. I'm just a bizarre, broken woman who can't even act normally in a room full of people.'

'Violet, please—'

'You cannot fix me, Ash.' She lowered her head, afraid to look at his face. 'I know that's what you've been trying to do all these weeks, so I can be a proper marchioness.'

'Oh, for God's sake.' He placed his hands on her shoulders gently. 'Violet, look at me. Please?'

'No.'

'Violet. Look. At. Me. Or we shall stand here all night. Because I'm not letting you go until you do.'

Slowly, she lifted her head to meet his gaze—and his smile. Her heart gave a little flip-flop when she saw the crinkles at the corners of his eyes.

His real smile.

'You are absolutely right, Violet,' he began. 'I cannot fix you. I can't because there is nothing to fix. *You are not broken*. And I love you just as you are.'

Her heart stuttered. 'You…you can't.'

'Of course I can.' Cupping her chin, he brushed her thumb across her cheek. 'I love everything about you.'

'No, it's not possible. You and I…we don't make sense. You're you and I'm me.'

He chuckled. 'I wish I could find a way to explain it in a rational way, like the way you do when you speak of numbers. Mathematics can explain everything—but it can't explain why I love you. It can't tell me why you are the first thing I think of in the morning and the last before I fall asleep. There's no formula to calculate how much I love you or show me why the days seem longer when we are apart and time spent with you always seems so short. The real, universal truth I know is that you mean everything to me. Violet, please believe me when I say I love you.'

Violet could only stare at him for the longest time. She scrutinised every inch of his face in an attempt to catalogue the expression there. Had she seen it before? Perhaps, but maybe only in small doses. She recognised the longing in his eyes, as well as the hope behind them.

'Violet, please say something.'

'I can't.'

'Why not?'

'I don't know how to come up with a parallelism that could possibly be greater than what you just said. Anything I say would simply pale in comparison,'

His smile reached from ear to ear. 'Just tell me you love me.' A line appeared between his eyebrows. 'I mean, you *do* love me, don't you?'

'Of course I do.' She lunged at him, wrapping her arms

around him and slotting her lips against his for a long kiss. 'I love you, Ash,' she sighed against his mouth.

While she hadn't been able to name the emotion earlier, she was absolutely certain now.

'And I'm glad your analogies have improved.'

'I love you.'

He smiled—a real smile.

'Now, if you will let me, I would very much like to take you home and make love to you all night long.'

'Yes, please.'

After a lengthy, passionate lovemaking session that evening, they lay together in bed with Violet curled up against Ash's side.

'Ash?'

'Hmm…?' He opened one eye. 'What's the matter, darling?

She bit her lip. 'I have a question.'

'What is it?'

Disentangling herself from him, she sat up to face him. 'What if I don't get pregnant in time? Or at all?'

He shrugged. 'Well, what if you do?'

'But what if it's a girl?'

'But what if it's not?' he countered.

'But what if it is?'

'Confound it—'

With an impatient snort, he pulled her down once again to his side, cradling her in the crook of his arm as he stroked her back.

'Then I shall tell you the truth, darling. Our life will not be as we know it now. We will have to make our own way in the world. I won't have all the material things I'm used to, but I will have *everything* that matters.' He kissed her temple. 'I will have you, our lovely daughter or son, and other children I may be lucky enough to have with you. Unfortunately, the only thing you get is me, darling. But if you are satisfied with just me, I promise I will do everything I can to ensure your happiness. Does that answer your question?'

'Yes,' she said. 'But what—'

'Violet—'

'I was joking.' She kissed his shoulder. 'I love you, Ash.'

'And I love you, Violet.'

And that, perhaps, was the most incredible thing of all.

Epilogue

Hertfordshire,
1851

'Papa, tell us a story.'

'Once upon a time there was a very pretty and very smart girl.'

Nicholas Gregory St James, Viscount Gilmore, wrinkled his little nose. 'Ugh… Papa, why is this story about a girl?' He stuck out his tongue. 'I don't want to hear a story about a girl.'

'Why not?' cried Lady Charlotte Anne. 'Papa, girls can have their own stories, can't they?'

Ash looked from his son to his daughter. 'Of course they can, poppet.' He tapped her pert little nose. 'Girls can do anything, don't you know?'

'Like Mama?' she asked.

'Yes, just like Mama.'

Ash looked at his son. 'May I continue my story?'

Nicholas nodded. 'All right.'

He cleared his throat. 'Once upon a time, there was a very pretty and very smart girl. One day she was waiting for her carriage when a handsome prince came riding by. He saw the girl and instantly he fell in love with her.'

Nicholas made gagging sounds. 'Ugh…love and kissing.'

'Some day you may not mind kissing,' Ash told him.

'Papa, the story!' Charlotte tugged at his sleeve.

He cleared his throat. 'So, the handsome prince fell in love with her, and she with him, but unfortunately a witch came upon them and put a curse on the prince.'

Charlotte gasped. 'What curse?'

'She turned him into an ugly beast.'

'Then what happened, Papa?'

'Well…' He thought for a moment. 'The very pretty and very smart girl decided—because she was indeed very smart—that the ugly beast was still her handsome prince, no matter what he looked like, so she married him just as he was. The end.'

'What?' Nicholas exclaimed. 'That's it? But it's so short.'

'You didn't ask for a long story, did you, now, Nicholas?'

The boy let out an exasperated grunt, then fell back on the carpet. 'But I wanted dragons and fighting and soldiers.'

'Well, next time you should be more specific.' He chuckled, then lunged for the boy, tickling him until he was screaming and laughing in surrender.

'Papa, stop!'

Ash let him go. 'That'll teach you, you little munchkin.'

'I liked your story, Papa.' Charlotte climbed onto his lap and laid her head on his shoulder.

He kissed her head of golden curls. 'Thank you, poppet.'

'I like it too, but I think it has some inaccuracies.'

Ash's heart stuttered at the sound of the low, husky voice. He turned his head and saw his wife in the doorway of the nursery, leaning against the jamb.

'Inaccuracies?' he scoffed. 'What inaccuracies? I'll have you know my stories are based on real life.'

Violet padded over to them and sat down next to Nicholas, cradling him on her lap. 'Well, there was just one inaccuracy, really. The prince wasn't handsome.'

'He wasn't?'

Light blue eyes twinkled at him. 'No, he was *beautiful*.'

Before that fateful night he'd met Violet, if anyone had ever told Ash that he'd find himself happily married to the love of his life and have two wonderful children, he would have told them to go to the madhouse.

But here he was, living in marital bliss in the countryside, and he couldn't ask for more. He had everything he could want, a beautiful family, a big house, and a thriving estate.

And that last one was all thanks to Nicholas, who'd had the foresight to be born exactly one day before Ash's thirty-first birthday. About a year and a half later, he had been joined by his sister, Charlotte.

'What are you doing here, by the way?' Ash glanced at the clock. 'It's two o'clock. You should be working.'

Aside from being a partner at Mason & Wakefield Railway Works, Violet also pursued her own interests in academia. She was currently working on her third paper, and preparing to speak at the Paris Academy of Sciences next month.

'I know,' she said. 'But I missed you and the children.'

'But your routine—'

'Can be broken.' She grimaced. 'But only once in a while, on special occasions.'

'Ah, I see.' It was his birthday after all. 'Shall I call Nanny? So you and I can head up to our bedchamber?'

He flashed her a lecherous smile.

Violet leaned forward. 'She's already waiting outside. And I have something for you.'

'A gift?'

'A surprise.'

Ash licked his lips. 'All right, children, playtime is over. It's time for your nap.'

'But, Papa,' Nicholas whined.

'No buts—and you opened your presents yesterday, Nicholas.' He grinned at Violet as she helped him up. 'It's time to open mine.'

He swatted her on her behind, making her laugh, then followed her outside.

'Wait.' She placed a palm on his chest. 'Care to make this a little more interesting?'

'What do you have in mind, darling?'

She slipped her hand into her pocket and retrieved a long strip of cloth.

'A blindfold, Violet? Hmm… I like it.'

'Put it on, then,' she said, handing it to him.

Once he'd secured the blindfold, she took his arm and led him away. Ash tried to guess where they were going, but she seemed to be leading him in circles.

'Violet, where are you taking me?'

'I told you—it's a surprise.'

'You know, it's not fair that you can surprise me, but I can never surprise you,' he pouted.

'Oh, don't be a baby. You're worse than Charlotte.'

She stopped, then he heard a door creak and she gently pushed him forward.

'We're somewhere on the ground floor,' he guessed, since they hadn't climbed any stairs. 'Are we in a linen closet? Do you want to play master and chambermaid? Because I'd be very interested. You can pretend you're dusting the dresser and then I'll bend you over and—'

'Ash!' she warned.

'What—did you want to play the master instead?'

With an exasperated sigh, she whipped off the blindfold.

Ash blinked as his eyes adjusted to the light. 'What the—'

'Surprise! Happy Birthday Ash!'

When his vision cleared, Ash let out a gasp. There, inside the ballroom, all their friends and their families were gathered, laughing and clapping as they threw confetti at him.

'This is your surprise?' he asked Violet. 'A party?'

'Yes, you numbskull.'

'But where are the peacocks? The fire-eaters? The jugglers. What kind of party is this?'

Violet scowled at him.

'I'm jesting, darling. I love it.' He gave her a quick kiss on the lips. 'Thank you, Violet. And thank you, everybody,' he called out to the room.

'Yes, thank you, Violet,' Ransom said dryly. 'For stopping Ash before we—including all the children—heard any more of his depraved fantasies.'

'You loved it,' Ash said, then waggled his eyebrows at Persephone. 'Don't tell me you've never played master and chambermaid with him?'

Her eyes sparkled behind her spectacles, and she placed a hand over her protruding belly. 'I'll never tell.'

'And that means yes.' He winked at Ransom, who only glared at him. 'Thank you for coming. I know it's a lot to ask, with you being busy at The Underworld and the twins.' He glanced over to the two boys, who were running around playing tag with Nicholas.

'Anything for my best friend,' Ransom said.

'Hey, I thought *I* was your best friend.' Cam came up to him and enveloped him in a hug. 'Hey, old man, nice to see you. Happy birthday.'

'Cam, I can't believe you came all the way here for me. I'm utterly flattered.'

'I didn't come here for you. We're down here for Christmas, remember?' He jerked his thumb at Maddie, who was currently wrangling three little girls of varying ages while she balanced a one-year-old boy on her hip. 'Oops, I think Maddie needs me. Excuse me.'

Ash looked around, frowning. 'And where's—'

'Sorry we're late,' Kate called as she rushed over to them. She was still wearing her coat. 'That weather is brutal. Oh, no,' she clucked her tongue. 'We missed the surprise.'

Sebastian helped her off with her coat, then handed it, as well as his own, to Bennet. 'Sorry about that…the carriage took for ever.'

'Papa, we're going to play!' Henry announced as he scampered past them, his little brother and sister trailing behind.

'You know,' Ash said as he accepted a hug from Kate, 'you wouldn't have to take a carriage all the way here from London if there was a railway line. If only we knew somebody who owned a successful rail works company.'

Rail travel had boomed in England in the last seven years, and there seemed to be no stopping it. And at the forefront of that industry was Mason & Wakefield Railway Works. Kate's first locomotive engine, dubbed *The Ice Queen*, had been a smashing success and, thanks to her, goods and people were now moving around faster and farther all over England.

Kate rolled her eyes. 'You're one of our investors, Ash. Take it up at the board meeting next week.'

And thank goodness he had thought to invest the last of his money in Mason & Wakefield just before Nicholas had been born. Even though Violet had been pregnant, there had still been the chance she would give birth to a girl, so he'd decided to risk it all and invest in Kate's company. Violet had been worried, but since she'd already joined the company he'd told her that he knew it was a smart invest-ment—or rather, *she* was a smart investment. Even if Nich-olas had been a girl and the Canfields had taken away the lands around Chatsworth, it wouldn't have mattered, be-cause Ash had become a very rich man.

'Well, now everyone's here,' he declared, 'where's the cake?'

Everyone gathered around the table set up in the mid-dle of the room, laden with goodies and a cake, singing as Ash blew out the candles. After that, the festivities contin-ued with more food and merrymaking, and because there were nearly a dozen children in attendance, tears, fights, and scraped knees.

'Are you all right, darling?' Ash placed an arm around Violet. 'Is the noise too much?'

She shook her head. 'No, I'm still fine, but maybe I'll go and lie down in an hour.'

He pressed a kiss to her temple. 'If you say so. But don't feel you have to stay because it's my birthday. I already have my wish. You don't have to suffer because of me.'

'I'm not,' she replied. 'Dare I ask what the wish was?'

'I can't tell you. You know that.'

She rolled her eyes. 'That doesn't make sense. How can a wish not come true just on the basis of it being told.'

'My lovely, logical Violet.' He glanced at his children, then back at her. 'You know what my wish is.'

'Jugglers?'

He burst out laughing. 'No, my love. Ah, here they come now.'

Nicholas and Charlotte bounded over to them, holding a wrapped present. 'Open it, Papa.'

Kneeling down, he unwrapped the gift. It was a miniature portrait of the two of them. 'Thank you, I love it.'

'Mama helped,' Charlotte said. 'Can we go back and play now?'

'Yes, you may.'

Ash watched his children run off, then turned to his wife, who was watching the children intently. Her lips were pursed and her eyebrows were furrowed together.

It was a look he recognised.

'What expression of the children's are you cataloguing this time?' he asked.

'I'm not cataloguing, exactly.' She turned to him and cocked her head to one side. Then her lips curved into a smile. 'Ah, just as I thought.'

'And what is that?'

'I *have* seen that expression before.'

'On the children?'

'No.' She planted her hands on his chest. 'On you. I saw it for the first time seven years ago.'

'And what, pray tell, is that expression?'

'It's love.'

* * * * *

If you loved this story,
be sure to pick up one of
Paulia Belgado's other
great Historical reads

May the Best Duke Win
Game of Courtship with the Earl
The Lady's Scandalous Proposition